THE

NOEL FORDHAM

First published 2014
Copyright © Noel Fordham

ISBN-13: **978-1499189261**

Author's Note

This is a work of fiction that takes place loosely in contemporary times. However, for the sake of the story and many of its characters, there is no smoking ban and capital punishment is due to make a return. I have also excised any reference to mobile phones, personal computers or anything regarded as 'social networking'. No great conspiracy, they just don't belong in this story.

N.F.

1

Endings are never easy. That exact moment, the cut-off point where everything stops and there is nothing more left to say or do or think, can be almost impossible to pin down. Almost. Allen Wyngarde stared down the polished metal shaft of the World War Two service revolver at his sixty-two year old reflection in the small square mirror on his writing desk. It wouldn't be long before the manuscript, his parting shot to the literary world, indeed the world around it, was wrapped up and ready for Henry Meyer. He studied the revolver, running his left index finger along the barrel and down to the tip of the trigger. His father, the Captain, had never fired a single round from the gun during wartime. He'd given his only son the speech about the futility of violence and had chosen the pen over the sword after retiring. But his new ambition as a writer had been cut short in the United States during a holiday devoted to research for his first work. He collapsed waiting for the elevator at the Grand Central Station in New York and died before his head hit the floor. That was three years after the war when Allen was too young to rationalize the loss that his mother felt. That would come later.

He drained his glass of Cognac and leaned back heavily in his chair. His eyes burned as usual; a symptom of always continuing to write long after the natural light had faded. Lighting up his millionth cigarette of the day, he considered the manuscript on his desk and allowed himself a smile over his almost complete suicide note. Henry Meyer would soon take notice. Recently, his literary agent had hardly been enthused at Allen's latest venture. Indeed, he got the feeling that the damn upstart was going cold on him in favour of some other young, up and coming talent. Fuck you, Henry, he thought.

He placed the service revolver back in the top drawer of the desk and walked over to the window of his overstuffed and, until a year ago, underused study and peered through the browned, untidy blinds down onto the street below. Sometimes he missed Barbara, sometimes he missed their Dee. He allowed himself a thought or two of his dearly departed wife and his estranged daughter. After a heavy drinking session, he would always tell himself to call Dee, but then he always convinced himself it was just the hangover talking.

Two doubles later, he answered the phone.

'Allen,' said the grotesquely familiar noise on the other end.

'Hello Iain,' said Allen, sparking up another cigarette.

'I know it's late, Allen. Not interrupting at all?'

Allen breathed smoke into the receiver. 'What can I do for you, Iain?'

'How are you fixed tomorrow? Only I thought you might care to come and have lunch at the Club.'

This was unexpected. One of the country's most well respected playwrights and, on a more personal level, a premier pain in the arse, Iain Gwynne was making a play for his attention. Instinct told him to discontinue the phone call at once. It wasn't so much late as *early*, and he had two chapters left to complete. Deciding whether or not to honour a luncheon date with Iain Fucking Gwynne should have been a no-brainer.

'What time were you thinking?' said Allen.

'Shall we say noon?'

'Okay. Iain, is there any special reason why you're inviting me over?'

'You'll see, Allen. It's a surprise.'

Allen felt a chill flash across the back of his neck. He should have discontinued the phone call after all. It was painfully obvious to him that Iain had found out about Ursula.

'Try not to be late, old boy.'

Iain Gwynne discontinued the phone call but Allen barely noticed. He stood by the desk, receiver still balanced between his ear and his shoulder as he topped up his glass. Shit. He knows about Ursula and I. Shit. Allen dropped the receiver in its cradle and massaged his neck while downing the Cognac. Ursula couldn't have confessed, *could she*? The whole thing had pretty much been engineered by her in the first place. Allen considered himself to be just going along for the ride. For three years or more, he and Ursula Gwynne had enjoyed their secret, no holds barred trysts in every shape and form behind her husband's back. Allen had asserted early on that Ursula, sexy and neurotic in equally exciting measures fucked him because, although by no means conventionally good looking, was far more conventionally good looking than Iain. Allen didn't just fuck Ursula because of the usual symptoms of an illicit affair - the thrill of keeping secrets, the dangers of being found out, the back tracking and message wiping - it was also because it was something that he knew he could get *done*. In a life of loose ends and failed personal commitments, sex with Ursula Gwynne was an exercise in successful maneuvering and hedonistic ambition. But most of all, Allen just loved having one over on someone like Iain Fucking Gwynne.

But now, as far as Allen was concerned, the cat was out and scratching at the door. He thought about trying to contact Ursula, but for all he knew, she could be sitting there, right next to Iain on that huge leather sofa of theirs in the drawing room; her with a remorseful tear rolling down her puffed up, guilty face, he with one eye on his expensive set of golf clubs.

Allen put out his cigarette, slumped into his chair and lit another cigarette.

Lubricated by a volume of alcohol befitting an establishment such as the Otto Club, Allen slipped into a black cab at his end in West Ealing and directed its driver towards Mayfair. He smoked a cigarette when the traffic welded itself together at White City. As the cab did slow motion kangaroo jumps towards a set of red lights, the driver's mouth slid sideways around his face towards Allen.

'The rozzers have got their work cut out this time.'

'Sorry, what?'

'Rozzers. The Albion Snatcher. This'll be number four.'

Allen shifted in his seat. He hadn't noticed the latest episode in the ongoing manhunt for the child snatcher. Between working on his masterpiece and being screwed by Ursula, he'd allowed himself to remain blissfully unaware of the tabloid headlines baying for the blood and guts of the so-called "Albion Snatcher".

'Seven years old,' said the driver, 'makes you grateful we got a government with big enough fuckin' balls to get capital punishment back.'

'Yes,' said Allen.

A middle aged woman, possibly of Eastern European extraction, tapped at the driver's window with a bouquet of failing red flowers. The driver wound the window down.

'Flowers for your sweetheart,' she said from under a heavy headscarf. It had gotten quite windy outside.

'Fuck off, luv,' said the driver, his elbow nudging the sad bouquet back.

She looked in the back of the taxi but Allen turned away and stared out the window into the traffic. The lights changed and the cab jerked forward. Allen half-listened to the driver telling him about how he and the other cabbies were always extra vigilant nowadays. He also explained in great deal what they would do if they caught the Albion Snatcher. It wasn't enough that the government had pushed through the reinstatement of the death penalty in England, as part of the New Directives. People were more excitable than ever; the death sentence hadn't been carried yet and certain sections of the public were feverishly anticipating the first execution. The Albion Snatcher had become the nation's favourite for capital punishment. The *England 24* red top tabloid had been running a readers' poll on suitable candidates for execution for several months now. A disgraced gravy train MP here, a television presenter there. It seemed every week a public figure was being put through a trial by media. Allen was glad he didn't indulge the tabloids and that they left him alone. They hadn't been interested in him for years. He paid the driver and stepped out on to the pavement.

'Iain Gwynne,' said Allen to the non-stick face behind the counter. The concierge placed a finger on the large open book between them.

'Sign the register please, sir,' the perfect enunciation rolled out of the concierge's mouth like all good *faux* upper class accents should. This man, whose name Allen read as Gibbons, carried himself with the self satisfied grace of somebody who thinks they've made it; rubbing shoulders with the high and mighty, the movers and shakers who occasionally look them in the eye. People like Gibbons sadly lacked the self awareness of their position in life. People like Gibbons kept the elite's mojo oiled.

'Would you tell him Allen Wyngarde is here.'

'Please follow me, sir.'

Allen followed Gibbons down the long, wide corridor into the nucleus of the Otto Club. It was a gigantic, vile throwback to an Empire the world outside had forgotten about. In here, patriotism raged like a spoilt child throwing a constant tantrum. The vast, smoky hell known as the Atrium was decorated with three piece suits and broadsheets, the smell of expensive booze mixed effortlessly with the sound of many influential voices influencing each other. Gibbons led him to a secluded part of the room, near the bay windows that overlooked a private outside square built in the centre of the club. Iain Gwynne sat alone in an oversized leather chair at an undersized teak table. He had his back to them, and Allen could see he was reading *The Edition*, the paper people read to give themselves mystique and ambiguity. Allen hated his full head of hair, untouched by grey without appearing dyed, and self consciously ran a hand through his own widow's peak. Gibbons leant in and spoke in a low, pompous tone directed into Iain Gwynne's right ear. Allen prepared himself for what would follow. The game was up and he would just have to take whatever his lover's husband had planned for him. The Otto Club no doubt held some dark, secret fraternity room somewhere in its bowels; its purpose being for rendition and humiliation.

But like so many of his plays that Allen had put himself through, Iain Gwynne told him absolutely nothing. He placed his paper on the table next to his drink and rose casually to his feet, turning to face Allen with a pleasant, amiable smile. He looked great, well-fed but in no way fat, his three piece suit moulded perfectly on to his physique. He extended a hand and as Allen shook it he realised that this man was impossible to read.

'Hello, Allen,' said Iain. 'So considerate of you to come over at short notice.'

He released his grip on Allen's hand and waved him towards the vacant chair opposite.

'Send the steward will you.'

'Certainly, sir.'

Gibbons dissolved into the hazy atmosphere and Allen steeled himself. Iain folded *The Edition* and slid it to one side of the table. He studied Allen for a few moments. Allen smiled through pursed lips.

'Everything alright, old boy?' said Iain.

'Yes,' replied Allen, although he didn't think it sounded at all convincing.

'Good good. Nobody appears to have seen or heard

much of you lately. Gone to ground, eh?'

'I've been working.'

'Really?' Iain's eyes lit up a little. 'Excellent. Another telemovie is it?'

Allen almost winced at the word. Since Barbara's passing, he'd mainly made his money writing and editing films scripts that were made for television. They invariably starred industry no marks, weighted down by an actor or actress who'd seemed promising a decade earlier.

'No. I'm writing a novel.'

'Splendid.'

'Yes.'

Iain shifted forward in his chair and leaned across the table.

'I wanted to talk to you about something.'

'Alright, Iain.'

'I thought you were the one to come to.'

'Alright.'

The steward, an older, not disagreeable chap, arrived.

'Another large Black Juneau for me,' said Iain.

'Certainly, sir,' said the steward.

'Allen?'

'Cognac. Large.'

'Yes, sir.'

The steward vanished and Allen removed his cigarette case from inside his jacket. As he placed one between his dry lips, Iain produced a gold lighter and held it out. Allen lit up and gratefully inhaled.

'Allen,' said Iain in a measured tone, 'I want to give you something.'

Iain reached down under his chair and produced a

large envelope that contained something thick and heavy. He put it on top of the paper and brushed the top side with his right hand.

Allen leaned forward and studied it.

'Is that a manuscript?'

'That's right, old man.'

'A new play?'

'No,' said Iain, trying to suppress a grin. 'A novel.'

The steward brought the drinks and they sat in silence as he set them up on the table. When he'd gone, Iain slid the envelope across the table.

'I want you to read it, Allen.'

'Me? Why me?'

Allen realised that he had sounded a little too reluctant and that Iain had picked up on it.

'What's the matter, Allen?'

'Nothing. Sorry, Iain. My mind has been a bit out of sorts recently. Deadlines, that type of thing. Well, you know.'

'Yes,' said Iain, raising his glass, 'I know. Cheers.'

They clinked glasses and drank. Someone behind Allen had nodded off and was snoring peacefully into their port and lemon. Allen noticed that the envelope was sealed.

'I really would be very grateful if you'd give it the once over, Allen. Truth is, I've been a great admirer of your work and I thought you'd give me an honest opinion, what with it being my first novel and all.'

Allen swallowed some Cognac and balanced his cigarette on the edge of the large glass ashtray. He picked up the envelope and held it in his hands, as though the weight would tell him something about what was inside.

'Just my opinion?'

Iain smiled and ran a finger across his eyebrows.

'I almost feel embarrassed for asking, but I could use a little help with the ending too.'

'The ending?'

'Yes. I haven't been able to get it quite right.'

'Right.'

'Like I said,' Iain looked Allen straight in the eye as he spoke, 'I really would be very grateful.'

Allen Wyngarde returned home later that afternoon and drank a lot. Again he thought about calling Ursula, but dismissed it. He put the envelope on the desk and sat in the chair, smoking a cigarette and watching it as though expecting something to suddenly jump out of it. After half an hour he took it to the wall safe in the bedroom and locked it in. Five minutes after that, he took it out of the safe and dropped it in the waste basket beneath the desk. He poured himself another drink, got hard thinking about Ursula, then felt guilty about it and locked the manuscript in his desk.

Allen went to bed early, drunk and as unsettled as a condemned man.

2

A few miles east, in the heart of *The Edition*, the call came through to Trent Seether just as he was about to wrap up his South America story and deploy himself for yet another night down in The Cloisters bar in Aldwych Circus. He took the call as he pulled on his sports jacket.

'Seether. You have five seconds from now.'

'Trent,' came the familiar voice on the other end.

'*Christ*, Super G,' sighed Trent. 'You're all I need right now.'

'I've got something really big for you', said Super G feverishly. Trent could almost feel his breath coming through the earpiece.

'Again? Christ, what could be so important that I'm standing here on the phone to you instead of trying to get in a copy girl's knickers by midnight?'

There was an audible inhale, the kind Super G always gave when he was about to unload a usually unreliable tit-bit on Trent.

'I've been looking upwards towards the heavens,' said Super G in a low, hushed tone. 'And I have seen the light.'

Trent ran a hand through his thick, tight blonde hair and checked the pockets of the sports jacket for his keys and cigarettes.

'You're not going all religious on me are you, G?'

'I need you to come over,' said Super G hastily, as though pre empting a hang up.

'Where, your place?'

'You must come over now, Mister Seether.'

'You must be joking,' said Trent. He was eager to

end the call immediately, but he hated being rude to Super G.

'It really is very important.'

'Can't you give me a clue over the phone?' said Trent politely as he checked his watch. Shit.

'I've been looking up towards the heavens--'

'Yeah, yeah, alright,' said Trent. 'I'll come over later.'

'Really?' said Super G with a touch of uncertainty.

'I promise,' said Trent as he turned his desk lamp off. 'But if this turns out to be another steer I'll shatter your bollocks.'

'Please hurry,' said Super G and promptly hung up.

Trent placed the receiver into its cradle and contemplated his brief conversation with the man who was, for the most part, the bane of his journalistic life. What the bloody hell was it this time? *Seen the light*? Trent ruled out the Second Coming; no self-respecting saviour would visit this cesspit of a town.

After necking three swift fixes of Black Bug in The Cloisters and failing in a half-hearted attempt to charm the new copy girl, Trent Seether launched himself into a cab and headed east towards Stepney, where he knew Super G would be waiting anxiously for him to arrive. The murkiness of Adam's Brook Road did little to raise his spirits, and as he paid the driver he looked up to the fourth floor of the Victorian house that was now home to several failing flats, Trent wished for all the world that he'd blown this particular acquaintance off and made more of an attempt with the copy girl. If he could get this over and done with, maybe he could rush back and take another shot before Brendan Hunter's several large Martinis kicked in and he moved in on her.

'Come up,' said Super G over the intercom.

The stairs creaked louder when the sun went down, even more so as Trent charged all the way up and swung through the doorway into the top flat. He closed the door behind him just as he heard Super G call him from the back room. Trent, filled with tired resignation, walked down the shabby, stained hallway that led into what would normally have been a bedroom. In the case of Super G, it was where he seemed to spend the majority of his life. He constantly watched the stars from the large glass window he religiously cleaned. The oversized telescope that he had modified himself over the years covered at least a third of the room. It sat amongst piles of recording and monitoring equipment. Trent sat on a small office chair in the corner and watched Super G printing out sheets of paper with charts and numbers on them.

'Come on,' said Trent testily, 'what the hell is all this about?'

'Just a minute...' said Super G, his protruding eyes burning through his spectacles and into the papers in his hands. He flicked the top sheet and stumbled over to Trent, dropping the pages in his lap. Trent lifted them to read.

'What am I looking at here exactly?'

'Don't you see it?' said Super G, leaning in and trying to read the printouts from Trent's perspective.

'I see a nervous wreck who could use a make out session with a toothbrush.'

'That reading there, those *lines,* they're the

anomaly.'

'Listen,' said Trent, losing his patience, 'are you telling me you've got some type of evidence of extra terrestrials or something like that? *Again*?'

'It's the *North Angel*,' said Super G.

Their eyes locked.

'The *North Angel*,' said Trent.

'That's right.'

Trent's shoulders collapsed and he pushed the bundle of papers into Super G's hands. Then he stood up and walked over to the telescope and peered out of the window into the night.

'Why do you bother with all of this, eh? There's a whole world *below* you that you haven't experienced yet, never mind above you. Why don't you go out and make a friend, get yourself pulled off by a brass, place a bet, buy some coke or a pop record? Why do you put yourself through all this?'

He turned around and saw that Super G was sitting on the office chair, curled over his printouts. You poor, skinny little fool, Trent thought.

'Look,' he said after a while, 'a few bits of paper are nothing to go on. And nobody upstairs is going to declare anything are they?'

'I know what I have here,' said Super G quietly.

'That's not good enough.'

'I'm going to try and get something converted onto a tape for you.'

'You do that,' said Trent, deciding it was time to leave. Super G didn't get up. Trent stopped at the doorway to the hall and looked back. 'When was the last time you ate something substantial?'

'I get by.'

'That's not what I asked.'

Super G didn't say anything else so Trent made his way back down the hall. As he opened the front door he debated briefly whether or not to leave some money just inside. But he decided against it; Super G probably wouldn't even notice for weeks.

After he struck out with the copy girl, who decided to "go on somewhere" with Brendan Hunter after the last orders bell, Trent Seether took a cab home to his flat in Putney and collapsed fully clothed and face down on his bed. He lay in the crucifix position for several minutes until the hazy blackness began to shroud over him. A second before it covered him completely, the phone on the bedside cabinet thundered into his ear.

'Seether,' he mumbled.

There was no reply. Instead, he heard a click, followed by a wave of tinny static noise. Trent dragged his free arm up the bed and dropped it over his face.

'Super G,' he said, struggling to raise his voice, 'fuck off.'

Trent hung up and passed out.

3

At that moment, in the north of London, a black cab swung in along the kerb and idled outside 77 Vancouver Hill. Harry Brewer exited awkwardly onto the pavement with a battered suitcase and surveyed the property at the end of the overgrown garden path. This was the first time he'd laid his eyes on the family home in well over a decade. Now it was empty of life and there was so much that had to be done. He pushed through the wooden garden gate and trudged tiredly up to the front door. He wondered, as he pulled the keys from his long overcoat pocket, whether any curtains were twitching at his presence there on the doorstep of the late George and Caroline Brewer. Finally showing his face is he?

His foot slid on the post just inside the front door, and the second he closed it he wished he'd left it until the morning to come around. He didn't feel especially sad for the loss of his parents, tragic though it was for them to die. He had been too disconnected from them and their world that it just made him feel hollow inside. The house still contained all their possessions, their *things*, just as they'd been left when his parents locked the front door for the final time and marched on down the garden path to their destiny, laid out on a wreckage-strewn hillside in South America. At least all the curtains were drawn.

Harry left the suitcase in the hall at the foot of the stairs and went into the front room. He found the light switch in a second and when the room lit up, for a fleeting moment he thought he could hear his parents' voices disappearing through the walls. The house was cold and he made a direct line towards the antique globe drinks cabinet which he gratefully found to be fully stocked. He poured himself a generous dose of bourbon and sank it, letting it warm his insides one inch at a time. He ran a finger along all the spines of the books on one of the shelves of one of the bookcases in the room and then took the bottle and his suitcase up the stairs to his old bedroom on the third floor at the back of the house. The bed was still there, pushed sideways up against the wall under the window. Harry went and sat on it, remembering the last time he had done so. He'd been much slimmer and better groomed then. He'd also just dropped out of university halfway through his first year, convinced that he could make it on his own terms and not those of his peers. He'd been wrong of course; all of those good friends had gradually left him for the sunnier shores of like-minded know-it-alls with their low slung man bags and identical accents. Harry meanwhile had succumbed to the necessity of getting by on hard sell legwork and an uneasy alliance with cigarettes, alcohol and pornography. He'd lived all over the city, along every compass point, and now he realised that the whole time he'd just been circling the family seat, casting a scornful eye on the failed family endeavour. And now they'd gone and left him the bloody lot.

Harry drank from the bottle and looked at the bare, painted walls where the girlie posters had hung. The only other item of furniture in the bedroom was the old wooden wardrobe, against which he'd received head from Jenny Blake before she'd lost patience with his lamentable attempt to return the favour. This bedroom, indeed the whole damn house, was a ghastly reminder of how little he'd achieved in his thirty eight years. He allowed himself a grim smile that he was now right back to square one.

'Cheers.'

He drank some more and wandered out onto the landing into the bathroom to pee. He left the light off so that he could avoid seeing himself in the bathroom mirror to the left of where he stood. Every few years, since he was a teenager, his reflection would catch himself out somewhere and he'd momentarily realise that he wasn't quite sure who he was looking at. Subtle changes, more widow's peak, more weight around the cheeks, a dimming of the light in the eyes to match the dimming future. By now there was almost nothing left of him to see.

He went down a floor and opened up his parents' room. The furniture was different to how he remembered. He drank some whisky as his eyes fell on their personal effects; the make-up, clothes, alarm clock and the loose change scattered on one of the bedside cabinets. Harry placed the bottle on the dressing table and stared up towards the top of one of the wardrobes. He stood on his toes and tentatively reached a hand up over the lip. His fingers brushed against something but it wasn't the porn magazines he'd hoped to find. He pulled down a small leather diary and thumbed through the pages with a passing interest. Amongst the scrawls, one name printed on a business card. It had been underlined with red ink.

'Anastacia.'

Harry slipped the diary into the back pocket of his trousers and lay back on his parents' vast bed. The sheets and pillows were crisp and cold and for a moment he had the oddest notion that they were still here, lying under the sheets, waiting for him to sweep them back and find them hiding from him. He'd been six years old when he'd pushed open the heavy door and climbed up onto the king size to begin shaking the seemingly fast asleep figures under the thick duvet. They hadn't been asleep of course, and he'd felt the square box between them that had contained his birthday present. Caroline had smiled her functional, multi-purpose smile as she let him have it, George had propped himself up on his right elbow and looked on; disconnected, disaffected, a passing interest just because he happened to be there when it was occurring. At any rate, Harry had exceeded all of his father's expectations by driving his brand new Radio controlled jeep straight down the stairs less than two hours after un-boxing it and inserting the batteries. George had said nothing, had had an unconvincing tinker about with the circuit board before placing it back in the box and leaving it on the dining table before going out.

Harry had a few more drinks and kicked off his shoes. The bed sheets and pillows started to warm up a little. No, they weren't here.

He awoke later when a sheet of sunlight illuminated galaxies of dust across the bedroom. Harry sat up and realised he'd let the whisky bottle slip from his hands and spill all over his trousers.

'Shit.'

Harry pulled himself off the foot of the bed and stumbled out of his trousers and underpants. He squinted at his watch and saw the time was just coming up to six o'clock in the morning. He sucked the alcohol from between his fingers and removed the rest of his clothing as he padded across the landing and into the first floor bathroom. He knocked the water on and piled his clothes up next to the lavatory basin. He found the towels in the towel drawer where they'd always been and draped it over the shower screen as he stepped in. He didn't so much wash as linger there under the water, occasionally pushing his hair back over his head. He didn't know how long he stood there, warming up and driving the cold tide of alcohol-induced grogginess from his knackered body. He ran a handful of cream over his chest and paunch, meandered around his genitals and the tops of his legs, and gave a cursory salute to his ears and face. He dried off and smoked a cigarette while perched on the lavatory clipping his neglected toenails and shaving the three days' worth of stubble off his tired, worn out face. He tapped the hair out of the end of the electric razor and left it on the windowsill before pulling some clean but un-ironed trousers, shirt and V-neck sweater out of his case. After dressing, he fetched himself another bottle, his cigarettes and went up into the loft. He pulled on the light switch and saw that the key was still in the lock at the end of the wooden walkway that led to the roof terrace. He stepped into a glorious morning, and pulled his shirt collar closer to his throat as the bite of fresh air greeted him. He walked towards the edge of the terrace and looked down into the back garden stretching back, unrolling itself in flowerbeds and green belts peppered with grey stone squares. He saw the greenhouse and shed at the very rear and immediately remembered hiding there when he'd put the back door window through with a cricket ball.

George had sniffed him out, of course. You could still get away with giving your kids a bloody good hiding in those days, of course, before the so-called chattering classes got their way and outlawed it. Thank god for the government and their New Directives.

Harry settled down on to the floor of the roof, propping himself up against the coarse brickwork of the chimney stack. He pulled on a pair of sunglasses from his trouser pocket and poured himself a large whisky. He felt the incremental warmth of the sun as it climbed the clouds to the top of the sky. Harry gently blew cigarette smoke at it and decided he'd stay at the house until the weekend. After that, he'd go back to the rock he'd crawled out from under and forget about this place and everything that went with it. He'd find a private few moments to mourn George and Caroline Brewer at a later date.

He heard the scraping sound first. The sound of heavy plant pots being dragged across a stone surface. Then it was accompanied by the light, floating melody of a female voice semi singing. Harry leaned forward, his dark red pullover reluctantly peeling from the brickwork. The singing was coming from down below in the garden to the left of where he was facing. He gently placed the bottle on the floor and crept towards the edge of the terrace. The garden walls were built high on all the houses on Vancouver Hill. Harry rested his elbows on the low, foot high brick wall that ran along the edge of the house and straight across the roof of the adjoining house. He couldn't see anybody at first, but as he slid himself along closer to the central dividing line between the two properties, he caught his first glimpse of her.

The woman was bent over a waist high ceramic plant pot that was full of soil. She was wearing nothing, except for a large floppy sun hat. In the shade of the garden wall, Harry could see the contours of her body and estimated her age to be around late forties. He based his assumption on the evidence of the slight yield to gravity of her figure, although it still possessed that cuddly, fuckable quality that Harry looked for in older women. He raised his sunglasses onto his forehead as she pottered about in her garden, moving smaller plant pots aside to make room for the larger one. Harry exhaled smoke as he watched her breasts, slightly downturned, shake as she gave the flowerpot a sharp thrust. Then she stood back and stretched her arms out above her head. Then she removed her sun hat to reveal long, mousy hair tied up in a loose ball behind her head. As she pulled a forearm across her brow she raised her head and stared straight up towards the roof. Harry ducked back behind the low wall and extinguished his cigarette out in the whisky.

Down below, in the quiet sanctuary of her private garden, Deborah Flaxman pulled her sun hat back on and picked up the glass of sparkling water at her feet. As she drank, she allowed herself a brief smile.

'Like father, like son,' she said to herself.

4

Special News Update: *The family of missing schoolchild Patience Sweetlove has taken part in a search of the local area. As well as officers of the New Metropolitan Police Service, members of the local community also worked in shifts throughout the morning. A famous face in the crowd was singer Crispian Bull, who took some time out from promoting his new single to lend his support. Asked about his involvement, Mr. Bull said he wanted to "give something back to the community that would be buying his new album due out at the end of the month". He also confirmed that if Patience, aged seven, isn't found by the time his English tour commences, he will dedicate the opening track,* Pretty Little Lost, *to her memory.*

In an attic in deepest, most affluent Surrey-Annexe, Detective Inspector Valentine Kibber, having spent the best part of an hour squinting through a pair of high power binoculars, suddenly sat back and unscrewed the cap from his hip flask.

'Fuck,' he growled as he took a big nip of brandy. He coughed into his greying moustache and took another nip for good health. He loosened his tie and rubbed the bags under his eyes.

'Fuck it.'

'The brandy won't help, Sir.'

Kibber replaced the cap on the hip flask and turned to see Detective Sergeant Samuel Keady sitting on the foldaway chair next to him. Kibber looked his junior up and down before turning his attention back to what was happening at the other end of the binoculars; which at this time of day was precisely nothing.

'And what would you have me do, Sergeant?' said Kibber as he rested his forehead against the thick rubber shield of the binocular lenses. 'They've had me up here for ten bloody weeks now. *Ten bloody weeks!* And for what? To watch that bloody big bollocks billionaire down there. And what's he doing? How the bloody hell should I know? Haven't seen the cunt since I got here.'

'Isn't that what surveillance is all about, Sir?' said Keady.

'You're not going to go all *New Metropolitan Textbook* on me are you, Sergeant Keady?' said Kibber wearily.

'No, Inspector,' said Keady.

'Good, because that's the last thing anyone bloody needs.'

Kibber surveyed the grounds of the sprawling estate that was the primary English residence of Gregory Gem, the most successful media mogul in the history of monopolies. Kibber had read the file with an ingrained rage. He'd never been much into music, not since the better days of those twinkling pop starlets that had caught his eye as well as his ear. He didn't recognise anything that came out of the radio these days. This omnipresent force, Gregory Gem, seemed to have full control of just about everything that was commercially released. That in itself didn't really matter to a fifty three year old like Kibber. What did rankle was the fact that he'd been given the "special assignment" of monitoring Gregory Gem's every move and compiling a report for his superiors. He'd been given all the "not on a need to know everything" bullshit, but as Kibber had been brought in from Vice, he figured that Gem was probably into something dirty. So far, the media tycoon had yet to show one single, over tanned limb. Kibber had snapped everyone else that had come and gone; a publicist here, a fashion icon there. It meant little to Kibber personally, but he kept watching, with only his faithful sergeant and his hip flask for company.

'It's been three days now, Sir.'

'Since what, Sergeant?'

'Since that little girl went missing,' said Keady. 'Patience Sweetlove.'

'Yes,' sighed Kibber, 'and no doubt there'll be three more days, and three more days after that.'

'You don't think we'll find her, Sir?'

'*We?*' said Kibber, pulling away from the binoculars and turning again to his sidekick. 'What's all this "*we*" business? Do *we* look like we're going to find the poor little sod? Stuck up here in this fucking attic in the heart of Trillionaires' Toy Town?'

'I meant it in the sense of the community, Sir,' said Keady. 'Everyone seems to be pulling together, you know, making the effort to bring her home safe and sound.'

'Yeah, well,' said Kibber, 'all I'm getting at is that it doesn't look like there's going to be a happy ending this time either.'

'You think it's him again?'

Kibber sighed and stared through the binoculars.

'Yes, Sergeant, I think it's *him*.'

'The Albion Snatcher,' said Keady in a hushed tone. 'Who was it that gave him that name again, Sir?'

'Some gobby smart arse at *The Edition*,' replied Kibber gruffly. 'Trent Caesar or something.'

'Rather glamourises him, Sir, in my opinion.'

'That's the name of the game, Sergeant Keady. Even the scum get the PR treatment these days.'

'Well, Sir, I've got a feeling about the whole thing this time.'

'Really, Sergeant,' said Kibber flatly. 'You'll excuse me if I don't join in with your positive, mental exercises.'

'Yes, Inspector.'

They sat in silence for a while. Kibber heard the pages of his newspaper rustle.

'Oh, bad luck, Sir.'

'What is it now, Sergeant?'

'The Pelham Juggernauts crashed out of the division last night.'

Kibber sighed again. He hadn't watched his team play the previous night; he'd been out of it by seven.

'I heard,' he said.

'Newtown Medico came through on aggregate, Sir.'

'I'd forgotten that's your team.'

'That's right, Sir. Man and boy.'

'Is there anything to eat?' said Kibber. He didn't feel especially hungry; he just wanted to offset the brandy a little.

'I don't think so, Sir,' said Keady. 'Would you like me to go and pick you something up from the deli on Twist Street?'

'No, don't worry,' said Kibber, waving a hand. 'I need you to stay here.'

Kibber rose to his feet, grimacing slightly at the

stiffness in his knees.

'Sir?'

Kibber pulled his suit jacket from the back of his chair and stuffed himself into it, then repeated the same action with his rain mac.

'I have to go out to my A.A. meeting, Sergeant,' he said, dropping his hip flask into the inside pocket. 'I won't be very long.'

'How's it all going, Sir?'

'Alright,' replied Kibber without commitment, 'this week we're discussing the relationship between alcohol and guilt.' There were no A.A. meetings anymore and he'd made sure of that.

'It sounds fascinating to me, Sir,' said Keady.

'I thought it might,' said Kibber, closing the attic door behind him.

Detective Inspector Kibber stepped through the discarded vegetable waste and crossed the street market on Concertina Street. He pulled the rain mac collar up as he sidestepped the traders and wooden crates stacked up on the road. He mounted the pavement on the opposite and walked up to the door stuck in between the two foreign wholesale companies. He gave a cursory glance left and right before removing a key from his trouser pocket and letting himself into the building. As soon as he pushed the door shut, he could smell her scent. He smiled involuntarily and followed it down the threadbare, unfurnished corridor and up the bare wooden floorboards of the stairs at the end. Once at the top, he looked straight into the small and very dead camera lens protruding from a crack above the door to her apartment. He rapped his knuckles on the door and ran a heavy hand through his thinning hair.

Claudia opened the door after a moment and said nothing. She stepped aside as Kibber walked in and stood in the middle of the room. As she locked the door, Kibber took a good look around the apartment. Claudia wrapped herself tightly in her lace dressing gown and climbed onto her leather sofa. As she lit her cigar, she heard him relieving himself in the bathroom, door wide open as usual. The toilet flushed and then he was back there in the room, an imposing figure with his belt still undone.

'I wish you'd wash your hands,' said Claudia, brushing ash from her dark skinned leg.

'Shut up,' muttered Kibber and went straight for his hip flask.

'There's scotch on top of the fridge,' said Claudia.

Kibber gave her look, and then chuckled to himself as he went into the kitchen. She heard him drag the bottle off the fridge and twist the cap off.

'Who's this for then?' she heard him say.

'Who'd you think?' she said, raising her voice slightly.

Kibber was suddenly back in the room, a half pint glass half filled with scotch.

'You tell me.'

'Then we'd have no secrets,' said Claudia.

Kibber took a couple of steps towards her, and Claudia felt that first tiny shudder inside her.

'I don't want you to have secrets from me, darling,' said Kibber.

He sank to his knees in front of her and placed his free hand on her bared leg. She pulled it a little closer to her, but not too close.

'Do you really want to know about all the others?' she said.

Kibber began to squeeze her leg, but then he let go and stood up straight. Claudia watched him empty his glass and walk over to the window.

'I don't want you to say things like that to me, darling,' he said.

'You know what I am,' said Claudia, tapping her cigar into the ashtray on the small table next to the sofa. 'If you don't want to know about it, then don't talk to me about it.'

Kibber turned to face her. He had started to sweat.

'I need you to be mine,' he said, 'right now.'

Claudia extinguished her cigar and stretched herself out on the leather sofa. She let the dressing gown slip open to reveal her silk brasserie underneath. She held her arms open, beckoning him to come to her, just like she'd done so many times since he'd first got involved with her after arresting her in a swoop operation in King's Cross two years earlier. So for two years this battle damaged, rotten worn out Detective Inspector had been climbing onto her spider web and immersing himself in her. She knew that he had fallen for her, the same way others had. In return for what she gave him, what she let him have, he gave her protection from the men who were beneath even him, and he paid her for it. He had also insisted on having keys made for him so that he could get in if ever there was an emergency. She had tried to talk him out of it, and later had tried to ask for the keys, but he had refused, as she knew would be the case. So she'd dropped it and worked around it. He also bought her things, things that she wouldn't look twice at herself but she told him 'thanks' and wore them, or used them when he wanted her to.

Kibber rested his head on her chest and listened to her heart beating beneath. He closed his eyes, forgetting everything for a moment while he inhaled her scent. He felt her fingers stroke his hair. He felt her lips lightly brush against his forehead.

'Do you want to go to my bed honey?' whispered Claudia.

'Here,' said Kibber.

'What do you want honey?'

'I don't know.'

'Tell me honey.'

'I don't know.'

Claudia reached down and took his right hand, bringing it up and gently laying it on her breast. She watched his hand sit there, motionless, the fingertips barely making contact with her flesh.

'Do you want *the other stuff* honey?'

His head gave a barely perceptible nod.

'Then you will have to let me get up honey.'

He shifted slightly, as though pretending to be asleep. Claudia dragged herself free and went into the bathroom. She removed her clothing and looked herself over in the mirror above the sink. She knew she was prettier than most, her dark exotic features showed no signs of fading yet. She still had time.

Claudia flushed the toilet and went back to where he was still lying. He's straightened himself out face down on the sofa, eyes still closed. She sat on the edge of the sofa and ran her hand down his back, gently tugging at the rain mac.

'Do you want me to undress you honey?'

He grunted a reply. Claudia inwardly sighed and began to pull his clothes from his body. He raised his pelvis a little as she undid his trousers and dragged them from his legs. He said something unintelligible, into the sofa cushion.

'What was that honey?'

His right hand snaked towards her knee. She moved in, lying on his back so that her fingers were holding his waist and her cheek pressed against his. Kibber's eyes flicked open.

'You keep *the other stuff* for me,' he said.

Claudia kissed his ear.

'It's only for you honey,' she whispered and she knew he believed her whenever she said it. She moved back behind him, sighed inwardly, and then began to slide her tongue down his spine.

Forty minutes later, Kibber did up his shirt and listened to Claudia as she turned off the bath taps and get into the water. He stood the other side of the door, inhaling the bath salts. He slipped on his jacket and tapped the door.

'I'm going.'
'Alright, honey.'
'It's on the dressing table.'
'Thanks.'
'Can I come tomorrow?'
'Not tomorrow, honey.'
'The following then.'
'Alright, honey.'
'Same time.'
'Same time, same place.'

Kibber almost told her there and then, but he managed to restrain himself. He put on his rain mac and left the apartment, locking both doors behind him as he went.

Kibber made stops at The Cloisters, Hardy's and The Royal Seal, sinking several large measures, before ringing New Scotland Yard to requisition an unmarked squad car to drive back to the attic room down in Surrey-Annexe. When he got to the top of the stairs he saw that the door was unlocked and that Sergeant Keady was nowhere to be seen. He slumped heavily in the seat in front of the binoculars and put his face to the eyepiece. The grounds around Gregory Gem's gigantic palace seemed to be deserted. He picked up the notebook and pencil and proceeded to write in his untidy scrawl.

14.22 / MINIMAL ACTIVITY RECORDED. POSSIBILITY OF ACTIVITY INDOORS. NO VISUALS ON GREGORY GEM OR ANY OF HIS KNOWN ASSOCIATES. FUUUUCK. FIT THE FUCKERS UP WITH SOMETHING. FUCK IT FUCKIT FUCK.

Kibber erased the entry and took a nip from his hip flask. He left the attic room, locking the door behind him. Then he drove the squad car east to Walworth and pulled up outside 119 Angel Avenue. A light shower tapped across the windscreen as Kibber stared out at the warm, inviting glow seeping through the curtains. A slight chill in his bones made him get out of the car and walk up to the dark blue front door. He hesitated before knocking. He heard her voice telling the children to go and watch the television before she opened the door.

'Hello, Ruth.'

Ruth, looking tired and flustered, sagged against the door frame, which she held half open. She looked him up and down with instant revulsion.

'What are you doing here?'

'I…'

'I told you never to come here again.'

'Have you seen Sam?'

'Just leave me alone.'

'He wasn't on the job when I got back this afternoon.'

'I don't want you to come around here again. I don't want the kids seeing you, stinking of booze. Never come back.'

Ruth shut the door calmly but firmly, leaving Kibber stranded on the doorstep. He thought about knocking on her door again, but instead he decided to exercise a modicum of self restraint and got back in the car. He drank from his hip flask and as he did, he saw the dark shape of someone peering out at him from behind the curtains in one of the upstairs windows. Kibber started the engine and pulled slowly away from the kerb.

Upstairs, Ruth stared down at the car from the front bedroom window. The children had made the connection between the dirty man at their door and their father and as she trod wearily down the stairs she once again told them their daddy wasn't coming home tonight.

5

Interplanetary Terrestrial HQ, Greenwich (X 11 Clearance)

'We've got partial, Ma'm.'
'How far?'
'Further than we thought, Ma'm.'
'Can you give me any amplification, Walter?'
'Not really, Ma'm. There's just a lot of distortion at the moment. McRae is seeing if he can neutralise it.'
'McRae?'
'Here, Ma'm.'
'It's not your present location I'm concerned with at the moment, McRae. What can you tell me about the North Angel?'
'There's a sonic anomaly in the noise that definitely matches the North Angel's signal, Ma'm.'
'And what are they telling us?'
'Too much interference to make it out, Ma'm.'
'Ma'm?'
'Talk to me, Walter.'
'Beijing and Paris want to go on conference.'
'I'll bet they do. Tell Janet to ice them for now.'
'Yes, Ma'm.'
'McRae?'
'Yes, Ma'm.'
'If you so much as think about moving your arse off that chair, I'll personally impale it on the Interplanetary Flag.'
'Yes, Ma'm.'

Harry Brewer showered for an hour and a half before working himself into his dark blue three piece suit. He was aware that the extremities of his body didn't seem to fit into the corners properly but he took the bus to and stepped into The Cloisters just after eight pm. After nearly ten minutes of standing at the bar clutching a folded tenner, he finally became visible to one of the bar staff who delivered him a pint of best and a whisky chaser. He was jostled by some suits at the bar talking over each other and found a little cubby hole to sit with his drinks. It wasn't long before he had his eye on an extremely attractive twenty something standing near a fruit machine holding a cocktail in one hand and an unlit cigarette in the other. Either side if her, two potential suitors had strategically positioned themselves to take the advantage over the other. Harry drank his drinks and watched, wanting her to suddenly see him sitting there and break away from those two goons without a word to come and sit by him. The one suitor was drawling heavily into his pint, seemingly oblivious to her lack of interest. The other man was sensing his advantage. He casually ran a hand through his heavy, blonde hairstyle and let his arm drape across the top of the fruit machine, just above her head. Harry lit a cigarette and placed his lighter on the small round table directly in front of him. Any second now, he thought, she was going to come over and ask for a light.

As it turned out, the blonde guy was distracted by someone tapping him on the shoulder and the minute his back was turned, the girl said something to the other guy and they both moved away into the crowd. Harry watched the blonde guy turn back and smiled at his expression when he realised he'd lost the advantage. He went through his pockets before noticing Harry sitting there.

'Sorry, mate, can I borrow your lighter?'

'Sure,' said Harry.

A few more drinks later and the noise in the pub became too deafening. Harry took a black cab back to 77 Vancouver Hill and took a bottle of bourbon into the darkened kitchen. He sagged heavily against the breakfast bar and drank two fingers in sorry silence. As he turned to face the window, he saw the homely glow of the subdued garden lights illuminating the top of next door's garden wall. Harry, perked up by the thrill of expectation, took the bottle upstairs and stepped out onto the chilly roof terrace. He put his bottle down as quietly as he could on the floor, nearly losing his balance. He steadied himself with his fingertips and crept towards the ledge. Dropping to his knees, he witnessed the woman next door slowly moving around her garden. She was dressed only in a pair of dark green Wellington boots and she was softly calling a name into the shadows.

'Sara...'

There was no reply. She made some low kissing sounds and Harry realised she was calling for a cat. Harry squatted there for as long as she was out there, admiring her mature figure and wishing it was he who she was calling to take inside to the warmth of her home. Her back door locked and Harry, rock hard with nowhere to put it, retreated back downstairs and found his father's diary. He found the card with the number for this Anastacia bird and dialled the number. He was drinking from the bottle when a female voice came on at the other end.

'Hello?'

Her voice was soft with a slight accent to it. Just that one simple word seemed to trickle through the receiver into his ear.

'I'm terribly sorry to call at this hour,' said Harry, immediately feeling he was already completely out of his depth here.

'Who is calling please?' Her voice was calm and even.

'I was hoping to speak to Anastacia actually.'

'Yes, you are through to Anastacia. Who is calling please?'

'My name's Harry.'

'Do I know you?'

'I'm afraid not--'

'Then, I'm very sorry but I cannot be of any help to you.'

'Well, I've come across your er, business card, you see,' said Harry quickly. 'My father is George Brewer. I believe you know him.'

He heard a lengthy sigh on the other end.

'Listen, whatever you want to know you'll have to take up with your father. I don't want to become involved in anything.'

Sensing she was going to hang up, Harry got in quick.

'Wait, you don't understand. I'd like to book your services. My father's no longer around and I'm here all on my own.'

There was nothing but silence on the other end. Harry tried not to breathe too loudly. Finally she spoke.

'Did something happen to him?'

'Yes,' said Harry. 'They both passed away recently. Look, I've got some time and some money and I could do with the company.'

Another pause.

'You know my rates?'

'Fill me in when you get here. If you're coming, of course.'

'You are at your father's house?'

'Yes.' *Fucking hell*, the old bastard shagged her in the family home.

'One hour I will be there. Cash only in advance, okay?'

'Okay.'

The line went dead and Harry replaced the receiver. He drank some bourbon and went upstairs to his bedroom. He checked in his case and pulled out the thick envelope of money he'd brought with him and estimated he still had just over two grand in there. He sBrewerped off and decided he'd have to come before she arrived. After hurriedly finishing himself off on the bed, Harry quickly showered and put the three piece suit back on. He smoked a cigarette while he paced up and down the floorboards, then swallowed some mouth wash before going into his parents' bedroom. He couldn't bring himself to lead her to this room. He checked out the other two guest rooms, pleasant looking and functional with a double bed in one and a single in the other. Neither seemed fitting somehow so he turned all the lights out settled into his father's armchair in the front living room, trying to moderate his intake of bourbon.

There was a tap on the door just after ten and Harry, his body tense since he sat down, suddenly exhaled loudly and got to his feet. He went over to the bay window and ventured a peek through the curtains. He saw her standing in the doorway, back to him. She was wearing a long black coat which went down to just below her knees, revealing stockings and high heels. He answered the door as casually as he could.

'Hello,' said Anastacia politely. She was slim beneath her coat and her dark brown hair was tied up behind her olive skinned face.

'Hello,' replied Harry, immediately feeling awkward.

'Will you invite me inside? It's getting quite chilly out here on your doorstep.'

She smiled, a little unsurely, Harry noted.

'Sorry, of course, come in.'

He stepped aside and let her pass him into the hallway. He closed the door and saw her looking around and up the staircase. How many times had she stood there with George when his mother was away, he wondered. Anastacia turned lightly on her heels to face him.

'Can I get you anything before…' Harry faltered.

'Before…?'

Anastacia smiled at his nervousness and placed her handbag on the table, next to the telephone.

'You can take my coat if you like,' she said.

Harry dutifully took her coat and hung it in the cupboard under the stairs. Anastacia was wearing a sleek, dark green dress that was cut low around her cleavage and just where it ended, the he could see the suspender clips holding up her black stockings.

'Right,' he said, 'shall we go into the living room? What would you like to drink? I've probably got everything, you know.'

Anastacia followed Harry quietly into the living room and watched him fumble over the globe drinks cabinet, randomly selecting and replacing bottles.

'Let's get the business side out of the way first,' she said.

'Right,' said Harry, 'with you.'

'It's three hundred for two hours,' said Anastacia, 'eight hundred if you want me for the whole night.'

'The whole night?' said Harry. He hadn't planned that far ahead.

Anastacia studied him, noting his indecision with quiet amusement.

'It's really up to you, Harry.'

'Right,' said Harry. 'Shall we say three hundred for the two hours and then how about we see how it goes after that? I mean, if that's alright with you that is. Sorry.'

'Do you have the money?'

Harry excused himself and raced up the stairs and into his bedroom. He counted eight hundred out in fifties and shoved five hundred into his jacket pocket. He returned and passed the remaining three to Anastacia. She had poured them both a gin and tonic and she handed him a glass.

'Cheers,' she said and they clinked glasses.

'Cheers,' said Harry, trying to take a small sip. He noticed she was looking him up and down.

'You know,' she said, 'you don't look like your father too much. Not physically anyway.'

'No,' said Harry. George had been quite a bit taller than he was. He'd taken more after Caroline in that department.

'But I can see him in you,' said Anastacia. 'I'm sorry your parents passed away, although as you might expect, I never met your mother.'

'No,' said Harry, 'thanks.'

What to do now? Anastacia seemed to read his mind.

'Would you like to go upstairs, Harry?'

Harry thought about telling her he'd wanted to do it downstairs, in the living room. Now all of that didn't seem to matter.

'Okay. That'll be nice.'

'*Nice?*' Anastacia giggled and put a hand to her red lips. 'You're really quite strange, Harry.'

She took his free hand and led him out of the living room, down the hallway and up to the stairs. She was about to lead him into his parents' bedroom when he slowed down. She turned around and saw the hesitant expression on his face.

'I'm sorry, Harry.'

'No, no, it's alright. I just think, you know. Well, my old room is just in here.'

She saw the open door and so she led him into the dark room. Harry turned the ceiling light on and closed the curtains. He saw Anastacia surveying the small bed under the window. She rubbed her shoulders.

'It's a little cold in here, don't you think?'

'Sorry,' said Harry. He'd had enough to drink to not notice something like that. 'I can turn the central heating on.'

'Don't worry about that,' said Anastacia, placing her drink on the small shelf above the headboard. 'I'm sure we'll warm up.'

She turned her back to him.

'Will you unzip me?'

Harry delicately pulled the zip down her back and noted the absence of a bra strap. When he reached the bottom, Anastacia pulled it down over hips and let it fall to the floor. Then she turned to face Harry and took his hands in hers.

'Just relax.' Anastacia put his hands on her breasts and flicked her tongue in his ear. 'Just relax...'

Harry felt her hands sliding down his paunch, undoing the buttons of his waistcoat before slowly undoing his flies. For a moment, he experienced silent panic as he realised he wasn't hard. He cursed himself for drinking as much as he did. But the second she touched it, it reacted and by the time she had it out in the open he was fully erect. She looked knowingly into his eyes as she stroked him back and fore with her right hand. Harry massaged her breasts, a little too workmanlike at times, he thought.

'Just relax...'

Anastacia's left hand moved to the suspender belt where she pulled a small foil packet from under the strap. She let go of him and opened the packet, before deftly rolling the condom over his hard-on. The whole issue of protection hadn't crossed his mind up until that point. Again, he panicked, only for a second. He'd lost momentum before during the brief downtime of safe sex enforcement. *"Sorry, baby, I just don't like the texture of rubber, that's all..."*

But Anastacia was quick; the second it was on she had sunk to her knees and taken him to the back of her throat. He held on to her shoulders as his head began to feel fuzzy from the alcohol and when he turned his head up towards the ceiling light and shut his eyes, he thought he was going to topple over. He looked down at her, her head sliding back and forth. He was glad he'd prepared himself earlier. After a couple of minutes, she pulled away and looked up.

'Do you want me to carry on?'

'Hmm?'

'Do you want to come now or we have sex?'

'I don't mind really…'

She carried on for a little longer before standing up and unclipping her stockings from the suspender belt. She pulled off her lace knickers to reveal her hairless crotch. She saw him watching her.

'Take off your clothes,' she said, sitting herself down on the edge of the bed. Harry pulled at his clothes and cursed his socks as he launched them into the corner of the room. She took hold of his hard-on and pulled him down onto the bed so that he was sitting next to her. She took his hand and slid it up between her legs. He tentatively inched two fingers inside and she gently eased him back onto the bed. She straddled him and put him inside her. He watched her begin to bounce up and down, slowly but steadily. She placed her hands on his chest for support as she gradually increased speed. Her soft moans gradually became louder and louder still, finding keys with the buzzing in his ears. Harry's fingers crept along her waist and onto her arse, feeling the soft inlet at the top. He closed his eyes, the warm feeling of the alcohol wrapping itself around his head as she wrapped herself around him.

On the other side of the wall, Deborah Flaxman lay in bed, listening to the sound the girl was making at number 77. When it ceased, suddenly and without any notable increase in tempo, she smiled to herself, switched off the table lamp and rolled over into a deep, comfortable sleep.

6

Inspector Kibber emptied his glass of scotch and slid the glass away from him across the counter. The Cloisters had emptied slightly as a lot of the office wankers moved on elsewhere. He fumbled around in the pockets of the rain mac until he found what he was looking for.

The small velvet box contained a gold ring with a small solitaire diamond. He'd bought it not long after he'd fallen for Claudia. He balanced the ring carefully on the tip of his little finger and realised that his hands were shaking. Tomorrow he'd go to her apartment and make Claudia his forever.

'Another?' said the barmaid.

'Yeah, another,' said Kibber. He saw her clock the ring and quickly turn her eyes away from him. She gave him his seventh large scotch and he downed it, wiping his moustache. He put the ring back on its red silk bed and put the box away in his coat.

Tomorrow.

'Fuck tomorrow,' said Kibber and left the bar.

He parked the squad car on the street outside the door to Claudia's apartment and let himself in. At the top of the stairs, outside the second door, he straightened his tie and ran his hands through his greasy hair. He'd make her his forever and then he'd *make love* to her, proper sensitive and caring, like. He unlocked the second door and stepped into the pitch black apartment. He found the light switch on the wall next to the door and lit the room up. Closing the door quietly, he heard a stirring sound coming from the bedroom, followed by a sigh. He moved as silently as he could towards the open door and saw her sleeping figure stirring in the bank of light from the front room. He entered and crossed the lino to her side of the bed. Then he got on his knees and gently shook her shoulder.

'Claudia,' he said.

She stirred but didn't wake. He shook her again.

'Claudia,' he repeated louder.

'You're back.'

Kibber got to his feet and dragged back the duvet, throwing it onto the floor. The pale girl in the nightie who suddenly jerked up saw Kibber and screamed. Kibber saw red and lunged forward, placing a huge sweaty hand across her face to muffle her voice. Her eyes were wide with fear and as he grabbed her short, red hair he pulled her head close to his face.

'Where's Claudia?' he growled.

The girl was frozen in terror. She began to whimper and Kibber felt her nose running into his fingers.

'If you scream, I'll snap your fuckin' neck in two. Do you understand?'

He felt her try and nod in his grip. He removed his hand from her mouth and she barely moved.

'Where's Claudia?' he said.

'Out,' the girl whispered.

'I can see that you cunt. Where is she?'

'She's working--'

Kibber tightened his grip on her hair.

'Where?'

The girl started to say that she didn't know and Kibber gave her a swift backhander. He didn't let go of her red hair.

'What's your name, cunt?'

'Scottie.'

The girl brought a hand up to her raw cheek but Kibber slapped it away.

'What are you doing here?' he said.

'Nothing--'

Kibber dragged her by her hair off the bed and into the front room. He threw her onto the leather sofa and she huddled into a ball. He stood in the middle of the room, panting and sweating heavily.

'If she's out on a fuckin' job, you're gonna tell me where that fuckin' job is. Understand, cunt?'

The girl was shaking so much, he couldn't tell whether she was agreeing to his demand or not. He went into the kitchen and poured himself a scotch from the bottle on top of the fridge. He saw the two flute glasses and the empty sparkling wine bottle on the draining board. He also saw the note pinned under a fridge magnet depicting a tropical sunset. Written on it was a telephone number along with the words : *If you need me. Call you when I'm leaving. Put the chain on the door. Xxx.*

Kibber threw his glass and it smashed into the empty bottle. He heard sudden movement in the front room and walked in to see the girl was off the sofa and running for the door. He caught up with her as she got it open. He grabbed her by the neck and tried to restrain her, but she wrenched herself free and lost her balance, sending her first into the wall directly outside the flat and then toppling down the stairs, tumbling heavily until she hit the bottom and lay there motionless like a rag doll, face down with one arm pointing accusingly back up the stairs at him. One leg twitched at an awkward angle.

'Fuck,' said Kibber.

He went down the stairs and picked her up. He slung her over his shoulder and carried her back up to the flat, dumping her on to the leather sofa. Then he picked up the telephone.

'New Metropolitan Police Service, Vice Office.'

'This is Detective Inspector Kibber.'

'Hullo, sir. Danny Valour here.'

'Danny, I want the address for the phone number I'm going to give you.'

'Wake up, Harry,' said Anastacia.

The second Harry opened his eyes, he knew he hadn't come.

Anastacia was sitting on the end of the bed, dress on, fixing her hair. Harry saw he still had the condom on, melting like a little orange snowman on his navel.

'What time is it?' he said, sitting up on his elbows.

'Nearly midnight,' said Anastacia, standing up. 'I did try and wake you, Harry. Perhaps you shouldn't drink too much.'

'I'm sorry,' said Harry humbly. 'Why don't you stay the night and we can work something out?'

'Work something out?' she giggled. 'You say very strange things, Harry.'

She straightened her dress and Harry stood up and stretched.

'Look, I'm wide awake now.'

Anastacia gave him a peck on the cheek and squeezed his hand.

'Listen, Harry,' she said calmly, 'your father was a kind man. Kinder than most, really. But he was sad inside, deep down. You may not resemble him much in the flesh, but I see part of him there in you.'

'Did he used to fall asleep during all this too?'

She smiled.

'Perhaps I should be offended, Harry?'

'Please don't be. Look, seriously, why don't you stay? You can have the full eight. Just stay for a bit longer and let me make it up to you.'

Anastacia laughed, 'There's nothing to make up for, Harry. But you're very sweet. And still drunk, by the way.'

Harry trailed her down the stairs where she retrieved her coat and slipped it onto her shoulders.

'Would you mind if I called for a cab?'

'Alright.'

Harry watched her order the taxi and when she was done she turned and looked him over.

'You should perhaps think of taking that off,' she said, pointing at the condom he was still wearing. 'Unless you're planning on saving it for the next lucky lady of the night?'

Harry looked down and frowned. 'Maybe I'll hold on to it. Something to remember you by.'

Anastacia gave him a curious smile, as though unsure if he was being serious or not, before opening the front door.

'I'll wait for the cab outside.'

'Would it be alright if I called you again one day?'

She paused in the doorway.

'One day.'

Then she was gone, closing the front door softly behind her. Harry slumped down onto the stairs and let out a silent, heartfelt wail.

Kibber turned the steering wheel of the unmarked squad car into the street almost too late, very nearly colliding with the black cab that was heading towards him. The taxi swerved and beeped its horn as it passed.

'Fuck off!' yelled Kibber and parked up badly between two saloons. He switched the engine off and got out of the car. He walked along until he found number 77 Vancouver Hill. He stood at the head of the garden path, letting his rage stew inside him. Then, sufficiently angry enough, he marched up to the front door and rapped loudly upon it. He saw movement through the tiny pane of frosted glass and the door opened slowly. The man who presented himself was in his late thirties, out of shape and naked except for a condom which was hanging off a flaccid penis. He stank of booze and sex.

'Police,' said Kibber.

'What?'

'We've had reports of suspicious activity in the neighbourhood. Do you live at this property?'

'Police?'

'Answer the question.'

'Well, yes, but--'

'Mind if I come in?'

Kibber shoved past the naked man into the hallway and closed the door behind him. He looked him up and down in disgust while listening for anyone else in the house.

'Are you alone?'

'Yes.'

'You're quite sure of that?'

'Yes.'

'No one upstairs in any of the bedrooms?'

'Well, no--'

'Then may I ask why you're naked apart from a rubber contraceptive?'

'Oh, yeah. I was entertaining a lady--'

'So there is someone else here then.'

'No, she's just left actually.'

'Just left?'

'Caught a cab.'

Kibber considered this information. He walked into the living room and the man followed. Kibber positioned himself in front of the fireplace while the man sat on the arm of the sofa. Neither man spoke for a few uncomfortable moments.

'Look,' said the man, 'I don't know where all this is going--'

'Take the fuckin' johnny off,' barked Kibber.

The man jumped slightly, then pulled the condom off and, unsure what to do with it, draped it on the back of the sofa.

'What's your name?' said Kibber.

'Harry Brewer.'

'And you own this property do you?'

'Kind of.'

'What does that mean exactly?'

'I've just inherited from my dead parents.'

'Like I said,' continued Kibber, 'we've had reports of goings on in the neighbourhood. Hookers, pimping and soliciting, that type of carry on. Know anything about that?'

'Certainly not.'

'And this lady friend of yours that just left?'

'What about her?'

'Hooker?'

'Err, no…'

'I've got intelligence that suggests otherwise.'

'Okay she's a hooker. But seriously, it's not what you think--'

Kibber grabbed him and threw him face down on the sofa. He got on top of him and held his wrists while pressing his knee into his back.

'Now,' snarled Kibber, 'tell me what I think.'

'For Christ's sake, I didn't even bloody *come*!'

Kibber, bemused, relaxed his grip.

'You a bloody fruit or something?'

'What?'

'What kind of man screws a brass and doesn't even have the decency to come? Mind on other things was it?'

'No! I--'

'Or maybe women don't do it for you, eh? Maybe you're into something else, eh? You a *pretty boy*?'

'Pretty boy?'

'Or maybe you're into something else different again? We've been looking for this Albion Snatcher for a while now. I'm starting to think I've just found him.'

'Wait a second--'

Kibber produced his regulation handcuffs and snapped them onto his wrists.

'Get up!'

Kibber dragged him out of the house, down the path and over to the squad car. After throwing him into the boot he jumped in the driver's seat and sped off down the road.

Harry writhed uncomfortably in the enclosed space of the car boot, cursing several times as something underneath him kept rubbing against his exposed spinal column. The cop was driving like a fucking maniac and it was all he could do to brace his feet and shoulders against the sides of the car. After a while, he heard the noise of the city fade away outside and Harry's already fragile state of mind shattered completely all over the carpet of the boot. He was being taken into the wilderness, the backside of nowhere never to be seen or heard of again...

The engine stopped suddenly and Harry took another dig in the spine. A few moments passed before the boot sprung open and the policeman, reeking of booze, hoisted him out by his armpits and dropped him onto damp grass. Harry struggled to his knees and the first thing he saw was the distant skyline and the Telecom Tower. They were on Hampstead Heath.

'Time to get things out in the open,' said the Inspector, taking a drink from a hip flask.

'What are you planning on doing to me?' Harry blurted. Since they were getting things out in the open.

The Inspector reached into the boot of the car and pulled out a white paper body suit.

'I'm going to remove your handcuffs,' said the Inspector, waving a key between his thumb and forefinger. 'If you try and run, I promise that you won't get very far.'

The handcuffs came off and although he considered making a break for it, Harry knew that he was in no shape to get very far. The Inspector threw the suit at him and told him to put it on. It was cold and coarse, but at least he was covered up now. He could smell the drink on the Inspector, alcoholic radiation that made Harry's mouth water. He also desperately craved a cigarette, but based on the evidence so far, it appeared that he'd had his collar felt by the only non smoking psychopathic policeman in the entire New Metropolitan Service.

'You scared?' said the Inspector.

'Yes,' replied Harry. 'I'm also quite thirsty. You wouldn't have anything to drink by any chance?'

'Why yes,' said the Inspector. 'Matter of fact, I have a magnum of champagne in the fuckin' glove box.'

The Inspector shoved Harry hard in the chest causing him to fall back heavily into the back of the car. Harry let out a groan as the Inspector placed his jaw in a tight grip of the hand.

'People like you think you can swan about sticking your pricks in anything you fuckin' fancy, don't you, eh? What's the matter, not enough slags floating about the West End for you, eh?'

'I didn't think that much of it really,' said Harry through the Inspector's fingers, who promptly released his grip and dropped him back on the grass. He heard the unscrewing of the hip flask and the Inspector taking a long pull from it. Harry shifted his position on the grass so that he could rest his head against the number plate. The Inspector got down and rested on his haunches.

'Would you say you were a religious individual, Mister Brewer?'

'Not especially, Inspector.'

'Don't believe in God then?'

'God?' shrugged Harry. 'Not especially.'

'Probably just as well. God's got fuck all business in a city like this.'

Harry looked beyond his tormentor and down the hill at the shimmering artificial skyline, quiet and malevolent, wrapped tightly in it's sea green scarf of bad air. The psycho had a point, he conceded. He remembered the fall from grace of the Anglican churches; first the money-grubbing synods had signed the deal making Gemstone Events the official sponsor of Christian religious festivals and occasions. The epidemically proportioned multi media corporation had then got its feet in so far under the lectern that it now had a say in church policy, all for a nominal fee.

'What do you believe in?' said Harry.

The Inspector let out a heavy sigh and placed a finger on his heavy moustache.

'I suppose I should believe in right and wrong. I am the good and the fuckin' just and you are the bad. The *shit*. It should be my duty to make people like you more like me. Rehabilitation after a suitable period of punishment.'

'*Should?*'

'The government's New Directives are what everything is about, aren't they? The new toughened fabric that holds society in check. No more slapped wrists and naughty steps for the wicked no more, eh? Not with the return of the maximum penalty.'

'The people voted for it, Inspector,' said Harry, who had voted for it.

'They did,' said the Inspector. 'And now see how you all protest.'

Harry hadn't protested.

'Well,' the Inspector continued, 'we'll see how

much the fuckin' liberal fags protest when I bring in the Albion Snatcher.'

The Inspector flashed a knowing look at Harry and Harry felt his sphincter twitch.

'Wait!'

The Inspector exposed his coffee coloured teeth in a nasty gurn of a smile.

'What's the matter? You want to make a confession? I've got my notebook and pencil in my pocket. You can start at the very beginning with the first child. You do remember her name, don't you?'

'I'm not the Albion Snatcher,' said Harry. He realised his weak protest came across so unconvincing that he had to tell himself he wasn't the Albion Snatcher just to be sure.

'Her name was Melody Robbins. She was eight years old.'

'I don't remember.'

'You don't remember? What, you didn't keep any trophies? I suppose seeing as she was the first, it might not have occurred to you. I reckon you made up for it on the next ones though, eh?'

'What next ones?' said Harry, acutely aware that he just might evacuate his bowels at any moment as the psycho began to slowly pace back and fore, his heavy, unpolished boots treading heavily into the wet grass, flattening it into mud.

'The girl who you say was in your house.'

'What about her?'

'What was her name?'

Harry thought about her suddenly. Would he be betraying her if he gave the policeman her name? Was it even her name anyway?

'She called herself Anastacia.'

The Inspector stopped pacing and threw Harry a suspicious, sideways glance.

'Anastasia?'

'Anastacia. With a "c".'

'How do you know she spells it with a "c"?'

'I saw it printed on a business card--'

Harry tried to stop himself but then decided if he was going down then he may as well take his father's reputation down with him.

'Where was it, this business card?'

'In a diary belonging to my father.'

'Hmm,' said the Inspector, nodding his head slowly in understanding.

'So you see, Inspector,' said Harry, 'I saw the name and number of this Anastacia and decided I felt like a bit. I know it's all illegal and punishable but in my defence there are mitigating circumstances that must be taken into consideration.'

'Really.'

'Yes,' said Harry, committing himself to the punt. 'I've recently lost both my mother and my father in a plane crash on the South American continent. My head's fucked, Inspector. If truth be known, I'm so *fucked* that I couldn't even properly *fuck* her.'

The Inspector's eyebrows raised and he knelt in close to Harry's face.

'What do you *mean*?'

Harry tried to swallow but his throat was too dry.

'Well, what I mean is that I fell asleep. I didn't cross the finish line, so to speak.'

The Inspector stared blankly at him for a moment or two. Harry felt like closing his eyes. He was finding it very hard to keep an eye out for a clenched fist coming his way *and* to make sure he didn't shit himself. The Inspector's face broke out in a big, ugly grin, his unkempt moustache extending like an exercising slug. He got to his feet and, with his back to Harry, let out a throaty roar of laughter into the night. Harry struggled to his feet, his legs having gone numb in the chill and the damp. He rested himself against the boot of the car.

'Well, well, well,' said the Inspector as he approached Harry. 'You really are a useless, pathetic little shit, aren't you?'

'You wouldn't be the first to address me like that, Inspector,' said Harry, shivering against the cold paintwork.

'I'll bet,' said the Inspector. 'Well, on behalf of the New Metropolitan Police Service, I would like to thank you for assisting us with our ongoing investigation into the Albion Snatcher.'

Harry frowned at the Inspector's sudden change of direction.

'I'm not under arrest?'

'I'm going to let you off with a caution,' said the Inspector sternly. 'And I advise you to take it.'

'Alright,' said Harry weakly.

'Stay away from the brasses, Mister Brewer. Some of the most powerful people in the world have lost everything for the sake of getting their ends away. Be good.'

'I will, Inspector.'

Harry felt the bile rising in his throat, an acidic burning sensation. The Inspector took the hood of the paper suit in his grip and made Harry stand up straight.

'I hope you're not thinking of puking all over this beautiful squad car.'

'No, Inspector.'

'Good boy.'

The Inspector straightened out the paper suit. Harry tried to smile gratefully. Then the Inspector got in the car and started the engine. Harry went to open the rear passenger door but by the second his fingertips touched the silver door handle, the squad car was roaring away down Hampstead Heath hill. Harry stood there for a while until the sound of the engine melted into the ambience of the city below. Then he double up and was violently sick all over the muddy grass.

Claudia reached Concertina Street and put her key in the lock. She silently cursed Scottie for not taking any notice of her note about locking the door properly. She let herself in and as she made her way up the stairs she experienced the sensation that not all things here were well. She got to the second door and her hand began to shake as she turned the key first, then the handle.

She found Scottie dumped on the leather sofa as though she'd been dropped there from a great height. There was blood on the sofa and on Scottie's face and a web of coughed up mucus hung from her mouth, stretching down her throat onto her nightie. Bruising had started to form around the eyes and the left side of her head. Claudia, on the brink of losing all control, clutched Scottie's face carefully and spoke her name several times without receiving any response.

'Emergency Hotline, please state your preferred department.'

'Ambulance please.'

'Location please.'

'93 Concertina Street WC1.'

'Redirecting you to Gemergency Metropolitan Resources. Hold please.'

Claudia cradled Scottie's head in her lap as the latest chart topper played down the phone.

'Gemergency Metropolitan Resources. You're through to Miranda.'

'Please send an ambulance,' said Claudia, pensively stroking Scottie's short red hair. The phone conversation had already begun to dissipate her hope.

'What is the nature of the emergency?'

'My partner has been attacked. She has an injury to the head.'

'Is your partner conscious?'

'No, I don't think so.'

'An ambulance will be despatched to you as soon as possible. I would just like to do an assessment first.'

'Please hurry.'

'Is your location situated on a busy high street or quiet residential area?'

'The first one.'

'Ground floor, first floor or higher?'

'First.'

'Any pets?'

'No.'

'Any minors, that is, anyone below independent age?'

'No.'

'Any slippery surfaces?'

'No.'

'Any wet surfaces anywhere in the property?'

'No.'

'Is the property currently on fire?'

'No.'

'Thank you. An ambulance is being despatched to 93 Concertina Street, WC1. Estimated time of arrival is thirteen minutes. Please be aware that Gemergency Metropolitan Resources reserves the right to cancel or alter service as stipulated in our Customer Care Handbook.'

The line went dead and Claudia sat in silence, holding the motionless figure of Scottie close to her and silently wishing she could remember how to cry.

7

Special News Update: *At nine o'clock this morning, a press conference was held at the Associated Press Lounge of the New Metropolitan Police Service as part of the ongoing investigation into the disappearance of missing schoolgirl, Patience Sweetlove. The seven year old has not been seen for several days and is widely believed to have become the fourth victim of the Albion Snatcher. Seated at the top table were Patience's parents, Jackie and Mitch. Both appeared distressed. Seated either side of the duo were several high ranking officers and officials from the New Metropolitan Police Service :- Chief Superintendant Annabelle Stoking, sporting standard issue two-piece uniform; Assistant Commissioner Irvin Brownstone; Deputy Chief of Public Relations Brian O'Toole, who last year received the Media's Choice Award for Best Liaising In A Crisis; Detective Chief Inspector Marion Hood, a firm favourite amongst the Pro-Death Penalty campaigner; and Detective Inspector Charlton Huddlestone-Hughes, ahead of the pack to succeed Chief Superintendant Stoking should the tumour make a sudden return. During the press conference, Mrs. Sweetlove appeared stoic and at times seemingly unmoved by the proceedings. Mr. Sweetlove spoke when asked direct questions from members of the press gallery, but otherwise the principle dialogue came from Chief Superintendant Stoking and colleagues. Everyone at the conference was in agreement that the media coverage thus far had been proportionate to other news coverage. Mr. O'Toole stressed the importance of keeping the* *moniker "Albion Snatcher" in the public eye, stating that it was in the public historical interest to distinguish the perpetrator from other similar offenders of recent years. He also maintained that the proposed negotiations for the subsequent telemovie would help to keep the investigations in the public consciousness. It was during his speech that Mrs. Sweetlove visibly cracked. She was assisted by an unnamed WPC, who provided her with a glass of iced tea.*

Ursula Gwynne checked her make up in the gold compact that her husband had given her on their second anniversary all those years previously. She had made herself up just the way Allen wanted. The exacting nature of his tastes suggested to her that she should remind him of someone. She knew about Barbara, although not from Allen himself. That information came courtesy of Iain. Poor Barbara, thought Ursula.

'Just here, driver.'

The black cab pulled up alongside another car and Ursula stepped onto the pavement just as she felt the first spots of rain in the air. She looked up at the window to Allen's study and smiled to herself.

The front door buzzed open within seconds of her pressing the button to his flat and when she reached his study, she found him pacing up and down, cigarette in one hand and a large brandy in the other. He looked like he'd been drinking for a while.

'You should open a window, darling,' said Ursula, placing her handbag and coat on the hat stand by the door.

Allen Wyngarde stubbed out his cigarette and finished his drink. He hadn't been sleeping or shaving by the looks of things. He crossed the room and threw his arms around her in an overzealous bear hug.

'Darling,' said Ursula, trying to prize herself from his grip.

'Don't say anything for a moment,' said Allen, resisting her attempts to break their bond.

'What's wrong with you today?'

'I'm a deeply troubled man.'

'So I see. But I'm here now, darling and I don't really want to waste time exchanging this sort of affection with you.'

Allen sighed and relinquished his grip on her. He poured them both a brandy and lit himself another cigarette. She watched him slump into his chair at the desk. She sipped her brandy before sidling over to him. He watched as she hitched up her skirt and straddled him on the chair.

'Want to talk about whatever it is that's bothering you?'

'I'm not sure,' replied Allen.

'What does that mean?'

'I'm in a bit of a quandary, Ursula.'

'A quandary?'

Christ, thought Allen, she makes the word "quandary" sound positively filthy.

'Yes,' he said as she began to kiss his neck. 'It's about your husband, actually.'

Ursula stopped kissing and looked him in the face.

'Iain?'

'Yes.'

'Darling, you know the score. We don't talk about my husband while we're having sex.'

'It's not that easy, Ursula. He's given me something.'

'*I* want to give you something…'

'He's given me a manuscript.'

Ursula gave him a bewildered look, 'So bloody what? He's a writer.'

'He's a *playwright*, Ursula. There's a difference. What he's given me is a manuscript for a *novel*.'

'Again, Allen: So Bloody What?'

'I'm too frightened to open it. I'm too apprehensive about what may lie within those pages.'

'I can cure you of all your apprehension, Allen,' purred Ursula. She locked her forearms behind his neck and began nibbling at his cheek.

'Ursula…'

'Uh-huh…'

'Do you know what Iain's manuscript might be about?'

'Why would I know…?'

'He's your husband.'

Ursula stopped nibbling and looked squarely at Allen.

'And *you're* my lover,' she said calmly, 'in case you'd bloody forgotten.'

'I'm sorry,' sighed Allen, 'let's have a drink. It might loosen me up a little bit.'

Ursula's lips split into a naughty grin.

'I've got something far better than alcohol.'

She jumped off Allen's lap and retrieved a little white bottle of yellow pills. She returned to her place on Allen's lap and held one between thumb and forefinger.

'Stick out your tongue, darling.'

'I'm not sure about this, Ursula,' said Allen. 'All these strange narcotics you bring with you, they do funny things to me.'

Ursula laughed and squeezed the pill between his lips and put a hand over his mouth.

'You silly old fool,' she said. 'They're supposed to do funny things to you. Now be a good soldier and swallow it for me. Then we can start to have some good, hard dirty fun while we still have the time.'

Allen swallowed the pill and tilted his head back as he unbuttoned his shirt. He could see Ursula, in his peripheral vision, twirling around his study, hands in the air. She'd put some music on and was asking him to get up and dance. He pushed himself to his feet, trying to flick his shoes off at the same time. Ursula had a drink in her hand and he tried to take it off her but she held it above her head. He put his hands on her breasts and she turned around, rubbing her backside up against his crotch and he wrapped his arms around her waist, slowly kissing her neck. She told him to take his trousers off and he fumbled with the belt, telling himself he would move onto braces any day now. He sat on the floor and negotiated the trousers over his knees and feet. Then he lay back and he felt Ursula climb onto him, shrouding him, clouding him, urging him forever on.

'Maybe I shouldn't take any more of your magic pills, Ursula,' said Allen.

It was three hours later and he was curled up on the small sofa in his study while Ursula straightened her dress and fixed her hair by the window.

'Darling, you were insatiable,' she said.

'Really?' said Allen, it was all still a bit vague as far as he was concerned. 'I wasn't, you know, too rough or forceful was I?'

Ursula finished with her appearance and walked over to him. She sat next to him and kissed him lightly on the lips.

'Darling, you were exactly as I wanted you to be.'

Allen smiled at her and she stood up, checking her handbag.

'I have to go,' she said. 'Can you take care of that?'

She was referring to the used condom wrapped up in tissue on the little table next to the sofa. She always left it to him.

'Stay for a drink,' said Allen lazily.

'Iain's not at the club tonight.'

'Give him my regards,' said Allen.

'Funny,' said Ursula.

Allen watched Ursula from the study window as she passed between the parked cars lined up along the kerb below and made her way up towards Uxbridge Road. He poured himself a drink but he could only sip it. Allen didn't know where Ursula got hold of these recreational drugs and he didn't want to know. It had never been a big thing for him, not like alcohol and tobacco, but when Ursula had walked into his life he'd allowed himself to be opened up to many different feelings and impulses. His life with Barbara had been safe, solid, loving, unexciting. It broke his heart to think of his life with her on those terms but it was an inconsolable truth.

He pulled out Iain Gwynne's manuscript and set it on the desk, next to his own. Then he took a deep breath, downed his drink and passed out.

8

Harry's entire body was screaming at him to wake up and eventually he did. He ached in ways that almost made him want to cry the second he opened his eyes. He was stiff, sore, chafed and shivering. He slowly sat up and realised he'd collapsed onto the living room sofa when he finally managed to return home from Hampstead Heath. He'd walked the entire way, avoiding members of the human race wherever possible, enduring their stares and jeers when forced into their vicinity. At least that psycho had let him keep the paper suit, for all the credibility it gave him. It had got torn near Mill Hill Broadway when a couple of drunks had started on him, tearing the suit down the front, exposing his paunch. He'd managed to slip free and run faster than he thought possible. His bare feet felt black and mangled and he suddenly considered the fact that he might need to go for tetanus. Then he remembered climbing over the garden wall down the left side of the house and retrieving the spare key hidden in the water of the bird bath in the back garden. He remembered gazing up at the house next door, wondering what the gorgeous woman was doing while he was standing in the middle of the garden at nearly three in the morning, semi naked and semi torn. He remembered having another drink and, frustrated by his failure to perform with Anastacia, had embarked upon a solo session only to pass out soon after.

Harry poured himself three pints of ice cold water from the kitchen tap and took himself up the stairs to the bathroom where he poured himself into the shower for ninety minutes, trying to wash the shame and embarrassment from his body. At the end of it, he still felt damaged and unclean. His feet throbbed and smarted, his wrists had thick red rings around them where the cop's handcuffs had rubbed away the first layers of skin. What was it the Inspector had told him? *Be good.* Be good? Harry allowed himself a shivery laugh as he delicately dabbed himself with the bath towel. He wondered whether he should phone the police and complain. But what did he remember? He didn't remember the name; the car he was driving wasn't a regulation police car. What if he wasn't even a policeman in the first place? Harry shuddered as he spooked himself with the thought that he might very well have had a narrower escape than he'd first realised, up there on Hampstead Heath, just the two of them.

He dressed in dark brown trousers, deep purple v-neck and white shirt, then he took a strong cup of coffee upstairs onto the roof, along with the thick cushioned footstool from the living room. The sun was remarkably bright for the season and not at all cold. In fact, there seemed to be a slightly warm current flowing in the air that late afternoon. Harry placed the footstool up against the chimney brickwork and sat himself down on it; sipping his black coffee and listening to the breeze thread its way through the trees in the gardens below. He let his eyelids drop as the sun rolled through the clouds and drove some of the chill from his body. He wanted to drift off but it wouldn't happen and he knew it. Lazily, he dragged himself across the roof towards the ledge and lay flat on his stomach with his arms supporting his head so that he could see into the garden next door. The garden was a serene vision of plants, flowers and pathways. A small tortoise shell cat sniffed around one of the large ceramic plant pots, rubbing itself up against the side before wandering onto the grass and lying down flat. There was no sign of her.

'You're looking in the wrong place.'

The voice made Harry jump. He turned to his left and there he saw the lady from next door. She was lying back on a sun lounger just behind her own chimney stack, again wearing nothing but her large floppy sun hat and sunglasses. An opened newspaper was draped over her midriff. She raised a glass of iced tea and smiled.

Harry shifted so that he was sitting on the low ledge.

'How do you know I was looking?'

The woman sipped her ice tea and placed the glass on the floor beside the sun lounger. Harry watched as she stood up and folded the newspaper neatly under her arm.

'I think I've found your cat,' he said.

'The tortie?'

Harry nodded.

'She's not mine. Sara's a black cat.'

'Sorry.'

'You look terrible,' she said, placing one hand on her hip. Harry tried but he couldn't take his eyes off her. She was a different kind of beautiful to Anastacia; fuller in figure, less groomed and cultivated and one hundred per cent natural.

'Yeah, well,' he said, struggling to get to his feet, 'I had a rough night.'

'I can only imagine.' She held out her hand. 'My

name's Deborah.'

Harry stepped forward and shook it, 'Mine's Harry. Did you know my parents?'

Deborah let go of his hand and tilted her sun hat back a little.

'Yes, kind of. They seemed like nice people.'

'Yes,' said Harry, 'a lot of people said that about them.'

Deborah studied the worn out figure standing awkwardly before her.

'Harry?'

'Yes?'

'Have you had breakfast?'

Harry hadn't eaten French toast since he was a child, on a weekend break somewhere tepid and impersonal, with his parents and an obscure aunt and uncle who he never laid eyes on again. It tasted brittle in his mouth and he loosened it with the remains of the coffee he had brought down from the roof terrace. He ate at the large square breakfast bar in the centre of the kitchen while Deborah looked on from the window. She had altered her wardrobe by forsaking the sun hat and shades for a long white blouse and a pair of sandals. She stood, leaning casually against the dishwasher the other side of the breakfast bar, silently watching him eat. Harry pushed the plate of dark crumbs slightly away from him.

'Thanks for that,' he said.

'You're welcome,' said Deborah. 'You really don't look healthy. Do you feel ill?'

'No,' replied Harry, wishing he could lie down, 'not really. It was just one hell of an evening last night.'

'You had company?' she said. Harry somehow detected a knowing twinkle in her eye. Had she spied on him like he had spied on her?

'A friend,' he said, 'a lady friend. She didn't stay. And then I went out. With another friend.'

'What do you do, Harry?'

'*Do*? You mean, as in work?'

'That's right, Harry,' said Deborah, picking up his plate and slipping it in the dishwasher.

'It's complicated.'

Deborah faced him and considered the slightly strange, probably screwed up individual sitting in her kitchen. He had that quietly bubbling inner torment about him, as though any moment now he would either burst into tears or make an ill-executed pass at her.

'Does that mean you don't want to talk about it?'

'You don't mind?'

Deborah shook her head.

'What about you?' said Harry.

'I'm a freelance journalist.'

'That sounds great,' said Harry cheerfully.

'It can be,' said Deborah, 'when it pays. The trouble is, there's not much to write about these days that is worth someone else's time reading. Not in this city anyway.'

'Oh, I don't know,' said Harry as he stood up to stretch his stiffening legs.

'Really?' said Deborah. 'You think there's plenty more fascinating stuff to titillate the public, do you?'

'There must be.'

'Tell me then.'

Harry saw Deborah's eyes narrow and her features

melted into a challenging expression.

'Alright,' he said, sealing his mouth with his index finger for a moment and pacing the floor in a narrow circle. Deborah watched him, waiting for him to surprise her. Then he stopped and clicked his fingers: 'The missing girl!'

'The missing girl,' repeated Deborah. 'You mean Patience Sweetlove?'

'Yes,' said Harry, 'that's right. She is still missing isn't she?'

'As far as I am aware, yes.'

'Well, there you go. That's something to write about. The missing girl, Patience Sweetlove.'

'She's already being covered by our wonderful media.'

'So?'

'There's no new angle there, Harry. Try again.'

'The Albion Snatcher?'

'The Albion Snatcher?'

'The one who's taken the missing girl.'

'How do you know the Albion Snatcher took Patience Sweetlove?'

'Well, he must have done. It makes sense, doesn't it?'

'Have you got inside information, Harry?'

'What do you mean?'

Deborah's eyes narrowed, 'Are you the Albion Snatcher, Harry?'

Harry suddenly felt very uncomfortable. He fiddled with his collar.

'Don't be ridiculous.'

'Oh look,' smiled Deborah, 'I've made you go all red. I was only joking, Harry.'

'Yeah, I know,' said Harry, slipping his hands into his pockets to give them something to do. 'She'll turn up, that Patience, anyway.'

'And the New Metropolitans will catch the Albion Snatcher and hang him from Westminster Bridge,' said Deborah, pouring herself a glass of filtered water. Harry picked up on the sarcastic tone.

'I take it you don't agree with capital punishment then?'

'Ah,' said Deborah, 'so you *do*.'

'Yes,' he replied, 'I suppose I do.'

'You *suppose* you do? What kind of a wishy washy stance is that to take, especially over something so serious?'

'Okay, I do.'

'Do you know for definite that the condemned men and women are guilty? Or do you just *suppose* they are? I *suppose* you haven't really given the matter a great deal of thought, Harry. I *suppose* you're quite at home floating on top of the logs drifting downstream. Am I right?'

Harry blanched, didn't quite know how to react.

'Sorry,' he said, 'where has all this sudden aggression sprung from?'

Deborah came over to him and placed her hands firmly on his shoulders.

'Harry, it's not aggression. It truly isn't. You really don't like being challenged, do you?'

'No,' said Harry.

'Oh, Harry, open your eyes and let your soul see the sunlight!'

'My eyes are wide open, Deborah,' said Harry defensively.

'Yes, but their staring into the dark, into *nothing*.'

'I get by, as there's *nothing* in my way.'

Deborah's smile faded and her hands slipped down to her sides. She sighed and left him alone in the kitchen with nothing but the smell of cold coffee on his breath. He heard her pottering around upstairs and, understanding that it wasn't a spur for him to make an advance on her; he went through to the living room. Along the whole one wall that backed onto his next door there were shelves from floor to ceiling; books, magazines, journals, scrapbooks. Harry worked his way along them, running a finger across the uneven spines. His attention was grabbed by one large, homemade edition. *"Press Cuttings."* Inside, he found clippings from newspapers or magazines all written by Debbie Flaxman, apart from the odd one where she was joined by someone called Trent Seether. The clippings were mainly music reviews with the odd essay thrown in for good measure. Harry didn't commit himself to reading any one piece in its entirety; for him music had always been a passing distraction, something other people took care of while he drank or fornicated. Deborah Flaxman, music journalist. As he turned one page over, a small card, about the size of a regular photograph, slipped out and landed on the carpet between his feet. The Kommune Club: *"Where Music Survives"*. That's all that was on it.

Harry heard running water and went to the foot of the stairs. A door closed heavily beyond the corner of the half landing and he put a foot on the first step.

'Deborah?'

There was no reply, but he could hear her in the

shower. He went up to the half landing, listening to her half singing to herself in a slight, high tone.

'Deborah?'

'What is it?' came the reply. She didn't sound angry that he had made his way up her stairs uninvited. But then again, she didn't sound overjoyed either. Harry decided to stay on the half landing.

'I was just wondering,' he said politely, 'what's the Kommune Club?'

'The Kommune Club,' said Deborah as she sat on the sofa, rigorously drying her hair with a towel, 'is a private venue where lovers of music gather. Ostensibly, it's a refuge where like minded people go to escape the soul-less.'

'The soul-less?'

'You must have heard of Gregory Gem.'

'Everyone's heard of him,' said Harry.

'That's part of the problem,' said Deborah, folding away the towel and dragging a reluctant brush through her locks. 'Everyone's heard of Gregory gem because there's *nowhere* on this planet to hide from Gregory Gem. His influence is felt in everything from pop music through to space exploration. It makes me want to puke.'

'So he's a successful businessman who's got a lot of fingers in a lot of pies,' said Harry, crossing one leg over the other on the ergonomically-tested chair opposite. 'If he puts money into things, what's the big deal? Mind if I smoke?'

'Yes,' said Deborah. 'The big deal, Harry, is what he gets in return for all his money.'

'What does he do?' asked Harry, longing for a

nicotine rush.

'He buys power and influence,' sighed Deborah. For the first time, a genuinely melancholic expression passed like a shadow across her features. She pulled her dressing gown tight around her as though shielding her person from something threatening in the room. It gave Harry a chill.

'Power to do what?' he asked. 'And influence over whom?'

Deborah slowly turned her head and looked into Harry's eyes:

'Anything and everybody.'

'Come off it,' said Harry, 'nobody has that much power and influence, Deborah. Not even North American presidents.'

'North American presidents are front of house,' said Deborah, tying her hair back, 'they don't stay behind the scenes, greasing palms and plotting coups. World leaders are figureheads, Harry. Or do you buy into the common thread like everyone else?'

'I make my own way on my own assumptions,' said Harry.

'That's part of the problem - *assumptions*. You assume too much, Harry. Like you probably assumed that, just because I let you ogle me while I was in my own garden naked, it means that at some point I might let you talk me into bed.'

'I never assumed that,' said Harry, even though he probably had. 'And anyway, isn't that an assumption about me?'

'It's a conclusion based on the evidence presented to me over the last couple of days.'

Harry decided he didn't want to talk about his

private thoughts on Deborah.

'You know, it sounds to me like you've got something deeply personal against Gregory Gem. Don't tell me; he's actually your father.'

'Don't be so bloody stupid,' said Deborah. She got up and went into the kitchen. Harry listened to her pouring more coffee. When she returned she handed him a cup and sat back down, lost in uncomfortable thoughts.

'Then what's your issue with him?' said Harry.

'My career,' said Deborah, 'or lack thereof.'

'How's that?'

'A few of us could see the way things were going in music. Every single, every "artist", every television programme, radio station and publication were gradually being geared in his favour. There's always been manufactured pop, of course there has. But nothing like this. It became as though you weren't experiencing anything, weren't *feeling* anything anymore. Like being tapped in an elevator that just goes up and down, up and down, up and down all day with that terrible, hopeless *muzak* continuously playing out of the tiny hidden speakers. Only it wasn't just music; TV, films, fundraising, research, medicine, public services, sport, food and drink, religion...everything, at some level no matter how visible or well hidden, has his influence in it.' She paused to sip her coffee so Harry did the same. 'I tried looking into it, tried playing at being a great investigative journalist and not just some teeth and tits bubblegum reporter. I guess I asked the wrong questions in the wrong ears as soon after that I got fired and never worked as a full time journalist again.

Now I eke out my living doing freelance reports on whatever I can get.'

'Do you regret it?' asked Harry.

'The investigating?'

Harry nodded.

'Never,' she replied steadfastly. '*I* know. There are others that also know. And so long as I'm not alone, I'll always know that I was right to try and do what I did.'

They drank in silence for a while. Then Deborah placed her cup on the floor and stood.

'Maybe I'll take you to the Kommune Club one night,' she said.

'Thanks,' said Harry, 'that'd be great.'

'Right now,' she said with a pleasant smile, 'I must ask you to leave.

9

No matter how hard she tried, Claudia could not block out the persistent "beep-beep" noise coming from the monitoring equipment that harnessed Scottie in its grip. The comatose redhead lay inert in a thin white smock; a pale terminal for tubes, wires, electrodes, masks and rubber patches. Claudia didn't know what a lot of it meant, only that they should be working harder to save her true love's life.

She was tormented by the images she conjured up in her mind; the struggle in the apartment, the assailant forcing himself on her, the severe beating and the fleeing from the scene of the crime. The vengeful nature of her people was always rising up from within her and she was finding it a constant struggle to keep it in check. She so very dearly wanted to meet this unknown attacker face to face to maim him, to drag it out.

The professionals knew nothing at this stage of course; they'd have a better picture to paint her later, after the thousandth obligatory corporate sponsored test. Claudia had heard stories about patients vanishing in places like St Marcus's Hospital. Acquaintances in The Profession had had other acquaintances that came in to one of these places to get checked out or stitched back up and simply disappeared. It made Claudia shiver and rub her bared arms. She still wore the dress she'd had on at George Brewer's house. She never thought she'd end up there again. While his son had been out cold on the bed, she'd had a look around just out of curiosity. Everything looked exactly the same and she even contemplated taking a quick tour of the roof terrace, just for old time's sake. It was on that roof terrace one humid summer night that George Brewer had insisted on doing his "*A-Levels*". Claudia recalled feeling as though somebody was watching them the whole time they were up there.

The intermittent "beep-beep" brought her back into the room, back to Scottie's side. Claudia felt the guilt returning, the guilt at having left her delicate flower alone to sleep in that horrible apartment. Why now, she asked herself, why now when we were so close to getting away from it all?

Claudia delicately took Scottie's upturned hand in hers and gently squeezed it, as though reassuring her lover that she'd be alright in the end. There was no return squeeze of "I know", of course, not like when Scottie had needed reassuring in the past. Claudia kissed Scottie's fingers and turned her head to rest her cheek there. The room lost its focus as she allowed her eyes to slowly close, blocking out the cold, clinical sterility of the environment. This wasn't a place for her, for them. This was a place of bad endings and messy exits, not happy resolutions and promising dawns. Claudia tried to sleep, as if doing so would bring her in tune with Scottie.

Interplanetary Terrestrial HQ, Greenwich (X 11 Clearance)
-"_ts___he_l___chr_"-
'Another partial, Ma'm!'
'Can you clear it up?'
'It's very faint.'
'Is it possible to identify the voice?'
-"_____res_h___"-

'It's female, Ma'm.'
'Probably Captain Blanchard, Ma'm.'
'Thank you, Walter.'
'Ma'm!'
'Yes, Adina?'
'We've drawn up a list of possible actions the North Angel may have taken-'
'And?'
'Well, Ma'm, based on the altering strengths of the signals and interference we've been receiving, we're pretty sure the North Angel has turned herself around.'
'So you're telling me the North Angel is on a return course?'
'We think so, Ma'm.'
'Well, that is irregular, don't you think? If your theory is correct, then our Captain Blanchard is ignoring protocol.'
'Yes, Ma'm. But maybe-'
'Be quiet, Adina.'
-"ff_____esth__gra____ssss___sca__d__"-
'Walter?'
'Slightly stronger, Ma'm. Still not much to go on.'
'Give it to Signal Analysis.'
'Yes, Ma'm.'
'Well, don't just sit there keeping your balls warm.'
'On my way, Ma'm.'
'Adina.'
'Ma'm?'
'Get me Director on my direct line.'
'At once, Ma'm.'

10

When Harry answered the door later that evening, he was surprised to see Deborah Flaxman waiting patiently on the doorstep. She was dressed in tight black jeans, heels and an oversized sweater under a short black leather jacket. Her hair was tied up behind her head. She looked him up and down. Since returning home from hers earlier he'd done precious little besides sBrewer down to a tee shirt and jogging bottoms, drink two bottles of shiraz and empty his balls half a dozen times.

'You've got ten minutes,' said Deborah, stepping into the hallway.

'Until what?' asked Harry as he closed the front door.

'Until I go to the Kommune Club without you. Can you at least try and make yourself presentable in that time?'

'You're serious?'

Deborah play acted looking at consulting her imaginary wristwatch.

'Okay,' sighed Harry, 'give me a minute.'

'I'll give you nine,' said Deborah.

Harry tramped upstairs and pulled an unpressed black suit on over an off-white shirt. He was just at that point when one more bottle of wine would have seen him nicely on his way, at least until the uncomfortable chill of the witching hour. Now he was about to paint the town red, or something.

'Very cool,' said Deborah as Harry came down the stairs. He paused to check he had the essentials; wallet, keys and cigarettes.

'Have we got time for a quick snifter before we go?' he said. 'I've got a lovely shiraz on the go.'

'No, Harry,' said Deborah. 'Now let's go.'

'Okay,' sighed Harry.

'And cheer up,' said Deborah, squeezing his arm, 'you never know; tonight might just change your life.'

Harry saw that Deborah already had a black cab waiting out on the street and she told the driver to take them to Spirit Street. They said nothing as they sat there in the back of the cab. Deborah sat quietly, looking out of her side. Harry played with his keys in his trouser pocket, feeling like he wasn't going anywhere on his own terms. He'd never liked being railroaded, shanghaied, steamrolled or coerced into doing things, even if he did actually want to do them. He balanced it out by telling himself he should probably be grateful that some people took the time to include him in their plans. After all, he didn't really have a plan of his own.

'Can you pull over here?' Deborah called out, reaching inside her leather coat and producing a solid looking brown purse. She paid the driver and we stepped out onto the pavement. There was a doorway to an unadvertised downstairs bar directly across the street and Harry stood and stared at it for a few moments before its tractor beam locked on to him and started pulling him slowly but steadily towards it.

As they descended the stairs, Harry could instantly feel the heat, hear the music and taste the sweat. They reached the bottom and Harry found himself in a large rectangular room with a bar running along the far side. The place was about three quarters full and he suddenly caught Deborah checking his reaction. She gave him a wink and he smiled. Then he followed her to the bar.

Harry seated himself on a stool, while Deborah was greeted by a barman who he heard her call Rick. The music was just the right volume. The song was something he hadn't heard before, or maybe he had, just a long, long time ago. Rick placed two creamy drinks in wide plate glasses on the counter.

'Brandy Alexanders,' said Deborah.

'You read my mind,' said Harry.

Deborah raised her glass and waited for Harry to do the same. They clinked, drank and then Harry lit up a cigarette with one of the complimentary packets of matches. He noticed that the packet was completely white, void of any information. Harry smiled and began to relax a little. No teenagers in this place. Good, he thought. Only for sophisticated bastards like myself. Some talent on display, too. Then he remembered that he hadn't shaved and realised he probably looked pretty bloody shocking from the shirt collar up.

'Harry,' said Deborah, leaning in and placing a hand on his knee, 'I'm going to leave you alone for a short while. I'm just going to go with Rick. You'll be okay, won't you?'

'I'm a big boy, Deborah,' said Harry, holding up his Brandy Alexander. 'Go ahead with Rick and do whatever it is you've got to do.'

Deborah gave his knee a gentle squeeze and she walked down to the far end of the bar where Rick was waiting for her. Harry watched them disappear through a door camouflaged amongst mirrors before turning to study the gathering crowd of the Kommune Club.

Harry's eye was caught by a woman sitting in an alcove at the far end of the room, directly opposite the hidden glass door. She was waving slowly in his direction. He didn't react immediately, but he realised she wasn't trying to get his attention, rather one of the waiters collected at the bar just behind him. One of them noticed her, nodded and gave her a subtle "thumbs up". Harry sipped his drink and watched her lower her head. He estimated that she was maybe very late fifties. She was wearing a very flattering green dress. The music that had been playing faded out suddenly and after a few seconds another song began. Harry, despite being pretty sure he didn't know this one, thought it sounded familiar, as though he'd always known it. The woman in the alcove raised her head and placed both hands on the table. She tilted her head towards the ceiling, eyes closed. Then, with no small amount of serene melancholy, she started miming to the female vocal.

She performed the whole song, her face full of melancholy. At one point in the song, Harry was certain that she stared straight at him through her thick eye makeup. A lot of the people in the bar didn't seem to be paying her much attention. But Harry was. Harry was paying her every last bit of attention he had.

Three minutes later, the song finished and the woman reclined back into the shadows of the alcove. A new song started and Harry put his cigarette out. He turned to the waiter behind him.

'What was that song called that played just then?'

The waiter looked him up and down curiously.

'It's called *Love Don't Fear Me* by Audrey Lee.'

'Right,' said Harry. As the waiter turned away,

Deborah reappeared at his side, drinking her Brandy Alexander. She read something in his expression.

'What's got you so excited?'

'What do you mean?' said Harry, lighting up another cigarette.

'You're having a good time then?'

'It's alright.'

Harry noticed a brown paper bag under her coat. She caught him looking and whispered in his ear:

'Rare imports. Practically contraband these days.'

'Rare imports?'

'Records. Very hard to come by. And *very* expensive.'

'I see.'

'I've got access to a secret pipeline.'

'Sounds great.'

'That's between you and me, Harry,' she said seriously.

'And Rick,' said Harry, exhaling a long stream of smoke above towards the ceiling lights.

'And I'd prefer it if it stayed like that.'

'You don't need to worry about me,' said Harry. 'I'm not sure I know anybody to tell.'

Deborah nodded and they drank in silence.

'Deborah,' said Harry as he finished his drink.

'Yes, Harry?'

'Have you heard of Audrey Lee?'

At the mention of the name, Deborah's face lit up in amusement.

'You've witnessed it then.'

'Witnessed what?'

'Audrey Lee's nightly performance.'

'*That's* Audrey Lee?'

'Sitting in that low lit alcove down there? Yes, that is Audrey Lee.'

They both stared down the long room to where she was sitting. Harry could make out her green dress, but her face was hidden in the shadows of the dim light. He placed a hand on Deborah's shoulder, left his cigarette burning in the ashtray and began to walk towards the alcove. Still her face remained hidden and as he got closer, another figure appeared, suddenly sitting upright opposite Audrey Lee. The figure turned and looked straight at Harry. He was a small, wiry man in a dirty, crumpled tuxedo. His face was a mask of malevolence. Harry was sure he heard the man growl like a violently disturbed dog and he stopped in his tracks. The man didn't take his eyes off Harry. Audrey Lee appeared to be doing nothing about it. Harry weighed up his options and decided to return to his place at Deborah's side.

'Who's that scrawny little prick with her?' he asked, tapping the finger of ash from his cigarette.

'Nobody really knows,' said Deborah as Rick placed two more Brandy Alexanders in front of them. 'His name's Gubbs apparently. He accompanies her here every night.'

'Her significant other?' wondered Harry out loud. It didn't feel plausible to him.

'I shouldn't think so,' said Deborah. 'What does it matter anyway?'

'Nothing, I suppose,' said Harry flatly. 'I just don't like the look of him, that's all.'

'I doubt you're alone in that,' said Deborah.

'What do you know about her?'

Deborah catches Rick's eye and he comes over,

leaning towards us across the counter.

'Yes, honey?' he said in a thick southern accent.

'Tell my companion about Audrey Lee will you?'

Rick gave Harry the once over, then rested on one elbow. Harry put on his best listening face.

'She was one of the Celebrations.'

'The Celebrations?

'The backing vocal group for the singer Perry Coolidge. There was Audrey, Juliet Scott and Martha Mann. Perry was an asshole. He got Juliet pregnant, but it was taken care of. He never liked Audrey because she turned him down and stood up for Juliet when he put her through what he put her through. He tried to kick her out of the Celebrations at every opportunity, but the record label wouldn't have it. Audrey was the most popular of the girls on that stage. There was something about her that none of the others could equal.'

'So what happened?' said Harry, getting on with his second Brandy Alexander.

'They were playing a gig in Paris, part of a six month European tour. There was this photographer at the front of the crowd snapping away. Perry noticed that this photographer was taking more pictures of Audrey than of any of the other band members and he didn't like it one bit. Every time this photographer aimed his camera lens at Audrey, Perry would jump in between them to block her out.'

'Very mature,' said Deborah.

'That's what the son of a bitch was like,' said Rick. 'Anyway, this photographer dude, Nigel St Davos, greased someone's palm to get a message to Audrey to come and meet him. She got away, met him and they spent the night propping up the bar at a local watering hole. He convinced her that she should go solo; quit the Perry Coolidge & The Celebrations and let him manage her. She took a little persuading but he eventually talked her around.'

'Could she do that?' asked Harry. 'I mean, just quit on the spot like that?'

'Rumour has it Nigel St Davos approached the group's manager, Geordie Skins. They cut a deal and Audrey was released from the Celebrations.'

'Just like that?' said Harry.

'Just like that,' said Rick.

'Then what?'

'Well, Nigel promoted her, they cut a single, the single did reasonably well. And then…'

His voice trailed off.

'And then?' pressed Harry.

'And then she dropped off the radar. That's where the biography ends. It doesn't pick up until she walked into this place a couple of years ago. She's come in here every single night since.'

'*Every* night?'

'*Every single night.*'

Rick left that with them as he went to serve a couple a few feet away. Deborah read Harry's thousand yard stare.

'You really are fascinated by Audrey Lee, aren't you?'

'And I'm not sure why,' replied Harry.

'See?' she said.

'See what?'

'I told you this place would change your life.'

'Hardly,' said Harry. 'I'm just interested in finding

out a bit more, that's all.'

'And then?'

'Nothing,' said Harry. 'Perhaps.'

Deborah smiled evaporated into the crowd to dance. Harry stared down the bar towards the alcove. But now it was empty. In the midst of Rick, Brandy Alexanders and rare imports, Audrey Lee and her pet Gubbs had left the building.

11

Detective Inspector Kibber entered the Eiderlands Boarding House in South West London. The proprietor, Mr. Sisk, was seated in his usual position behind the compact reception desk, wiping his hands dirty with a grubby towel. Kibber usually tried to avoid any kind of conversation with this overweight, sweaty blob. Mr. Sisk acknowledged him with a wave and a smile of dirty teeth. Kibber reluctantly nodded and approached the desk. He towered over Mr. Sisk, who barely made five feet two inches. There was never likely to be a friendship between them; Mr. Sisk tolerated Kibber because he had been a regular tenant for the last eight months who'd never been late with money and had never caused any trouble. Kibber tolerated Mr. Sisk because he did as he was told: he never asked any questions and he left him alone.

'Good evening, Mister Kibber,' said Mr. Sisk. Kibber flinched; he was always pronouncing his surname as "Kebber". Kibber noticed there were more tins of paint stacked up behind the desk.

'Still not finished decorating, Mr. Sisk?' he said.

'One day it will be done,' said Mr. Sisk cheerily. 'Perhaps I will invite you to the grand reopening.'

'You have high hopes, Mr. Sisk,' said Kibber. 'I don't suppose there's anything for me?'

'Nothing, Mister Kibber.'

'You didn't manage to come across any of your infestation during your renovations by any chance?'

'I'm sorry, Mister Kibber,' said Mr. Sisk, 'So far I have found only one rat. I'm sure to find more as I work.'

'Well, hopefully it was the one that was scratching all night last night.'

Mr. Sisk smiled to himself and ran a fat finger along his brow line.

'Lucky you take such strong *medication* to help you sleep.'

Kibber ignored the jibe and strummed his fingers on the desk.

'I'm going up,' said Kibber as he headed towards the staircase, 'and I don't want to be disturbed.'

'No problem,' said Mr. Sisk, waving him away like a fly.

Kibber reached his room on the third storey and let himself in. He locked it with the big brass key. He always left the curtains closed, whether it was day or night. He pulled the two bottles of whisky from the pockets of his rain mac and dropped them on the single bed, which he'd pushed up against the wall to give him more floor space. Then he produced his hip flask and took a long drink from it. He felt his body temperature rise from his chest outwards and he removed his rain mac.

After turning on the light, he set the room up exactly the way he wanted it to be for the rest of the night. He placed the two bottles of whisky in the centre of the floor, along with the glass tumbler from the sink, emptying his toothbrush into the basin. Next, he opened up the large towel and stood on it, removing his clothes slowly and stacking them in a pile behind him. When he was naked, he stretched himself as much as his battered body would allow and stared at the four walls of his room. Claudia looked back at him from almost every single photograph and Polaroid he'd put up over the time he'd lived at Eiderlands. Most of them he had taken himself, developing them in the evidence labs at New Scotland Yard. The first shots he'd taken of her, he'd just tried to re-enact the photos he'd confiscated over the years, the dirty swag from countless busts he'd taken part in with Vice. The little private library he'd been building up had been enough for him until he'd seen Claudia. After that, all those other photographs had become irrelevant, redundant. So the first shots he'd taken had been of her had been experimental, tentative, full of clumsy angles and encroaching shadows. Claudia had dutifully posed, always alone, baring everything for Kibber and his lens. After a while, she'd begun talking him into posing with her. His own self image was something that he always tried to avoid, but eventually she had dragged him into the frame, literally *pulling* him from behind the camera and onto her. He'd been uncomfortable and blocked his face. Claudia showed him how to use the delay on the camera; he'd gone out and picked up some dumb bells and worked out for an hour before realising that lifting weights was no substitute for the taste of the hard stuff.

Kibber let his eyes wander over the hundreds of pictures secured to the walls, filled the glass tumbler with whisky and emptied the glass in one go. He gently pulled one large, rectangular photograph from amongst the collection and set it down on the floor, between the whisky bottles. This was his favourite image of her; she was naked, but it was a close up shot of her head and shoulders lying back on the pillow looking up at the camera. He had taken it with one hand whilst propping himself up with the other, right at the moment he had come. This was *the* image of Claudia. He fell to his knees, drank more whisky and got himself hard. Her eyes stared back at him, just like they had when he'd taken the photograph, burning into him. He could feel the temperature in the room increasing and he drank more, feeling the tickle of sweat beads gathering on his forehead. He placed a hand on the photograph, touching her face and sliding his swollen fingers down the gloss until they felt the coarse lino underneath. He slowed down, determined to make it last all night. He had all night, all night to drink and be with Claudia. He would straighten out; he would pick up a suspect, one with form, to wrap up the attack on the redhead. He'd do good by Claudia; he'd do good *with* Claudia.

Kibber awoke several hours later, naked and in the foetal position, the towel sweat-soaked and crumpled up beneath him. He sat up, shivering, the smell of booze around him and over him where the second bottle had spilled over as he passed out. He put his fingers in his mouth and ran them along the inside of his mouth. His teeth felt thick and heavy between swollen gums. He heard the rats scratching above him, on the other side of the ceiling. He pushed himself to his feet and attempted to pull his trousers on. He got one leg halfway in before he lost his balance and crashed sideways on to the bed. And there he remained until Mr. Sisk gave him his morning wakeup call at seven fifteen.

12

***Special News Update**: Last night, amidst speculation that the New Metropolitan Police Service were preparing to wind down their investigation into the disappearance of schoolgirl Patience Sweetlove, a staff insider revealed that they would be extending their search into neighbouring woodland. The area, popularly known as meeting place for sexual deviants, is being earmarked as possibly containing an unmarked grave which may bring the investigation to its, some say, natural conclusion. Mr. and Mrs. Sweetlove were unavailable for comment, but released the following statement through the publicist Karl Kelvin of KKEye Publicists, who has so generously offered his services to the couple: "Mitch and Jacqueline would like to extend their deepest gratitude towards all the officers of the New Metropolitan Police who have been working around the clock with such dedication on their behalf. They are confident that the mystery of Patience's disappearance will be solved very soon. They would especially like to thank the several celebrities who have leant their support by offering to write and record a special charity single in memoriam of their beautiful little angel." Mr. Kelvin declined to offer any more information regarding the single, such as who will be performing on it, but it is likely to include several dozen acts that have featured on some or all of the previous twenty nine 'Good Cause Tracks'.*

Allen Wyngarde blinked hard and stopped watching his cigarette smoke winding lazily towards the ceiling light. He didn't know just how long he had been lying on the small, solid sofa in his study, but he was acutely aware of how much time he'd been wasting. He had an appointment with his own end that he was failing to keep since that phone call from Iain Fucking Gwynne. He took a final drag of his cigarette and crushed into the ashtray balancing on his chest. His hand slid to the floor and found the telephone where he'd left it hours earlier, the first time he had tried to summon up the strength to make the call he wanted to make.

He listened to the dialling ring for a full thirty seconds before it was answered.

'Hello?'

'Hello, Dee,' said Allen shakily, 'it's Daddy.'

'Hello Allen,' came the reply. Allen could almost taste the iciness in her voice. He shifted his position on the sofa, resting on one forearm.

'Listen, I was just wondering...' Allen sighed and scratched his forehead.

'Just spit it out,' said Dee.

'Well, I thought I might come over and see you, at your place. What do you say?'

'You did, did you?' said Dee calmly. 'You do realise that this is the first time you've called in over seven months?'

'I know--'

'And every single invitation I've extended to you has either been turned down or ignored completely.'

'I'm really tremendously sorry, darling.'

'Don't call me *"darling"*.' said Dee through gritted teeth. 'What's the matter? Your bit of fluff cancelled on you for tonight did she?'

'It's not like that.'

'And I suppose you're thinking of coming here because your place is still off limits, yes?'

'My place is in too much of a state, Dee.'

Allen was starting to get agitated. He fumbled for his cigarettes and managed to spill them all over the floor.

'Shit,' he hissed. He grabbed one and managed to light it as his daughter spoke.

'I don't think I want you to come over anyway. I still have a life that means something, even if you can't be bothered about it.'

'Yes, well,' snapped Allen suddenly, 'I might be bloody bothered if I had some grandchildren to come and bloody see!'

As soon as the words left his mouth, he knew he shouldn't have said them and he sat bolt upright on the sofa, hand stamped on his forehead. There was silence on the other end for an uncomfortable length of time.

'Thanks a lot, *Daddy*.'

The line went dead.

13

Harry dragged the blunt razor blade across his face towards an unsatisfactory shave, dropping lumps of shaving foam into the bathroom sink as he went. His head rocked from the Brandy Alexanders and the Shiraz that had followed it when he'd got home. He'd invited Deborah in but she had declined his offer. He hoped that she didn't think he was trying to make a move on her, as he was more or less sure that trying to make a move on Deborah was not on his agenda. In fact, all he could think about was Audrey Lee. Something about her fascinated him; not just the back story that had been given an airing by Rick, it was the very nature of her existence that struck a chord with him. Here was this little starlet in her striking, shimmering green dress miming - not even singing - but *miming* to her own song. And what a beautiful song *Love Don't Fear Me* was. Harry wiped the white residue from his face and ears with a hand towel and dressed in his dark blue three piece suit and black shoes. He stood in his bedroom smoking a cigarette and staring out the window into the garden below. He contemplated the rest of his stay at 77 Vancouver Hill. He hadn't planned on hanging around for more than a couple of days, but now that he'd met Deborah Flaxman, with her naturist persuasion and contraband records, and in turn witnessed Audrey Lee in all her tragic, might-have-been melancholy, Harry decided he would have to stick it out until something inside him had resolved itself.

He leaned across the bed and opened the window to feel how cold it was outside. The weather was quite mild, sunny even, and Harry heard Deborah calling for her cat. Harry threw his cigarette butt out of the window and went up to the roof terrace. Deborah was in her garden, dressed only in a pair of green wellingtons, a thick woolen scarf and a utility belt holding various small gardening tools. He watched her as she peered into the undergrowth, making squeaking noises to attract her pet. In the end, she sighed and stood up straight, running a finger around the inside of the scarf. She turned and looked up to see Harry watching her from above.

'Can't get enough of me, hey?'

'I wasn't spying, Deborah,' said Harry, squatting down close to the edge.

'Whatever you say,' said Deborah with a tired grin. She started walking towards her house.

'Deborah,' called Harry.

'Yes?' she replied, stopping just before she disappeared from view.

'I was thinking about going to the Kommune tonight. Can you come with me?'

'*Can* I come with you?'

'Well, what I mean is, I really want to go and I thought I'd need you to get me in there.'

'Relax,' sighed Deborah. 'Look, I've got stuff on later, but I'll call Rick and square it with him to let you in at the door. Good enough for you?'

'Thanks, Deborah,' said Harry, 'I really appreciate it.'

'You're going to go and pester Audrey Lee, aren't you?'

'I'm afraid so.'

'You should be afraid,' said Deborah and vanished

into her house.

Audrey Lee's immaculate and silent rendition of *Love Don't Fear Me* was reproduced to the crowded Kommune Bar just as Harry hoped it would be. He positioned himself at the bar, between a group of middle aged chin strokers and a merry band of pseudo revolutionaries. Rick recognised him and poured him a Brandy Alexander. After the song had finished and the club resumed its usual soundtrack, Harry indicated for Rick to come over.

'Yes mate?'

'I'd like to send a drink over to Ms Lee,' said Harry with as much sophistication as he could muster.

'What's her poison?'

Rick glanced down the bar towards the shadowy alcove and then back to Harry.

'She likes the Mint Sonata.'

'Never heard of it,' said Harry.

'Allow me,' said Rick and deftly began to mix the mystery cocktail.

'Could you also please convey a message to Ms Lee for me?'

'What message would you like me to convey?'

'Tell Ms Lee that her song has not left my heart or my head since I first heard it.'

Harry sipped his Brandy Alexander and watched keenly as Rick sent a waiter down the bar with the drink positioned on a silver tray. There were too many people in the way for Harry to see Audrey Lee's reaction. He saw the drink being placed on the table, then the long, slender hand slowly sliding across and the fingers circling the glass. But she didn't drink it;

the fingers twirled the glass around on the table, the index finger tapping the rim, as if considering its contents. Harry lit a cigarette and looked at Rick who gave him a shrug before attending to some customers. He faced the bar and downed his drink, ready for when Rick was free to top it up again. Being presented with drinks was something she was bound to be *au fait* with. He felt deflated; he'd been wasting his time and now he would get blind drunk, fall into a cab taking him to Vancouver Hill where he would knock on Deborah Flaxman's front door and attempt to seduce her with his vague charms.

'Excuse me, sir.'

Harry turned to see the waiter practically perched on his right shoulder.

'Yes?'

'Ms Lee has requested your company at her table.'

Harry stared at the waiter, blinked once, stared down the bar, and then stared at the waiter again.

'Okay,' said Harry.

The waiter stepped aside as Harry moved past him into the crowd. He felt his core temperature begin to rise as he cut through the dancers and the singers who knew every move and every lyric, who drank every drink, every brand of cigarette and every drug. He reached the end of the bar and as he got closer, the presence of Audrey Lee began to take shape, sitting there in that darkened alcove. He was no more than five yards away when Gubbs jumped from nowhere right into his path. In stature, he was barely as high as Harry's chin, but he let out a low growl from that evil, razor blade mouth. The eyes were black and dead, betraying a shrunken intellect unbothered by flair or reason, much less any self regard to dress in a half decent suit. Harry had never been looked at like that and he didn't much care for it. He was on the brink of shoving the nasty little runt out of the way when for the first time he heard Audrey Lee speak:

'Step aside, Gubbs, and let the nice gentlemen sit down.'

The expression on Gubbs' face at once changed. The visceral hostility was suddenly replaced by a nervy obedience of his handler's request. He shrunk away from Harry and reversed up against the corner of the bar. Audrey Lee indicated with her slender index finger for him to sit. He took his place at the table, directly opposite from the enigma in green. She leaned forward slightly and the ambient lighting revealed her features to him in for the first time in close up. She possessed a regal quality about her; an age ago she would have probably been the most beautiful creature on the planet. She wore her hair high and loosely fitted somewhere around the back, away from her neck. The eye makeup emphasised a sad, peculiar longing in her bejewelled eyes.

'Thank you,' said Harry, unbuttoning his jacket and smoothing out his tie.

'That's quite alright,' said Audrey and Harry detected the faintest of slurs in her voice. 'But perhaps I should be thanking you.'

'I don't think I've ever ordered a lady a Mint Sonata before.'

'I meant thank you for the kind compliment. It was really very kind of you.'

'Oh,' said Harry, 'you're welcome, Ms Lee.'

'What's your name?' said Audrey as the waiter

appeared at the table and set a Brandy Alexander down in front of Harry. Harry raised his glass to her.

'My name's Harry. Cheers.'

Audrey raised her glass and they clinked and drank. They didn't take their eyes off each other. Audrey regarded Harry the way an older woman regards a teenager whom she knows wants to take her to bed.

'You like my song,' she said.

'Yes,' said Harry. 'I mean, it feels familiar to me, but I'm not sure if I've heard it before. If that makes sense.'

'It is an old song,' said Audrey.

'Nevertheless,' said Harry, producing his cigarettes and offering one to Audrey, 'a good song is a good song. And *Love Don't Fear Me* is a great song.'

Audrey took one of his cigarettes and waited as Harry lit them both up.

'Hardly anyone in this world remembers it,' she said after expelling a long chain of smoke.

'I can't believe that.'

'You can believe it,' said Audrey as though she suspected Harry was merely humouring her.

'An injustice, if I may,' said Harry.

Audrey studied Harry's face until his throat began to run dry.

'You were here last night,' she said. 'You've never been here before that, have you?'

'I didn't even know there was a "here".'

'Then how did you find your way in here?'

'A friend.'

'Keep friends like that close by you.'

Harry suddenly, strangely, had an image of

Deborah in his mind; beautiful and serene, guarded but perhaps willing to give solace to him if and when he decided he needed it.

'I don't really have what others would call friends.'

'All the more reason,' said Audrey.

'I suppose so.'

They smoked in silence for a while before Audrey stubbed out her cigarette and drank her Mint Sonata down halfway.

'Well,' she said, collecting her handbag from the seat beside her, 'now that you've found "here", do you think you will stop by often?'

'Yes,' said Harry, 'I believe I will.'

Audrey stood up and before Harry could move, she stopped him by placing a hand tenderly against his cheek.

'Remember to shave properly the next time,' she said, sliding her hand down his face. 'You're not in some Dodge City saloon.'

With that, Audrey walked away from the alcove. Harry turned to watch her leave, but all he saw was Gubbs moving backwards into the crowd, pistol pointing at him with both hands and flashing him a menacing sneer that was substantially lacking in menace. Harry turned to his Brandy Alexander and downed it. He reached for the unfinished Mint Sonata and put it to his nose. He could smell the fragrance of her on the glass.

'Audrey Lee,' he said to himself, 'you're on my "to do" list.'

14

Interplanetary Terrestrial HQ, Greenwich (X 11 Clearance)
'I've managed to successfully dial back the interference, Ma'm.'
'And?'
'Should be coming through...NOW.'
- *"Interplanetary--"*-
'North Angel?'
- *"---"*-
'Christ!'
'Wait!'
- *"Interplanetary, do you read me?"*-
'YEAH!'
'Keep your voices down, this isn't Cape Canaveral. North Angel, can you hear me?'
- *"Yes, Ma'm, I read you loud and clear."*-
'Identify yourself please.'
- *"This is Captain Ione Blanchard, Ma'm."*
'Captain Blanchard, I request a detailed update on the status of the North Angel and her crew.'
- *"North Angel badly damaged. Crew have suffered mostly minor but several serious injuries. Chief Engineer Viktor Renko has sustained a heavy head injury but is stable in sick bay."*-
'Understood. What caused the damage, Captain?'
- *"---g--dffl--"*-
'What's happening? Why are we losing them?'
'I'm trying to re-establish contact, Ma'm.'
- *"---not as benevolent as we may have thought, Ma'm. The first strike disabled our shield defences."*-
'Say again, Captain.'

- "We've relayed visual and audio data to you."'
'Negative, Captain. That's a big negative - nothing's being received from any of your transmissions.'
- "---beautiful light---n-t--so beautiful after all---"-
'What is your current course, Captain?'
- "Don't have much time or power. Might just make it but---hope---if we fai---I-----hrhu---f----------h---"
'Get them back RIGHT NOW!'
'The North Angel's vanished again, Ma'm.'
'Ma'm?'
'What is it, Adina?'
'Director requests an update.'
'I'll bet he does.'

The Director for Interspace Programming, Sir James Swaffham, marched past the buttoned-up police constable and through the door to Number Ten. He allowed the bespectacled aide in his trendy tank top and tie to escort him down to The Box in the lower basement. The aide was making small talk but Sir James wasn't in the least bit interested. When they reached the outer office of The Box, the aide politely asked Sir James to wait before knocking once and entering the inner sanctum. Sighing in exasperation at the necessary infestation of admin ants everywhere he turned, Sir James sat back in the padded chair with its high sides and held the thick file of documents tightly in his grip. He hated the outer room, he hated the cold nothingness about it; a sterile neither here nor there holding pen for which he was too important for. Let the ministers of the Cabinet sweat it out here. Sir James Swaffham was too big for the outer room.

'The Prime Minister will see you now, Sir James.'

The aide was back in the room and holding the bullet proof door open just enough for Sir James to slip through. The heavy door closed behind him and the Director stood and watched as the Prime Minister finished reading a Top Secret document.

'Come and have a seat, Sir James.'

'Thank you, Prime Minister,' said Sir James politely and sat in the slightly larger leather chair with the slightly lower sides. The Prime Minister, spectacles removed, regarded the Space Director for a few moments and Sir James could see the words being arranged in that heavy, greying head across the desk.

'Sir James,' said the Prime Minister eventually, 'as I understand it, we have a problem of sorts *up there*. Would that be fair?'

Sir James shifted his position in the chair, 'Well, Prime Minister, we do have a slight problem with one of our expedition craft-'

'*HMS North Angel.*'

'Yes, Prime Minister, the *HMS North Angel*.'

'And what kind of problem are we talking about here?'

'Well, Prime Minister, it would seem that she failed to make rendezvous with the *Baltic Queen*. Greenwich has, however, been able to establish some contact with her.'

'What kind of contact?'

'Some audio, Prime Minister. It was patchy and mostly indecipherable, but they did manage to get a few words from the captain of *HMS North Angel*. The technicians down there are trying to clean up the recordings as we speak.'

'Ione Blanchard?' said the Prime Minister.

'Yes, Prime Minister.'

'General Blanchard's eldest, isn't she?'

'That is correct, Prime Minister.'

'Bloody tricky business if she dies up there, Swaffham,' the Prime Minister said gravely.

'Yes sir,' replied Sir James quietly.

'So is there some sort of explanation as to what's going on up there?'

'Well, Prime Minister,' said Sir James, 'I don't wish to jump the gun on this, but it would appear that Captain Blanchard and her crew may have run into something.'

'I see,' said the Prime Minister, reclining back behind the broad teak desk.

'Captain Blanchard did indicate that the craft had been damaged and that several of the crew had sustained injuries.'

'This is not an ideal scenario for us,' said the Prime Minister.

'No, Prime Minister.'

'A bad outcome in this affair and I may as well throw myself to the mercy of the media. And I'm not prepared to just lie down in front of that speeding train, Swaffham.'

'No, Prime Minister.'

'Any leakage so far?'

'Nothing to speak of, Prime Minister. We do, as you know, keep tabs on the usual suspects in the Press. So far, the only flag raised is for a brief eight liner in *The Edition*; no detail, all pretty vague really.'

Sir James pulled a printout from the document file and handed it over. The Prime Minister scanned it out loud.

'"Several instances of static interference have been recorded by a space enthusiast in East London. The Interplanetary Commission has explained that radio waves sometimes get disrupted by heavenly bodies, such as small asteroids and other debris. They said that in this instance, it could be one of the defunct Casper satellites still orbiting the Earth." Who wrote this piece up?'

'A journalist by the name of Trent Seether, Prime Minister.'

'Seether? I know that name, don't I?'

'Yes, Prime Minister, Mr. Seether is also the reporter who went after you over the South American affair.'

'Oh yes,' sighed the Prime Minister, 'that little shit.'

'Quite,' said Sir James.

'Who's this "enthusiast" he mentions?'

'A conspiracy theorist of sorts,' explained Sir James. 'He's been known to pester Seether from time to time. A nobody really, Prime Minister. Half the time, Seether doesn't even return his calls.'

'Could there be a problem with either of them in the near future?'

'Conspiracy theorists can be easily debunked, Prime Minister,' said Sir James greasily. 'Journalists like Seether, however…'

'What do you suggest, Swaffham?'

'We must avoid any of the Nationals picking up on any future tit-bits, Prime Minister. I suggest it might be prudent to bury any subsequent references under more *emotive* news.'

'Such as?'

'Patience Sweetlove, Prime Minister.'

'Patience who?'

'Sweetlove, Prime Minister,' said Sir James. Even he was a tiny bit shocked that the leader didn't immediately recognise the name. 'She's the schoolgirl that's currently missing, possibly another victim of the Albion Snatcher.'

Familiarity washed over the Prime Minister's face.

'Why do we have to sensationalise these murderers, rapists and nonces, Swaffham?' said the Prime Minister.

'It's the pursuit of celebrity,' said Sir James frankly, 'in all its grubby splendour.'

'You may be right,' said the Prime Minister dourly.

'Can I suggest you get in on the abduction story as much as you can, Prime Minister? That should keep the media focused away from our little space jaunt, at least until we know what we're dealing with and how to handle it.'

The Prime Minister nodded in consideration, 'I'll have a meeting with the Chief Whip. I'll have an official statement drawn up. Should be able to get it on the early evening news.'

'It might also be an idea to link it nicely with the reinstatement of the Capital Punishment program, Prime Minister. That'll keep everyone busy on the debating floors.'

'Then that's what I'll do,' said the Prime Minister, leaning forward and rapping the desk. 'The sooner any mention of this strange anomaly in space has vanished from the public consciousness the better.'

'I agree, Prime Minister.

'But make no mistake, Swaffham,' said the Prime Minister, suddenly becoming gravely serious, 'I want that space craft and its crew back. Do you understand?'

'Yes, Prime Minister,' said Sir James somberly.

'Then that's all.'

Sir James stood up and nodded before heading out of The Box. The aide was waiting for him on the other side to escort him back up. Inside The Box, the Prime Minister pressed a button on the desktop intercom:

'Put my Press hair on stand-by please.'

15

Detective Sergeant Sam Keady was sitting in the unmarked squad car when Kibber emerged from Eiderlands, pulling his rain mac tight around him to keep the weather from mixing with the alcohol in his system. He slid in behind the steering wheel and turned the engine over.

'Morning, Sergeant,' he said, letting the car idle on the wide driveway.

'Good morning, Sir,' replied Keady cheerfully. 'How was your evening?'

'Same as usual, Sergeant,' said Kibber with a shrug. 'As you'd expect when you're living in a guest house.'

'You visited Ruth,' said Keady.

Kibber sighed and gripped the steering wheel tightly, 'Yes, Sam, I did.'

'What did she say?'

'Not much. I'm not her favourite person am I. Don't worry, I won't go around again.'

'It's probably for the best, Sir.'

Kibber turned to Keady to read his expression, but the young sergeant was facing away, staring out of the window into the brusque morning. Kibber slipped into first and rolled the squad car down the driveway and onto the main road. He took the usual route down the bypass and onto the industrial estate to the greasy spoon they usually went to. Kibber ordered a full breakfast and a pot of tea.

'Not hungry again, Sergeant?'

Keady sat back on the cold plastic bench opposite his superior and flicked through his notebook.

'I've eaten already, Sir,' he said. 'You should probably think about eating that gunk so often, if you don't mind me saying so?'

Kibber poured the tea and topped it up with a nip from his flask, 'I don't mind, Sergeant. I think a few too many English breakfasts are probably the least of my worries.'

'Really, Sir?'

'Yes, Sergeant. But you don't want to hear about my problems.'

'I don't mind, Sir,' said Keady, closing the notebook to indicate his attention. 'If you want to talk about it.'

Kibber regarded his sergeant's words for a moment. 'I'm thinking about asking someone to marry me.'

'Oh, I see. Well, congratulations, Sir. Anyone I know?'

'Her name's Claudia.'

Kibber looked at Keady to see if there was a flicker of recognition. He couldn't be sure if the Detective Sergeant made the connection between the name of his potential significant other and the name of the exotic pro they pulled in several years previously. If Keady had made the connection, he didn't say anything to indicate it.

'I hope it all works out for you, Sir.'

Kibber said nothing, but drank his tea while he waited for his breakfast to arrive. He felt the alcohol burn in his chest. He felt a sudden nausea bubbling up inside of him and his head began to slowly throb. There was a copy of *The Edition* on the adjacent table and he reached for it. As he opened it, a narrow ribbon of cold tea dribbled down the page onto his crotch.

'Is there anything about the game last night?' asked Keady.

Kibber flicked through to the back pages.

'Newtown Medico are going after one of our players.'

'Oh really, Sir? Who?'

'Valdez.'

'Wow,' said Keady. 'That's a surprise, Sir.'

'Apparently the game the Juggernauts lost the other day swung it for him. Serves them right, I suppose.'

'Yes, Sir.'

Kibber's breakfast arrived and as he was about to probe it with the dirty fork, one of the staff turned up the television mounted on the wall behind the counter. A few customers turned to see what was on. The Prime Minister's face filled the screen and someone yelled at the staff to turn the channel over but no one did.

'The Prime Minister's talking about Patience Sweetlove,' said Keady.

'That'll be a great comfort to her parents I'm sure,' muttered Kibber as his knife cut through the film of grease on his plate.

'*...and as a result of my discussion with Chief Superintendant Stoking I have decided that extra manpower will be drafted in from neighbouring boroughs if necessary to assist with the search for Patience Sweetlove...*'

'That's a positive step, Sir,' said Keady without looking away from the television.

'The Prime Minister's a cunt,' said Kibber as he swallowed a mouthful of semi burnt mess.

'Nice hair though,' said Keady.

Across town, Harry Brewer, having been unable to drink himself to sleep on homemade Brandy Alexanders, shifted restlessly in front of the television as the Prime Minister waxed on about the missing schoolgirl. It reminded him of his encounter with the psycho policeman the other night. The thought of that bastard made him feel sick inside and he lit another cigarette and thought of Audrey Lee. He had been with older woman before and his conclusions had been largely positive. He considered what it would be like to sleep with Audrey, her hair starting to come away around her shoulders, that sparkling green dress hunched up around her waist. Unable to take things any further, Harry put his cigarette out and took a bottle of bourbon into the shower with him. He stayed under the steaming waterfall for over an hour until he felt himself starting to wrinkle. He dressed in trousers and a sBrewered blue shirt and went up onto the roof, welcoming the fresh air that filtered through the cigarette smoke in his lungs. Deborah was in her garden, calling for her cat in a childlike voice. She was wearing her wide brimmed sun hat and sunglasses and a light red sash wrapped around her waist which just revealed her round buttocks beneath.

'Still missing?'

Deborah stood straight and peered up.

'For the time being at least,' she replied cheerily. Her face was flushed above the outcropping of her breasts. Harry sat on the ledge of the roof terrace as Deborah approached the back of her house.

'I went,' said Harry. 'Last night, I mean.'

Deborah stopped by the door, 'Did you enjoy yourself?'

'I bought Audrey Lee a Mint Sonata,' he proudly replied.

Deborah smiled and Harry's amusing display of pride, 'I'm pleased you had a nice time.'

'I think she and I have this connection, you know what I mean?'

'Oh yes,' said Deborah, 'I know what you mean. I assume you'll be going back again then?'

'I'm going to go tonight.'

'Well,' said Deborah as she opened the back door, 'I hope you have a lovely evening.'

'Deborah?'

'Yes, Harry?'

'All those rare imports you get - from Rick I mean.'

'What about them, Harry?'

'Would you happen to have *Love Don't Fear Me* anywhere amongst them?'

Deborah, one foot resting on the doorstep and one hand on her hip, scratched her head under the rim of her sun hat.

'I'll dig out the 45 and drop it around later,' she said, disappearing inside and closing the door before Harry could say anything else. He finished his cigarette and crushed it into the roof terrace.

Several generous drinks later and Deborah dropped off the copy of Audrey Lee's song. She didn't come in, she didn't even knock on the door; Harry, head bent back over the arm of the sofa, heard the distant squeak of the letterbox followed by the gentle slap of a package landing on the inside doormat. He slid onto the carpet and crawled along the hall to where the record lay waiting to be played. He sat against the wall next to the telephone table and slipped the small piece of vinyl out of its protective cover. He massaged his eyes into focus and read the dark yellow label in the centre. *Love Don't Fear Me. Audrey Lee. (St. Davos-Lee).* On the other side, a song called *We've Already Reached The End. Audrey Lee. (St. Davos-Lee).* Harry placed the record on the turntable and carefully applied the stylus. As the warm crackling noise emerged from the two stereo speakers at either end of the living room, Harry positioned himself in the centre of the carpet, homemade Brandy Alexander in one hand, cigarette in the other and let the opening bars of the A-side penetrate his mind. Without the ambience of the Kommune Club, the song and Audrey Lee's voice sounded richer, darker and utterly compelling. He closed his eyes tightly and felt his body swaying, as though any second he would lose his balance and crash headlong into the wall. He could smell her scent, could see her eyes glistening through the shadows of the alcove. When he opened his eyes, Harry was lying on the floor; the room had gotten darker His throat and collar was sticky from the Brandy Alexander and the cigarette had burnt a long gash in the carpet.

16

Claudia silently cursed herself for falling asleep. She righted herself in the uncomfortable cushioned wooden chair and stretched her back. The figure in the bed had not stirred at all. Two uniformed representatives from the New Metropolitan Police Service had been and gone with the usual ineffectual low key routine she knew to expect. Claudia reached out and held Scottie's hand, squeezing it now and then as if each tiny amount of pressure would coax her into opening her eyes. She wished she could remove the thick white bandage from her head and stroke her hair just once. Her eyes wandered miserably across the stacks of electronic medical equipment that was keeping Scottie on the threshold of death's doorway. It wasn't making her better and it wasn't making her worse; it was just making her *exist*. Claudia was desperate for Scottie to awaken from her unconscious state. Claudia was desperate to tell Scottie that she loved her.

She rose from the chair and did some more stretching exercises. Her body ached from the lack of inactivity and she felt hunger pangs in her stomach. The room felt as though it were shrinking around her. It was airless and suffocating. Claudia went to the window and peered out through the vertical blinds. The corridor outside was quiet; a hospital porter pushed an empty, unmade bed towards the lift at the end, two sharp-angled nurses were discussing something over Styrofoam cups next to a notice board. At the far end, a doctor was writing up her notes behind the ward reception desk. Claudia looked back at Scottie, lying there in the cold, sterile bed and oblivious to anything around her. Claudia needed to get out of that room, just for one minute.

Claudia wandered aimlessly down the corridor, catching the eye of one of the gossiping nurses, who shot her a blank, apathetic glance. She walked towards the ward reception desk and rested her elbows on the surface, waiting for the doctor to acknowledge her presence. She waited the full minute.

'Can I help?' said the doctor, sitting back in her chair and clasping her fingers together.

'I'm a little hungry,' said Claudia. 'Is there anywhere I can get something to eat please?'

'There's a canteen in the basement,' said the doctor without any trace of personality.

'Thank you.'

'It's off limits to the general public.'

'I see.'

'The public eating area is currently under refurbishment. But there is a machine out on the stairwell. Nothing fancy.'

'Thank you,' said Claudia, barely raising a smile of gratitude. She was about to push herself away from the reception desk when something caught her attention. She had to look twice for it but there it was. On one of the doctor's folders, written in black ink, was that name: Cromwell Rouse. Claudia felt a shiver course through her. The doctor registered it.

'Is there something wrong, Madam?'

'No,' replied Claudia, regaining her composure. 'No, it's nothing, I'm fine. Listen, can you tell me if Dr Cromwell Rouse is working at St Marcus's today or tonight even?'

The doctor glanced at the small stack of folders and carefully slid them to one side.

'Why do you ask?'

'He's an old acquaintance of mine,' said Claudia, 'from a few years ago.'

'Really,' said the doctor humourlessly. 'Well, *Mister* Rouse will be on site later. If he ventures this way, I'll be sure to mention you, Ms...?'

'Guinevere,' said Claudia. 'Tell him Guinevere is here.'

Cromwell Rouse, chief consultant at St Marcus's Hospital for the previous two years, swung his big expensive classic car into his private parking space in the underground garage beneath the main building. He lowered the electric window and knocked his pipe out on the edge of the wing mirror before stuffing it into one of the front pockets of his thick brown blazer. He loved being at the hospital, away from Cressida, his wife of almost forty years. Just the size of that figure made him shudder. Good old doting Cressida. Good old faithful Cressida. Good old Cressida, mother to their five wonderfully well turned out offspring. What a lucky chap he was, that's how his friends saw it. Successful, wealthy, healthy and a solid family backing it all up. It was everything to everyone else and nothing to him.

Mistresses far and wide had come and gone since Rouse first sensed the rot setting in, first noticed the paint peeling from his immaculately constructed home life. He no longer made love to Cressida; she was still attractive at her age but unattractive to him. He slept with her from time to time but it wasn't making love;

it was mechanical, necessary the way sometimes it was necessary to defrost the freezer. Whether she still got anything out of it was something he had long since ceased concerning himself with. He assumed she just went along with it as he did, that during the act Cressida let her imagination run wild with thoughts of fucking her favourite crooner, her favourite actor, her favourite greens keeper at her country club. It didn't matter to him, not one damn bit.

Rouse took the lift directly to the seventh floor and unlocked the door to his private office. As he sat down behind his huge, sprawling desk and began looking in the top drawer for his diary there was a brief rapping on the door and he called for them to enter.

'Evening, C.R.,' said his fellow consultant, Mr. Mortlake.

'Hello Peter,' said Rouse. 'What's the death tally today so far?'

Mortlake grinned at the grim humour and sat down opposite Rouse.

'One more than you were expecting.'

Rouse stopped rummaging about in the drawer and looked at Mortlake.

'What do you mean?'

'You lost Billings this afternoon. Sorry old man.'

'Christ,' sighed Rouse. 'What happened?'

'It's those damn machines you sourced from the South Americas, C.R., they're a bloody menace most of the time, and bloody useless the rest of it.'

'Nonsense,' said Rouse with a dismissive flick of the wrist. 'Someone isn't doing their job properly.'

Mortlake sighed, 'Have it your way, old man. But the shareholders are screaming in the board's collective ear. They want answers, C.R. And only you can provide them.'

'Those impatient little shits,' said Rouse irritably. How he despised those faceless upstarts with their large balances and entry level intellect. He'd been one of the last to succumb to the corporate schemes and investment bodies but when he did cave in, he caved in as spectacularly as everyone else who cleaned up in the process. However, when it came to his "baby", Rouse had specifically warned the board and their bloody shareholders that there would be teething problems. Clearly they were all now suffering from selective memory syndrome.

'Little shits they may be,' said Mortlake, 'but without those little shits and their influence you'd never have got this program off the ground.'

'What side effects was Billings displaying before he died?' said Rouse, waving off Mortlake's defence of the board.

'The usual,' shrugged Mortlake as he lit a cigarette. 'Intense bleeding from the eyes, ears and nostrils, inflammation of the chest cavity. Oh, and an involuntary erection right before he flatlined, the lucky bugger.'

'It's unfortunate,' said Rouse. 'Billings was looking like the favourite to put into the next phase of the Treatment.'

Rouse paused for a moment to consider the next phase. This would see the machines built for him by Contact Chemicals that had thus far been semi successful in replicating the properties of the South American Hangman Beetle - the synthetic form of the insect's curious secretion, gradually be replaced by the real thing. Deals had been made, money and favours had been exchanged and questions avoided to bring a sufficient store of the rare insect into the country with the minimum level of fuss. The harvesting of the Hangman Beetle he would leave to others as they earned their exorbitant off-the-books fees in secret. This new, unheard of, natural wonder drug would be his legacy. Deep down he accepted that he had forced greater minds than his own out of the way in his fight for medical journal immortality, but he buried any guilt as deep as it would go. His colleague's voice suddenly brought him back into the room.

'You'll have to talk to the board, old man,' said Mortlake as he tapped ash into the black porcelain ashtray between them. 'Lord Riddenhurst's sphincter's quacking and you can bet your life he's dreaming up some big speech to throw you to the wolves.'

'Oh, sod Riddenhurst,' said Rouse, becoming visibly agitated by news of the setback. 'He's practically beyond his sell by date anyway. I'll prepare something for that lot, Peter, it'll be fine. Who's next on the candidate list?'

'This one's a property tycoon. His money's good and his body isn't. Forty seven years old and a fitness fanatic. Scuba diving accident three weeks ago left him in a coma. His wife has signed all the necessary paperwork.'

'Fine,' sighed Rouse, 'fine. Have his records sent up for me. Anything else?'

Mortlake put out his cigarette and with a 'no' he walked towards the door. As he opened it he paused and clicked his fingers.

'Reena said there's some woman on fifth who

knows you.'

'A patient?'

'No, but a relative of one, I think. Reena reckons she's European or Latino or some such. Attractive. Reena didn't like the look of her, but you know Reena.'

'Did this mystery woman provide a name?' said Rouse, only slightly intrigued as he went back to rifling his drawer.

'Reena said her name was Guinevere,' said Mortlake, finding the name amusing. He left without registering the colour Rouse's face had turned. Alone in his office, he got up and paced around the desk several times wondering to himself if it really was *her* down there on fifth. Obviously, he reasoned, it had to be the Guinevere he used to see. What was she *really* doing here at St Marcus's? Was she really visiting a sick relative, that old chestnut? Had she come back to him finally? Had she chosen him over all the others and raced to him with pounding heart and heaving bosom? Rouse realised that he may well be getting ahead of himself and he locked himself in his private bathroom for half an hour.

Claudia, her appetite in no way sated by three chocolate bars a tube of mints, was sitting back in the chair next to Scottie and re-reading a magazine article on the different homes owned by Gregory Gem when the door softly opened and in walked Cromwell Rouse. She said nothing; as the consultant closed the door behind him and leaned back against it, she replaced the magazine on the bedside cabinet and sat patiently with her hands pressed together in her lap. Rouse noted the expectant look on her face and diverted his eyes to the figure on the bed, the discoloured head almost completely obscured by tightly wound bandages. Eventually though, he had to bring his attention back to the beautiful creature he had known so often in the past.

'Hello Guin,' he said shyly.

'Hello Wellie,' replied Claudia.

'I'm sorry about Ms Scott. Is she…?'

'Is she a *close* relative?'

'Yes.'

'Yes. She was beaten up by an intruder and left for dead, Wellie.'

'I'm so sorry, Guin.'

Rouse moved into the room and examined the medical charts hanging from the foot of the bed. Claudia watched him with interest to see if she could tell whether or not he was genuinely reading the information that had been routinely logged over the past few days. The outlook consisted of a protracted semi recovery, full of tangled brain signals and involuntary discharges. He studied the broken and desperate expression on Guinevere's beautiful face and he almost succumbed to the feelings he'd succumbed to before. He didn't intend to make that mistake again and closed those thoughts down with a sudden injection of malice.

'Would it be fair to say that your past has caught up with you,' he said calmly, 'or at least, someone you actually seem to give a damn about?'

His eyes slid sideways to gauge her reaction. But she said nothing, just carried on staring at Scottie. Rouse put the medical charts back in order and stood directly in front of her. She didn't look up.

'Bitch,' he said. 'I was prepared to give up everything for you.'

'I know,' said Claudia, 'that was the problem.'

She slowly raised her head and their eyes locked. He couldn't look away and a heartbeat later he was hers once more. He sank to his knees and she accepted his long, balding head into her lap. He shut his eyes tightly and felt her hand stroking his scalp slowly.

'I missed you so much, Guin,' he whispered into the cloth of her dress. 'I didn't care about a bloody thing for so long.'

'Shhh,' whispered Claudia, '*shhhh*, Wellie. I'm back now.'

Rouse looked up. From above, she smiled at him with the warmth of a mother he had never known.

'You mean that?'

Claudia nodded, 'I mean it, Wellie.'

Rouse suddenly jumped to his feet and backed up to the door. Something wasn't right - *this* wasn't right.

'What's the matter, Wellie?' said Claudia, a concerned expression creeping across her face.

'No,' said Rouse, fiddling nervously with his tie, 'this is too weird. Too weird.'

'Wellie,' purred Claudia, gliding across the room and placing herself hard up against him. 'It can be like before, I mean *exactly* like before…if you can do one thing for me…'

She flicked her tongue in his ear and his knees nearly buckled.

'What?' he said without thinking it.

'I need Scottie to be made better again.'

She locked him with a different expression this

time. This time looked determined, serious. Rouse got his hands between them and slowly but firmly moved her to one side and positioned himself on the other side of the bed. He was stronger this time around, thought Claudia. But only just stronger. There was an uncomfortable silent tension in the room, bouncing back and fore between them. Claudia decided to throw her hand.

'I don't want to make things difficult for you, Wellie,' she said in a measured tone. 'But if I have to, if you give me no alternative, I promise you I will.'

Rouse's eyes narrowed in suspicion. What was this? A *threat*? Was she, this *whore*, actually threatening him? His momentary weakness was quashed by a growing unease and irritation.

'You're going to have to spell that one out,' he said, trying to mask his nerves.

'Very well,' said Claudia. 'I still have all of the photos we took together, and I mean...*all of them*. Just over one hundred, I would say. I'm sure I don't need to remind you of the content.'

Claudia paused to let her words sink in. She noted with quiet satisfaction that his complexion had started to pale as he recalled the many photographs they had taken in her apartment on Concertina Street.

'I don't believe you,' was all he could think to say.

'Yes you do,' she retorted softly.

Rouse believed her. She'd showed him some photos of her with others, when he tried to think of ideas but couldn't. He knew deep down that she would have kept pictures of him. But he immediately reacted over the fact that here was a glorified prostitute attempting to blackmail him.

'Who the hell do you think you are?' he hissed. 'Do you honestly think you can pull a stunt like this and get away with it? Do you know how many powerful and influential people I know?'

'Oh, I'm sure,' said Claudia. 'And I'm also sure they'd like to see you in action, Wellie. Let's see, how about a six by four of you masturbating on my sofa? Or perhaps a blow up of me inserting one of my dildos in your ass -'

'You shut up!' blurted Rouse, spittle looping over his bottom lip. His face had turned crimson in a mixture of rage and embarrassment. He took a few steps forward as though he was about to grab her. But Claudia didn't back away an inch. She placed her hands confidently on her hips and held her head high. Rouse's shoulders sagged and he tried a different approach. 'But, Guin, what can I possibly do? I've read the prognosis. How can I make it better?'

Claudia took one firm step towards the bed.

'I want you to give her the Treatment.'

Rouse's shoulders sagged even more, 'What?'

'The Treatment, Wellie. You know exactly what I am talking about.'

'I don't -'

'The kind of medical procedures you and your kind keep hidden from the general public. Don't try and deny it, Wellie. I know about these things.'

Rouse rested himself against the frame at the foot of the bed.

'How?'

'You talked sometimes, when you were drunk, or high,' replied Claudia candidly. 'How did you describe it back then? "A secret neuro-surgical breakthrough that would remain unavailable to the great unwashed who are over-eating and over-populating their way to oblivion." I didn't really pay much attention to its significance then. But now…'

She let the words linger in the air between them. She had Rouse beat into a corner for now. He straightened up, took a long, hard look at the unconscious figure in the bed before putting in his one gambit.

'You've got to give me something in return,' he said. 'I'm taking a very big risk if I put her through the Treatment, Guin. It's only fair, right?'

Claudia considered her options for a while, then looked at Scottie, lying peacefully unaware of what was going on inches from her. She sighed and realised that this man had to be kept on side as much as possible. She came up close to him and wrapped her arms around his neck. She raised herself up and whispered in his ear:

'What is it you want?'

Rouse placed his hands on her hips and half turned his head, smelling her hair.

'What will you give?' he said, his voice shaking at this physical contact.

Claudia took his hands in hers and slid them down over her backside, hooked up her dress and put them down inside her knickers. She heard him let out a tiny moan as his fingers kneaded her buttocks. She kissed his earlobe and, burying her physical repulsion deep, said:

'All that you are missing.'

17

'Tell me about The Celebrations,' said Harry as he lit a cigarette.

He'd been seated at Audrey Lee's table in the alcove for a little over three minutes, after she'd performed her special rendition of *Love Don't Fear Me*. He'd had enough to drink to feel bold enough to dive straight in. He wanted to know her thoughts on it, to apply flesh and blood to the bones of Rick's biography. It wasn't long before he realised he may have actually overstepped the mark.

Audrey Lee put down her Mint Sonata and sat back, saying nothing. Her face was in the shadows, the only movement came from the wisps of smoke she exhaled. Harry sat there, drowning in the uncomfortable silence of the alcove, unsure of where to look. He inhaled his cigarette into a dry throat and downed his Brandy Alexander clumsily, allowing a thin trail to roll out the corner of his mouth. He put the glass on the table and emitted a loud sigh.

'Look, Ms Lee,' he started, 'I --'

She cut him off by rising to her feet and walking away, only pausing momentarily to squeeze his shoulder in silent consolation. Harry remained seated at the table, alone and furious with himself, until he had finished his cigarette and the waiter had removed the glasses and emptied the ashtray. Then he got up and went down to the gents. As he descended the narrow stairwell, he tried to swallow away the bitter taste of squandered opportunity. Just who the hell did Harry Brewer think he was, encroaching on an obviously sad, isolated woman and assuming he had the technique and requisite charm to get her to open up about the good ole days? He shoved the door to the gents open and the three men standing at the urinals turned and immediately disregarded him in favour of their respective flows. Harry marched past them and splashed cold water on his face from the wash basin taps. He'd wandered blindly out of a blizzard of booze holding on to dreams and ideas unhindered by reason or pragmatism. He'd taken no care at all to prepare himself for the possibility that perhaps, *perhaps*, the lady wasn't interested in playing ball. He decided that he would just leave the Kommune Club, tail wedged firmly between his legs and never set foot in the place again. Places like the Kommune weren't meant for people like him, Harry decided. Places like the Kommune were for people who could live decadently so long as they had a back-up plan. Harry had no such back up plan; he'd set himself on a one way course into total oblivion, financed by a sum of money that wasn't, in the strictest of terms, *his*. It was too late for him to change that now...

The gents' emptied and Harry unzipped and readied himself at one of the urinal pods. He closed his eyes and realised how they stung from the potent mixture of smoke and tiredness. He began to slowly urinate in a trance-like state, eyes closed and head bobbing slowly up and down on failing shoulders. The sound of someone entering the gents snapped him out of it. As he was entering mid-flow, he suddenly felt a pair of hands grip his shoulders and violently yank him backwards, his bladder suddenly and very painfully locking down. Harry's shoes lost their grip on the damp floor and he went in reverse, arms flailing, back into the cubicle directly behind him and the area between his shoulder blades made heavy contact with the toilet seat within. As he struggled to get to his feet, grunting at the jabbing pain in his upper back, he saw Gubbs, his expression as hatefully repugnant as ever, clutching a dripping wet toilet brush with both hands like a sodden samurai sword. Gubbs raised the brush over his rat-like head and came at Harry. Harry kicked out wildly with his left leg and his foot caught Gubbs square in the chest, what there was of it. A blast of air was expelled from Gubbs' mouth and he dropped the brush. He managed to lock Harry's leg inside an elbow and Harry stretched forward and, grabbing him by the suit collar, pulled hard, sending them both toppling over into a heap. Then Harry broke free and was suddenly on top of Gubbs. They wrestled around on the gents' floor like drunken puppies for a few moments, each of them trying to commandeer the toilet brush lying just within their reach. Harry managed to twist Gubbs' arm back on itself and shove it into his face. Gubbs struggled to get free but Harry was too heavy for the smaller man. Harry's fingers got purchase on the brush handle and he threw it behind him, hearing it land in a toilet bowl with a splash. Harry punched Gubbs twice in the stomach and then got to his feet. Gubbs lay curled up, a scowling, growling unsavoury foetus at Harry's feet. Harry felt out of breath and distinctly out of shape. He wanted to knock Gubbs around some more to compensate for his own lack of fitness. He started to drag Gubbs towards the door of the gents by his shirt collar but gave up half way there and let him drop.

'I'll stand on your face next time,' he said in

between regaining his breath, 'you skinny piece of shit.'

Then he zipped himself up and walked out of the gents.

Harry crossed the crowded bar purposefully, determined to catch up with Audrey Lee. He could feel himself boiling over with frustration that she could think he was some kind of garden variety lurker, hanging around and hassling her at every opportunity. He darted up the stairs, his sudden impetus blocking out his creaking joints. Once outside on the pavement, he scanned the immediate vicinity, trying to pick her out in the throng of pubbers and clubbers. There she was, stepping gracefully into a black cab, her dark ankle length coat pulled snugly around her. Harry darted forward and caught hold of the handle just before the door clicked shut. Audrey looked taken aback as she saw him standing there, panting over the sudden burst of energy.

'Was that your idea?'

Audrey looked genuinely shocked to see him looming into the recess of the black cab. But she regained her composure quickly.

'What are you talking about?'

'Your little poodle trying to give me a makeover with a toilet brush.'

'Gubbs?' her eyebrows raised.

'Listen, Audrey,' said Harry, pointing a finger at her, 'all I was doing was taking an interest in you because I find you *interesting*. If you don't want to know, that's perfectly fine; I'm not one of these fucking weirdoes who can't take the hint. But at least have the decency to tell me so to my face, not have that little prick try and work me over. Okay?'

Audrey placed her hands in her lap and sat back in her seat. Harry didn't know what he was expecting; a slap, a stern rebuttal, the rough manhandling of the taxi driver.

'Get in,' said Audrey.

'What?'

'I said get in, unless you want another scrap with Gubbs.'

Harry followed Audrey's glance and saw Gubbs exiting the Kommune entrance. His face was filled with white range as he saw where they were. Harry jumped in the cab and slammed the door shut just as Gubbs skidded along the pavement, hands pressed flat against the window. The cab pulled away from the kerb. Gubbs kept up for the first few feet before disappearing into the headlights of the following traffic. They sat in silence for ten minutes and Harry tried to think of something to say.

'How much will Gubbs mind being left out?' asked Harry, making himself comfortable next to Audrey.

'I imagine he will mind an awful lot,' replied Audrey as she peered out of her side of the cab. 'It'll teach him a lesson about his appalling behaviour.'

'Good,' said Harry. 'So where are we going?'

'You know,' said Audrey as she began to touch up her lipstick in a small mirror, 'you will be the first person, aside from Gubbs, to cross my doorway in nearly seven years.'

'Seven years? I'm very flattered, Ms Lee.'

'You should be. I hope I won't regret it.'

Their eyes met briefly, both of them trying to see

what was crossing their minds at that very moment.

'How far is it?' asked Harry.

'Aren't we keen?'

'I know my bladder is.'

'How practical of you.'

'Unfinished business.'

Audrey leaned forward:

'Just here by the gates, driver.'

Harry and Audrey stepped out of the black cab and he peered through the gothic style gates that led to an old and expensive looking block of apartments. As Audrey entered a code on the stone wall and the gates clicked open, another black cab pulled up and out jumped Gubbs, sticky with torment and seemingly eager for another go. He slithered over and tried to position himself between Harry and Audrey. Harry was tempted to throw him into the nearest bushes.

'Oh, for goodness sake, Gubbs,' barked Audrey, 'just calm down will you?'

Gubbs backed off with a sudden obedience that intrigued Harry. They followed Audrey up the long, tree lined grounds beyond the gates. Despite her order, Harry maintained a wary eye on her poodle as they took a ride in the plush lift up to the fourth and final floor.

'Go to sleep,' said Audrey.

They were in the hallway of her apartment and Gubbs, without any form of protest, disappeared down one end, a door closing behind him. Audrey removed a pin from her silvery blonde hair and it swept over her shoulders.

'The room you're looking for is through there,' she said, indicating another door. 'Fix some drinks.'

Harry watched her enter the large, spacious lounge and cross into another room, closing the door behind her. Harry removed his overcoat and draped it on the back of a wide beige sofa. The whole apartment looked *old,* not ancient and shabby, just out of time, out of the present. Old furniture, old wallpaper, old pictures, fixtures and fittings. He walked down the hall, found the bathroom and had a satisfying burst. On his way back to the lounge, he caught a glimpse of Gubbs, that irritating little wanker, spying on him, his nose so obviously out of joint that it was folded around the door. Harry ignored him and located the drinks cabinet next to a large teak box that contained a television. He poured two vodka and tonics and regarded one particular photograph on the wall. It was an old monochrome picture of a much younger Audrey Lee on stage in some smoky club somewhere in history. Her eyes pierced the camera lens with the intense energy of mid-performance.

'Do you like it?' said Audrey, taking her drink from Harry's hand.

'Yes,' said Harry and drank.

'It was taken by a photographer named Nigel St Davos.'

'Right.'

'Have you heard of him?'

Harry knew what she was asking.

'I'm aware of him, yes.'

'How?'

'Rick.'

'Of course, Rick,' she said, sipping her vodka and sitting down on the sofa. Harry sat in a hard armchair opposite her. 'He likes to tell my story for me.'

'Sorry,' said Harry.

'For what?'

'I'm not sure,' said Harry with a confused look. 'Do you mind if I smoke?'

'Only if you're feeling generous,' said Audrey.

Harry lit up for both of them and passed one cigarette over. They sat and drank in silence for a few moments. Audrey studied Harry intently and he didn't mind.

'So,' she said finally, 'what's your life been all about?'

Harry hadn't had to answer a question like that for a while. He blew out a cloud of smoke and cleared his throat.

'For the last few years I was working as a rep for a medical solutions company in South America, not doing particularly well with it but enjoying the local nightlife and all its benefits. I discovered that one of my bosses was on the make, stashing aside a rather large sum of money. I had the opportunity to take it for myself, so I did and took the first flight out back to the homeland. Ironically, my parents were killed in a plane crash not a hundred miles from where I was living, just as I was flying over the equatorial line. So I came back to an empty house in England. Not much else I can say about it all really.'

'And this boss of yours in South America?'

'Will he come after me? I shouldn't think so.' Harry paused, seeing a chain of events in his mind's eye that he hoped were mere conjecture. And *yet*...

'In fact, my parents' plane crashing shortly after seems a little bit like a coincidence, don't you think? And the ironic thing is that everything my parents had has come to me anyway, so I don't particularly need the money anymore.'

Audrey considered what he had just told her over her glass, her eyes narrowed, trying to tell if he was spinning her a yarn. Harry sat back in the armchair and realised that that was the first time he had vocally acknowledged any of the grubby, illicit and tragic details of his recent history, including the matter of whether his parents' deaths were the result of his own greed. He blocked it.

'That was very candid of you,' said Audrey. 'You give the impression of someone who has just gotten something off his chest.'

Harry smiled thinly and tapped his cigarette over the huge glass ashtray on the coffee table between them, 'Over to you.'

Audrey rests her glass on the arm of the sofa and blinks slowly behind the smoke.

'I was a backing singer in a group called The Celebrations, but then I already know Rick told you at least that much.' She paused but Harry didn't say anything. He was content to just sit there and let her continue. 'The three of us, singing backing for Perry Coolidge, God's gift; not enough talent to stretch to the four corners of his ego, that's how Nigel described him the night we went out for the first time. Once, when we playing the clubs up in the north, he and I were alone on the tour bus. He decided that night that he'd make my life in the group a misery. The minute he pulled it out and told me what I should do with it and I refused, that was it. He knew he wouldn't have me, so he moved in on Juliet instead. She wasn't as...*familiar* with the way things worked back then.

She wasn't as resistant to the sexual coercions of snakes like him as I was. I'd grown up with it in my family and saw its effects. Juliet fell pregnant and Perry "took care of it", as the expression went in those days.'

Audrey paused while she emptied her glass and beckoned Harry to give her a refill.

'Anyway, I caught Nigel's eye on the Paris tour and he gave me a way out. He had the money to pay the right people off.'

Harry topped both their glasses up and handed one to Audrey.

'What happened to the group?' he asked.

Audrey stubbed out her cigarette.

'The day after I left, the tour bus collided with a truck on its way to Strasbourg. Most of them died at the scene, except Perry. Nigel and I went to the hospital where they'd taken him. He was burnt badly and didn't have long. But I wanted to see him. The way he looked at me, I thought he was going to ask me to make it alright between us. I shook my head to let him know it was too late for anything. Then I left him to die in a cold hospital ward alone. Do you think I was wrong?'

'No,' said Harry, matter-of-factly, 'I don't think you did anything wrong.'

Audrey ran a finger around the rim of her glass, seeing the past there within the circle.

'We wrote songs together, Nigel and me,' she said, the sparkle coming back into her eyes after the remembrance, 'and we took them into the studio when we returned to England. We recorded *Love Don't Fear Me*, of course and the song for the second side, *We've*

147

Already Reached The End.'

'I've heard it,' said Harry. 'I got hold of a rare copy, from a collector friend.'

'That song became somewhat prophetic,' said Audrey. 'I realised I wasn't ready to be a star in my own right, and never would be.'

'Why not?'

'Because I knew I'd never be good enough.'

Harry nodded in silent understanding: He knew that feeling.

'So, we recorded the first single and it scraped into the top thirty. One critic said I was five years too late. But I was suddenly a pop star. I did a national tour, sharing the bill with eight other acts. One dressing table mirror after another. It felt like I was never really there most of the time.'

Harry crossed one knee over the other and it started to cramp.

'After the tour finished, we were approached by a young and terrifyingly ambitious producer named Gregory Gem. He wanted to produce an album and we spent three weeks working on the songs I'd written with Nigel.'

'How did that do?' asked Harry. 'In the charts I mean.'

'It never saw the light of day. On the last night of recording, Gregory told Nigel about the fling he and I were having. All hell broke loose in the studio between them and Nigel stormed out. The master tapes went with him. I tried to get to Nigel for ages after, but I couldn't even get close. You want to know the best part of it? It wasn't even true; Gregory made the whole thing up just to get at him. And he fell for it.'

'His loss,' blurted Harry before realising that it somehow didn't sound appropriate. 'But whatever happened to the master tapes?'

'There was the inevitable legal battle; Gregory attempted to claim them but I don't think his heart was in it. He had the makings of a sneaky bastard and just look at him now. He controls everything. He let me run and I just kept on running. I dived for cover and went into a drunken meltdown. My starlet dream was over, and I was over with it. I've been pretending to be her ever since.'

Amid the melancholic ambience, Harry lit them both up again and suddenly he felt knackered. He felt as though he could fall asleep right there and then. He closed his eyes momentarily and when he opened them, Audrey's face was right in front of his. She was smiling at him and the room was darker.

'Did you come here tonight harbouring any secret agendas?' she said softly.

Harry shook his head without breaking eye contact.

'Then let's say our goodbyes for now.'

Harry felt cold as he hailed a cab twenty minutes later and a mile from Audrey Lee's apartment. On the journey through London, Harry recalled her story. She'd taken a way out of her life and yet she seemed to be still scratching at the door like a cat trying to claw its way back indoors on a stormy night. Right then, as he was feeling the long delay between his last and next drink, Harry had the genesis of an idea.

'Driver, can you stop at an off licence along the way?'

Deborah Flaxman searched the thick overgrown greenery of her back garden, taking extra special not to catch her exposed flesh on any of the thorns or nettles, but still her cat was nowhere to be seen. The battery was beginning to die in her torch and shaking it violently only made it blink erratically for a few seconds before the light continued to fade. She pressed her feet hard into her sandals and pressed on along the unkempt grass verge that led to the ghostly greenhouse at the far end. She swore to herself that she would throttle Sara when she eventually got her hands on her. She heard movement in amongst the giant balls of grass plants directly behind her and she spun around. She froze and listened intently.

'Sara...' she called softly in a high pitched tone.

The grass plants began to shake and as soon as something appeared in the shadows, she realised it wasn't her cat. An arm jutted out and Deborah grabbed the wrist with both hands and yanked as hard as she could. A blurry figure came stumbling out of the undergrowth and, powered by Deborah, went sailing across the grass into the pond. The figure flailed around until apparently deducing that the water was only sixteen inches deep. Deborah stood on the tiled edge of the pond and let out an audible sigh as the soaking figure sat up in the water.

'What the hell are you doing in my back garden at one in the morning?'

Harry dragged a hand down his wet face and looked up at the naked vision standing over him.

'I've had an epiphany,' he said, slurring his words.

'A lobotomy more like. How much have you had to drink?'

'Not enough,' said Harry as he struggled to get to his feet. 'Let's have a drink.'

Deborah grabbed Harry's arm and pulled him up on to dry land.

'You'd better get inside before you freeze to death,' she said, firmly propelling him towards the house.

'You must be freezing,' said Harry, looking her up and down. 'You want my overcoat?'

'No thank you.'

'You do know what season it is out here, don't you?'

'Get inside.'

Deborah closed the back door behind her and locked it.

'Take your clothes off,' she said in a matronly manner. Harry didn't say anything; he just did what he was told. Deborah collected a sweater and jogging bottoms from her airing cupboard and gave them to Harry to put on. She hung his wet clothes up to dry and found a half empty bottle of bourbon in the overcoat pocket.

'Classy, Harry,' she said as she passed it to his eager hands.

'You want a drink?'

'No. So what's this epiphany of yours?'

'Audrey took me to her apartment tonight,' said Harry as he took a large swallow of bourbon. 'She told me all about Nigel St Davos and Gregory Gem and the whole thing.'

'Really,' said Deborah. She was intrigued and kind of impressed but she didn't show it. 'So?'

'Nigel St Davos has recordings from her studio

sessions. I reckon if I can convince him to hand them over, we can do something with them.'

'*We?*'

'Audrey and I. But I need your help, Deborah, because you know about music and you know people who know about music.'

'I see,' said Deborah, crossing the room and slipping into a thick woolly cardigan that had been lying on the breakfast bar. 'You know, Harry, nothing's as simple as you like to think it might be. Say Nigel St Davos does still have all those recordings in his possession; what are the odds on him just handing them over to a complete stranger who turns up on his doorstep stinking of last night's booze?'

Harry looked a little put out at Deborah's cutting words and he put the bottle down on the work unit. He could feel his eyes beginning to close on him.

'I thought you could help me to persuade him,' he said meekly.

Deborah smiled inwardly at Harry's naughty little boy demeanour. What was it about this guy's personality that intrigued her so much? She was aware that he was fading slowly and decided to set him down before he fell down.

'Deborah,' slurred Harry as she helped him onto a sofa in the darkened living room.

'Yes, Harry?' replied Deborah as she pulled a blanket up to his neck.

'You don't need to parade about the place in the buff to look attractive, you know.'

Deborah put the back of her hand across her mouth to stifle a giggle and went upstairs to bed. Harry, his head spinning like a multi coloured top, imagined himself standing in the wings, watching Audrey Lee singing live to a crowd of thousands, hundreds of thousands. She took a bow and waved and just before Harry passed out, she turned to him and blew him the sweetest kiss.

18

Special News Update : *A spokesperson for the New Metropolitan Police Service has confirmed that an item of girls' clothing has been found in dense woodland near Hatcher's Rye, more commonly known as the "Trillionaire's Toy Town". It is understood that the item of clothing discovered was a shoe and that it was found by one of the search volunteers in a bin. The item of footwear - a pink Supertread XX - has been formally identified by Jackie and Mitch Sweetlove as belonging to their missing daughter, the schoolgirl Patience Sweetlove. Several dozen local businesses are sponsoring the police in their ongoing search and the spokesperson added that a special thank you is to be extended towards Cosmic Bicycles Ltd of Rudney Street for use of their latest Highground GL2 off road cycles which have come in great use to the search party. A review of the GL2's performance can be found on p47.*

Detective Inspector Kibber topped up his coffee with a nip from his flask and looked on as Sergeant Sam Keady sat next to him, patiently staring through the binoculars pointing out the window of the attic room towards Gregory Gem's estate. The drink gave him a sharp jab of heat as it went down, making him shiver in the chilly morning air of the attic. He was feeling it a little more this morning; he'd woken up naked next to the bed, sticky and disorientated and had screwed himself into his crumpled clothes before leaving Eiderlands. He'd successfully sidestepped a conversation with Mr. Sisk by swinging past the reception desk with a blunt "Urgent Police Business" which got him through the front door before the guest house owner could stick his nose in. Keady had been waiting for him outside, resting against the unmarked squad car that Kibber had yet to return.

'Sergeant,' said Kibber as he considered the under-furnished meat sandwich in his lap.

'Yes, Sir?'

'Do you think you have learned much from me?'

'Oh, yes Sir,' replied Keady affably.

'Really?' said Kibber, eyebrows raised. 'Such as?'

Keady sat back away from the binoculars and folded his arms, 'Well, Sir, I suppose I would have to say that you've showed me that it's possible to be an officer in the New Metropolitan Police Service and still have a conscience.'

'A conscience, Sergeant?'

'Yes, Sir.'

'You think *I* have a conscience?'

'Certainly, Sir.'

Kibber looked on as Keady smiled at him before returning to his surveillance. Kibber folded the sandwich back up in its wrapping and dropped it on the floor next to his chair. He drank his coffee and quietly regarded his Sergeant. The New Metropolitan Police Service seemed like such an unlikely career choice for someone like Sam Keady. His sensibilities seemed out of step with the organisation that glittered in England's heart of darkness. Ruth had told Kibber that she had never wanted Sam to enlist, that he should have put his degree in humanities to better use, but her husband was resolute; he had felt obliged to join when the government's New Directives were brought in.

Keady had confided in Kibber and told him that he was an objector to the reinstatement of the death penalty. Kibber had warned him to keep his mouth shut around other colleagues. The reinstatement of capital punishment had been one of the more favourable directives within influential circles and Kibber too had voiced his enthusiasm along with the rest of them. The nay-sayers were regarded as friends of the common criminal, left-wing bleeding hearts with too much faith in the rehabilitation of the wicked rather than justice for the wronged. Ruth saw Kibber as the representative of everything she hated. Kibber saw Ruth as an opinionated prat who filled her students' heads with right-on bullshit that made his job harder. Keady tried to smooth the way between them, but Ruth wasn't having any of it.

'Why do think I have a conscience, Sergeant?'

Keady turned to his superior, 'Because you're asking me, Sir.'

Kibber's eyes narrowed and he downed the rest of his coffee. 'Sergeant, you should have put your education to better use. You should have listened to your wife.'

Kibber got to his feet and stretched his arms up over his head. Keady said nothing, but sat writing on a notepad while looking through the binoculars.

'What have you got, Sergeant?'

'Two cars pulling up at the front of the estate. Several people getting out and going into the house.'

'Is Gem one of them?'

'Negative, Sir. I recognise a couple of them though, Sir; the singer Crispian Bull for one. And that looks like the band The Sick Driscolls, Sharlotte

Carney and several other people who look like aides. I think it may have something to do with that charity single for the missing girl, Sir.'

'Good for them,' said Kibber flatly and lay himself down on the old camp bed in the corner of the attic. 'I'm going to have an hour, Sergeant.'

'Yes, Sir.'

Kibber folded an arm across his face to block out his bleak surroundings and shifted his weight across the uncomfortable metal framework under the thin mattress. Keady made no sound at all.

19

'Don't fall back to sleep,' said Deborah.

Harry's eyes peeled open slowly, revealing a world beyond of hazy hues and morning aromas. The side of his head ached and he felt damp. Raising his cheek an inch off whatever he was resting on, Deborah came into focus. She was wearing a thin dressing gown and her hair was tied back loosely behind her head. She was sitting level with his head, a giant cup placed in both hands. His neck was stiff and as he struggled to get upright he realised he had been lying on the breakfast bar in the kitchen. There was a puddle of red wine on the surface that his head had been lying in.

'What's happening?' he mumbled.

'I guess you decided to help yourself to seconds,' said Deborah. 'Or thirds or fourths. Who knows?'

'Is it enough to say sorry?' said Harry, wiping the wet side of his face with a hand.

'I shouldn't think so,' said Deborah, 'but in light of your recent family history you get one "Get Out Of Jail" card. Good enough?'

Harry nodded, 'Good enough.'

Deborah went over to the percolator and poured out a large cup of steaming black coffee and handed it to him. Harry stared into the swirling liquid; his head rocked back and forth and he wished he could scalp himself to make the throbbing go away. He was trying to piece together yet another over-oiled night.

'I didn't try anything last night, did I? I mean, I didn't come onto you or something like that? Because if I did happen to act a little untoward then I really *am* very sorry about that.'

'Drink your coffee,' said Deborah. She leaned in close and whispered in his ear. 'It's from the South Americas.'

Harry took a big sip of the coffee and its strength nearly blew his head off. He watched Deborah get his clothes out of the tumble dryer and hang them up, and while he did he considered his master plan for Audrey Lee and the tapes in Nigel St. Davos' possession.

'Did I tell you my idea last night?'

'You did,' she replied as she hung his tie around the neck of a coat hanger.

'What do you think about it?'

Deborah finished arranging his clothes for him and padded past him into the living room.

'While you've been lying unconscious in my kitchen, I've been putting that time to good use.' She returned to the kitchen and dropped his cigarettes and lighter on the work surface. 'As you know, I used to be a music journalist back when there was music to write about. I have a friend that I used to work with and I've left a message with his office to give me a ring when he's free.'

'Wow,' said Harry humbly, 'I don't know what to say.'

'Well, save it until later,' said Deborah, 'my friend might not want to or be able to help. But, you never know, maybe we can try and get an audience with Nigel St. Davos.'

'This is great,' said Harry, suddenly feeling a bit of life pumping through his system. He got off the breakfast bar and put his coffee down, immediately wanting to hug Deborah. He refrained, unsure of where any boundaries lay. 'You're doing all of this for me, Deborah?'

Deborah regarded this slightly sad and pathetic out of shape figure standing in her kitchen and she decided she had no choice.

'Harry,' she said, 'you're trying to put something right, to make amends for something else. If this is what's going to help you then I'll help you too. Maybe then you'll think about straightening yourself out.'

'I will,' said Harry. He knew she was right and there was no point in denying it.

'I hope so, Harry. You don't get to roll the dice forever.'

Harry finished his coffee enthusiastically and began to collect his clothes from the hangers. They were still warm and felt very inviting. Without thinking he removed the clothes Deborah had given him and folded them up as neatly as his shaking hands would allow him. She sat at the breakfast bar and watched him wandering into his own clothes at near impossible angles. She found him fascinating for reasons she wouldn't find anyone fascinating; he was badly in need of some grooming, a neglected garden that offered the occasional glimpse of potential bloom. There had once been some kind of muscle tone there, but it had given way to puppy fat and well-executed self abuse. But, she thought, there was still something that on a very odd day she might have found inviting, attractive even. She watched as his naked figure disappeared reluctantly into that suit of his and marvelled at how he'd managed to achieve it without losing his balance and splitting his face open on the washing machine.

'So when do we start?' said Harry as he stuffed the

tie inside his suit.

'Why don't you let me concentrate on that for now,' said Deborah, gently assisting Harry out of the kitchen and down the hallway to the front door.

'Okay,' said Harry uncertainly.

'You go home, have a hot shower and climb into bed. With any luck you'll be sober by this time tomorrow. I'll be in touch.'

Before Harry could say anything else, Deborah had nudged him out onto the front doorstep and closed the door behind him. He did up one of his suit buttons and walked down the path. Inside, Deborah pressed her ear to the front door and listened to him whistle badly until that faded and she heard the key in the lock next door. After pouring herself another coffee with a drop of brandy for good measure, Deborah went up to her bathroom and immersed herself in hot water and scented bubbles while Harry showered and scrubbed with meticulous attention to detail.

20

Cromwell Rouse unhooked his surgical mask and scrubbed clean outside the theatre room. As he dried his hands he contemplated the inert figure of Guinevere's "friend" on the operating table. The Treatment had been administered as he had instructed and now the Scottie girl was lying in there, blissfully unaware of the deal that had been struck to buy her time. He threw his scrubs in the bin and thrust himself along the corridors of St Marcus's until he reached his private office where he found Guinevere sitting on the sofa, reading a magazine. She looked up at him expectantly but Rouse said nothing.

'How long until she can come home with me?' asked Claudia.

Rouse smiled as he sat down at his desk, 'She will require pills, twice a day for the next thirty days. But my dear, how did you know the Treatment was a success?'

'Because I know how good you are, Wellie.'

'Please,' said Rouse, holding up a hand in protest, 'there is no need to patronise me. I *know* how good I am. And I also know how good *you* are, Guin.'

'What do you mean?'

'Our deal.'

'You'll get what you want.'

'Not good enough, Guin,' said Rouse as he lit a cigarette and landed his feet loudly on the desk. 'Not nearly good enough.'

There was an icy silence between them for a few moments. Claudia rose to her feet and closed the thick blinds, shielding them from the ward outside. As she slowly approached the desk, Rouse felt himself becoming aroused. He had flashbacks of how it had been before with her. She came around the desk and positioned herself on his lap, letting her hand run down his chest to his crotch. She could feel him underneath, twitching at her touch.

'Take it out,' said Rouse.

'The pills,' said Claudia.

'After,' said Rouse.

'Before,' said Claudia.

They stared into each other, neither one daring to blink. Claudia gave his crotch a quick squeeze and Rouse gave in. He nodded and Claudia allowed him to get up and walk to a small refrigerated cabinet in the corner of the office. She watched him with growing impatience as he fumbled with his keys and opened it up. He took out a bottle of pills and held them in his outstretched hand. Claudia approached and took them off him. She examined the bottle and immediately she realised something was wrong.

'How many pills are in this bottle?'

'Thirty, my dear,' said Rouse, a smug grin spreading across his lips.

'You bastard.'

'My dear Guinevere,' said Rouse as he returned to his seat behind the desk, 'you really don't think that I could trust you to keep your word do you? I've got too much riding on this deal to simply allow you to slip away with your little friend.'

'And if she doesn't get the full course?'

'Then her recovery will only be partial. The Treatment will work up to a point, but she will be left immobilized, maybe for years, maybe for the rest of her life. The question is would you be prepared to wait?'

Claudia knew he had her in a corner for now. He held out his hand, beckoning for her to come to him. Claudia, feeling the sudden crushing weight of defeat on her shoulders, returned to her place on his lap. He snaked a hand up her back and gently gripped the back of her neck, pulling her face close to his. She could feel his stale breath invading her nostrils. His voice crackled in saliva.

'You must be prepared to honour your debts, Guinevere.'

'I am,' she said, trying to hide her disgust.

'Just the way it used to be?'

'Just the way it used to be, Wellie.'

Rouse licked her earlobe and placed her hand back on his crotch. 'And I want the photos and all the negatives. Every last one of them. Do you understand?'

'Yes,' said Claudia. 'Will you take me to her?'

'Later,' said Rouse.

Half an hour later, Claudia sat with her head resting on Scottie's right forearm, stroking her soft skin lightly with a finger. She couldn't take her eyes off her; she wished she would wake up so they could flee the hospital and start again somewhere, anywhere but here in this filthy metropolis.

Please wake up.

A nurse entered the room and scribbled on the medical charts, leaving without a word. Claudia's eyes burned with exhaustion and she let them close, imagining she was in a bed somewhere, cradling

Scottie's head in her arms. She felt a tear escape from the corner of her eye and for a split second she thought she could detect the slightest of movement in Scottie's forearm as the tear rolled from Claudia's cheek onto her love's skin. When Claudia opened her eyes, the room was in darkness.

21

Allen Wyngarde crushed his cigarette into the overflowing ashtray and swept away the accumulated smoke around the writing desk. He'd reached a decision, a plan of action, a method of attack. He'd rang an ex-police officer, who had been an advisor on some of the telemovies Allen had been involved with in the past, who'd retired years ago to the south coast and asked him, with fingers crossed, if he still had a contact number for a certain private detective agency he recalled being mentioned once. The ex-police officer, an old work horse policeman, had kept Allen waiting several minutes before coming back on the line with what he wanted. Allen answered several friendly questions concisely and politely - did he still write telemovies? Not anymore; Is Barbara cheating on you? No, she's still dead - and then he'd said "thanks" and put the phone down. Now he sat in his chair and read the number he'd written down several times. He picked up the receiver and dialled.

Nobody answered at the other end. Instead, an answering machine buzzed into life and delivered its message, narrated by a deep, male burr.

'You're through to K.D.A. All of the customer service lines are busy at the moment, but leave your name, contact number and brief reason for calling and one of our representatives will get back to you as soon as possible. Thank you.'

'Hello,' said Allen, wincing at the message. The diction of the recorded voice was poor and sounded like it had been an arduous session to achieve that "take". Nevertheless, despite hating the fact that he was having to commit himself to tape, Allen reluctantly committed his details to tape. But he chose to abridge his brief reason for calling:

'I wish to appropriate an expert in human tailing.'

Then he hung up and poured himself a stiff drink. Two hours later, just as he was on the fuzzy precipice of an afternoon stupor, the phone on his desk rattled into life and he reached for the receiver, shaking his head violently as he did.

'Hello?'

'Mister Allen Mackintosh?' came the garbled reply.

'It's Wyngarde actually.'

'I'm calling from K.D.A. Are you at liberty to continue with this conversation?'

'Yes.'

'We gather from your enquiry that you'd like to have someone followed.'

'Well, yes-'

'Tailing fees begin at one hundred pounds a day, with two hundred up front to cover booking fee and costs.'

'Right, alright.'

'Meet one of our representatives at Hyde Park Corner this evening. There's a bench just inside the eastern gate. Your contact will be seated there at sundown, reading yesterday's copy of *The Edition*. From there, the formal interview will commence. Is everything understood?'

'Yes, everything.'

'Bring all the necessary.'

The line went dead and Allen sat there, still holding the receiver to one ear as though wanting to continue the conversation. He nursed a cigarette from the packet on the desk and lit up before putting the phone down. What time was sundown these days? He checked his watch and decided he probably had around five hours to get his act together before he would meet K.D.A.'s representative. He went over to the safe and withdrew an envelope of money before running a dirty fingernail up a stack of old periodicals until he came to a particular edition from several years ago. He thumbed through it until he came to one of the special features. It was about Iain Gwynne, and there, in a box on the left hand page, was that photo of Iain Fucking Gwynne. Black and white, sitting there with a fountain pen in one hand, held like a cigar, gurning mirthlessly at the camera lens.

Allen cut the photograph out with scissors and put it in the envelope with the money. Then he stripped off, ran a bath and lay in it for the next three hours. But he didn't feel the slightest bit cleaner for it.

Allen Wyngarde found himself in Hyde Park, wrapped up against the wind, just as the sun was sinking into the dirty brown sky. He felt uncomfortable as he headed along the wide path, sidestepping everyone who entered his immediate vicinity. As he approached the eastern gate, there on the bench sat three people; an elderly couple who were picking over something in a Tupperware box, and a larger man next to them who had a newspaper held up in front of his face. Allen's fingers felt the outline of the envelope in his overcoat pocket and proceeded. He squeezed onto the seat in between its occupants and waited, unsure whether to start the conversation. He glanced sideways and noticed that the man's newspaper was *The* Edition and that the date printed at the top of the page was indeed yesterday's. After a minute or so, the man folded the paper and dropped it into the bin next to the bench.

'Did you bring the necessary?' he said without turning to face Allen.

'Yes,' Allen replied, reaching into his coat for the envelope.

'Not here,' said the man abruptly.

'We're going on somewhere?'

'That's right. Somewhere more private.'

Allen looked at the old couple, each one sucking on half a sandwich. 'Have you got anywhere in mind?'

Allen paid for the two pints of Black Bug and the two whiskey chasers at the bar of The Cloisters and took them over on a small tray to the cubby hole where the man was seated, staring at the backsides of two middle aged women at a fruit machine. Allen took a seat opposite, squeezing the drinks onto the small round table that was already fully laden with glasses and dog ends.

'Cheers,' said the man.

'Cheers,' said Allen, wishing they would get down to business.

'I've got plenty of experience in surveillance and tailing techniques,' said the man.

'Oh good,' said Allen. 'I was rather banking on that.'

'Who's the selected target?'

Allen downed his whiskey and pulled the envelope from his pocket. He removed the cut out and handed it over. The man held it between thumb and forefinger, regarding the image with detached dislike.

'Looks like a prick,' he said. 'Who is he?'

'His name is Iain Gwynne.'

'And what does our Mister Gwynne do?'

'He's a playwright.'

'And you're not a fan of his plays?'

'No, although that's not the reason I want him tailed. But no, I'm not a fan of his plays anyway.'

'I liked a bit of Pinter back in the day,' said the man, sipping his pint.

'Really,' said Allen.

'I could have taken up acting myself, I reckon. Seen enough amateur dramatics in the interrogation rooms.'

'Oh?' said Allen, lighting up. 'Were you in the police?'

The man hesitated and shot Allen a suspicious glance. Allen almost visibly recoiled from it.

'I mean, not that it matters.'

'This Gwynne,' said the man, 'anything else I should be made aware of?'

'Well,' said Allen, thinking into his pint, 'I've put his address on the back of the picture. He has a wife, Ursula, but no children. I would advise, if I may, extreme discretion. Iain Gwynne does have a certain standing in the literary world.'

'And can I ask why you want us to run surveillance on him? Is he knocking off your significant other?'

'Not quite,' said Allen, running a finger around the inside of his collar. 'I'd just like a detailed report of his whereabouts until further notice; where he goes, who he sees. That type of thing.'

'Hmmm,' said the man. He checked the address and put the picture in his jacket pocket. 'Now, the rest of the necessary.'

'Oh, yes,' said Allen. He put his fingers in the envelope. 'How much was it again?'

'The two hundred up front,' said the man as he watched Allen's fingers unsheath the cash, 'to cover booking fee and costs. Owing to cash flow - or lack thereof- I will need the first forty eight hours surveillance up front, Sir.'

Allen squinted at the man and received a hard stare in return.

'Right,' said Allen and handed over the money.

'Well,' said the man, sinking his pint and dragging himself out from the cubby hole, 'whatever Iain Gwynne stinks of, you can rest assured that I'll smell it.'

'And if I need to contact your office,' said Allen, 'who do I ask for?'

A novelty bell rang out and a cascade of silver change spilled into the gutter under the row of matching lemons, causing one of the women to clap her hands like a turbo-charged seal. The man, shoving the cash into his trouser pocket, did up the buttons of his rain mac and took one last look at their rear ends and grunted into his thick moustache.

'You can leave a message for Mister Kibber.'

22

The black cab swung in right outside the ambiguous topiary that adorned the unnecessarily wide entrance to *The Everglades Fulham* and out stepped Deborah Flaxman. She caught the eye of a couple sitting at a table outside, just in front of the long pane of glass on the left hand side of the entrance; the man gave her the well-mastered once over appraisal before returning to his cocktail menu. His companion, with her swollen mouth and suicidal beehive hair, regarded her with a mixture of claws-out intensity and suppressed admiration. Deborah straightened her deep purple dress down over her thighs and carried herself into the restaurant. The place was three quarters full; a vast chamber of vibrant sound and delicious scent.

'Yes, Madame?'

Deborah turned to see the tuxedoed *maitre'd* standing close to her, hands behind his back and his head emerging from his shirt collar like a banana being squeezed out of its skin.

'I'm meeting a friend here,' said Deborah, scanning the tables.

'And your friend's name please, Madame?'

'Seether.'

The *maitre'd* performed a quick check on his list and tapped the page in confirmation.

'Yes, Madame. If you would care to follow me.'

Trent Seether had been waiting just over twenty minutes when he saw the *maitre'd* leading her towards his table by the unused grand piano. He rose from his seat and flattened his tie as she made her final approach along the length of the *maitre'd's* outstretched arm. Neither of them spoke for a few moments, instead just looking straight into each other's eyes, searching for a way forward from now. It had been a hell of a long time.

'You look...' said Trent, trying not to look.

'Older?' said Deborah.

'I don't know what I was going to say.'

'Trent Seether stuck for words,' said Deborah with an ice breaking smile. She stepped forward and the second they connected in a tentative embrace, a whole kaleidoscope of good and bad times flashed in front of both of them. They separated and sat down at the table. Trent dragged a bottle of wine from an ice bucket.

'You still drink?'

'I do,' said Deborah, sliding her glass forward enough for him to pour.

'I imagine you know how surprised I was to receive your call.'

'You seem to have carved out a nice little career for yourself at *The Edition*,' said Deborah. 'How long have you been working there?'

'Too many years probably,' snorted Trent as they clinked glasses and drank. 'It's the kind of job that attracts cranks and other wonderful specimens.'

'Do you still get pestered from that conspiracy theorist?'

'Super G? Yeah.'

'What's his latest?'

'Big trouble in outer space.'

'How many inches did you give him?'

'Two. More than enough for his ramblings.'

'You love it,' said Deborah.

'I suppose I do,' said Trent as though realising it for the first time. 'But I loved it more working with you at *Undercurrent.*'

Deborah shifted in her seat, knowing that this conversation was bound to come along but still unsure about being willing to go with it. She played with her napkin and said:

'It was a good publication. I'm very proud of what everyone achieved there.'

'You gave it its *bite,* Deborah,' said Trent, leaning forward as though it was sensitive information. 'You should have been the editor-in-chief of *Undercurrent*, not Malcolm. That old sod let the paper die a slow death.'

'Times change,' said Deborah, 'and so do attitudes and tastes. If the public don't want it, we can't give it.'

'You don't believe that for a second.'

'It doesn't matter what I believe, Trent. It's the facts that matter. There's no room for anything with a little soul anymore. Haven't you worked that out yet? People no longer need anything with any meaning these days.'

'And you're happy with that?'

'Of course I'm not *happy* with it, Trent. But megalomaniacs like Gregory Gem matter more than people like me.'

Deborah hated saying that name and Trent visibly winced at hearing it.

'Do you still go to The Kommune?' he asked.

'I do.'

'Is it still in Camden Lock?'

'No. It still has to keep moving unfortunately.'

'So where is it now?'

'Well, I'm not sure I should divulge,' she said playfully.

'That's okay,' said Trent pretending his feelings had been hurt. 'I'm part of the machine now and therefore probably far to square to show my face at a joint like The Kommune.'

'Maybe I'll smuggle you in one day,' said Deborah. She immediately realised that that had sounded like an invite, a way in. Trent realised it too and subtly put his foot across the doorstep.

'I'd like that,' he said. 'It'd be nice to think I was subverting the Gem by going underground.'

The waiter appeared at the table before Trent could continue and Deborah could baton down her hatches. He left them to their menus and Deborah, without really looking, decided what she would have.

'The Moroccan Salad will be fine for me.'

'Is that all?' said Trent as he poured over the specials. 'You used to have such a marvellous appetite as I remember.'

'I had a large lunch.'

'I'll have the venison with all the seasonal vegetables,' said Trent to himself. He summoned the waiter with a raised hand and ordered for both of them.

'So,' said Trent, circling, 'how have you been?'

Deborah drank her wine and regarded Trent and his question.

'Are you asking me if I'm in a relationship with anybody, Trent?'

'I really am that obvious, aren't I?' he laughed. His laugh softened her up and she felt her shoulders loosen a little.

'I'm not seeing anyone,' she said. 'There's never

been anything serious since...' her voice trailed off, unable to describe what they'd had. Trent could see the shadow of their destructive past cross over her features. He downed his wine and replaced the empty glass carefully on the tablecloth.

'Deborah,' he said slowly, 'I'm sorry about everything. I probably said it at the time but I don't remember, so I'm saying it again. I'm sorry about everything.'

Deborah felt a knot tightening in her stomach, the scene of the tragedy.

'You did say sorry at the time,' she said quietly. 'It didn't mean much then though.'

'And now?'

'And now I know you mean it. But we were both stupid. The hedonistic lifestyle has many casualties, doesn't it?'

The biggest casualty for them had been Judy, their unborn daughter lost at almost full-term; a product of their supercharged passion and victim of their overindulgent lifestyle. Having gone a little bit too native with the rest of the rock and roll circus, Deborah had bled heavily and afterwards did little more than stare into the darkness of her future. There would be no other Judy; the damage was done, the removal irreversible, a blank canvas never to be troubled by tiny steps. Both she and Trent Seether came out the other side, a space between their parted hands that would never be filled. The space had grown at a rapid rate until Deborah could no longer hear what he was saying to her.

Trent knew exactly what she was thinking. He felt the scars on his body itch in remembrance. He poured them both some more wine.

'Not that I'm finding your company lacking,' he said lightly, 'but why do I find myself in your company at all?'

Deborah, relieved to be able to clear everything else away, rested her elbows on the edge of the table, folding her napkin several times.

'I need your help.'

Trent raised his eyebrows, 'Really?'

'I'm doing some research into old vocalists and musicians. I could do with some assistance with setting up interviews.'

'A kind of "where are they now?" type project?'

'Yes.'

'Interviews with whom?'

'Well, at the moment, I'm interested in just one person in particular. You remember Nigel St Davos?'

'He wasn't a singer. Didn't he manage?'

'He managed Audrey Lee.'

'Audrey Lee,' echoed Trent as he recalled the name. 'Christ, I remember her. Now there was a falling star. So you're after some background details from Nigel St Davos?'

'Something like that,' replied Deborah. 'What do you think?'

Trent considered his options, 'I suppose I could have a word with some of the showbiz guys at *The Edition*. It might prove to be impossible though.'

'Surely not,' said Deborah. 'I'm not asking for afternoon tea with Gregory Gem, Trent. Just see if there's a way to get in contact with Nigel St Davos. I can take it from there.'

'Alright,' said Trent. 'I promise I will see what I

can do.'

'Thanks, Trent. I really appreciate it.'

'What are friends for?' said Trent.

They ate their food, drank more wine and bounced small talk off each other before finding themselves standing on the pavement outside *The Everglades Fulham*. The small talk disappeared in their protracted goodbye; a melancholic thirty seconds punctuated by the realisation of wasted time. Impulsively, Deborah threw her arms around Trent's neck and kissed him hard on the mouth, lips closed and eyes burning. Trent wrapped his arms, barely touching her. Then Deborah pulled away, tears forming in her eyelashes. She turned and ran down the street, leaving Trent standing alone on the pavement, bewildered and exhiliarated at having been in Deborah's company again after such an uneasy, restless time apart. And now she had left him with work to do.

23

Special News Update: *Forensic researchers at the New Metropolitan Police Service have confirmed that the shoe recently discovered is that of missing schoolgirl Patience Sweetlove. The Prime Minister took time out from the South American Energy Crisis talks to again offer his sympathies to the girl's parents, Jackie and Mitch and to also sing the praises of the team behind the upcoming charity single. It is rumoured that television game show host Steve Stylus will feature heavily in the middle of the song performing specially written lyrics. His inclusion in the project is sure to appeal to the slightly older audience. Jackie and Mitch have already been approached by representatives of Gregory Gem to appear in the music video that will accompany the single, which will see them recreate key moments since their daughter's abduction, such as the press conference and the woodland searches. We predict a sure fire Number One!*

Scottie awoke suddenly, gasping in panic at her alien surroundings and the restrictive wires sprouting from her head and torso. Her right hand was caught under something warm. It lifted of its own accord and in an instant there was a face right over her face, a hand on her cheek.

'Scottie?'

Scottie stopped breathing just so she could hear.

'Claudia,' she said. Her voice was broken, barely more than a croak. She felt something touch her bottom lip.

'Drink some water, honey,' said Claudia, slowly tipping the plastic beaker. The first drops dribbled down the sides onto the white fabric of the surgical gown. Then Scottie got control and began to swallow.

'What happened?' asked Scottie in a barely audible voice when she had had enough.

Claudia replaced the beaker and held her hand tightly, 'You were attacked. At my apartment.'

'Attacked?' Scottie felt incredibly weak. She closed her eyes at the thought of it. She hurt all over; her brain had been turned inside out.

Claudia could see the discomfort she was going through. She knew she had to get the full Treatment from Rouse. Claudia also knew that Scottie had to rest and not have any unnecessary strain placed on her. But Claudia also knew that she *needed to know*. She gripped Scottie's fingers tightly and lightly kissed the nail of each one.

'Scottie,' she whispered. Scottie murmured something unintelligible. She was falling back to sleep. Claudia stood up and got close to her ear. 'Scottie.'

Another distant murmur.

'Do you remember who did this to you?'

There was no response for a full minute. Then Claudia noticed a gradual, subtle change in her appearance. The eyebrows seemed to invert themselves over tightly shut eyelids, the colour drained from her face like dishwater down a plughole; a film of sweat saturated the skin and Scottie began to visibly shake. Claudia realised she had pushed her luck and pressed the tiny red button on the wall above the bed. She held Scottie's shoulders, trying to subdue her.

She was letting out whimpers and growls, kicking her feet under the hemmed in blankets. Then the nurse was there and plunging a needle into a vein. The struggling subsided in dying waves until there was no more movement from her.

'How long has she been awake?' asked the nurse as she wrote something down on the notes at the bottom of the bed.

'A couple of minutes,' said Claudia, 'no more than that.'

'She's a long way to go yet.'

Claudia didn't reply and the nurse left her alone. She felt Scottie's grip momentarily tighten, followed by an exhale of breath that seemed to be beckoning her closer. Claudia put her ear to Scottie's mouth and heard the one word that made her blood run cold:

'*Kibber.*'

Interplanetary Terrestrial HQ, Greenwich (X 11 Clearance)

'Greenwich, do you read me loud and clear? This is Captain Ione Blanchard of the North Angel.'

'We have you loud and clear, Captain.'

'You've no idea what a relief it is to get contact with you once again.'

'What's the status, Captain Blanchard?'

'Ma'm, without wanting to sound too melodramatic, it isn't looking good up here.'

'Please expand, Captain.'

'We've seen something out there that I'm finding very hard to explain to myself, let alone to all of you down there.'

'Please do your best to entertain us, Captain. You

have a captive audience beneath you.'
'Ma'm, there is something else I must relay to you first. I regret to inform you that Warrant Officer Kyle Seato has taken his own life.'
'What did she say--?'
'Captain Blanchard; can you repeat that last transmission please?'
'Yes Ma'm. Warrant Officer Kyle Seato has taken his own life.'
'Explain.'
'Seato's personality began to change. He was becoming more erratic and unpredictable. I retired him from active duty and confined him to his quarters. Approximately three hours ago he informed us that he was going to go for a look around outside. He stepped into the airlock and ejected himself into space. Please acknowledge this transmission.'
'Transmission received and understood, Captain. Has Warrant Officer Seato's body been recovered?'
'Negative.'
'Adina?'
'Yes, Ma'm?'
'Are Warrant Officer Seato's family here?'
'His wife and two sons are up in the gallery, Ma'm.'
'Have they got sound up there?'
'The thirty second delay is set, Ma'm.'
'Well, for Christ's sake switch it off!'
'Yes, Ma'm.'
'Captain Blanchard?'
'Here.'
'What is the status of your remaining crew?'
'As before, but we are very tired and weak and the air is getting stale. I'm not sure we're going to make it

back. Ship's falling apart at the seams all around us.'
'I need you to tell me what you've seen out there, Captain.'
'------gh--'
'Captain Blanchard.'
'----------tge--'
'Ione…darling…'
'-'

24

Gubbs let out one long, continuous growl as Harry stepped past him in the hallway of Audrey Lee's apartment. The little self-appointed protector was watching Harry from his place on a small cushioned box outside his room. Harry crossed the living room to the large bay windows and stared down at the quiet avenue below. At some point it had rained and now the gutters were streaming with oily rainbows feeding into the city's underworld. He lit a cigarette and massaged his eyes. He was tired, but felt invigorated by his plan for Audrey. She was keeping him waiting and Harry began to get impatient. It was starting to get dark prematurely outside and he didn't want to hang around. He crushed his cigarette in the ashtray and walked over to the door which led to her private room. He knocked twice, resisting the temptation to place his ear against the wood.

'Audrey?'

There was no reply from inside. He tapped the door again, but still nothing. He heard movement behind him and he turned to see Gubbs in the room with him, pacing back and fore with his unblinking, piggy little eyes trained on him. Harry returned his attention to Audrey's door and knocked once more.

'Audrey?'

The door opened and Harry stepped back as Audrey Lee, in her shimmering dark green dress appeared before him. Her makeup was thick and glistening in the light of the room. She seemed to look straight through him as she came into the living room, slowly, regally, a dying queen. She sailed across the floor to the window and surveyed her darkening kingdom beyond. Gubbs stood in front of Harry and Harry ignored his malevolent stare.

'Audrey?' said Harry.

She turned around and looked at him with drink-drenched eyes.

'Hello, Harry Brewer. You've been smoking.'

'I was waiting for you, Audrey,' said Harry, feeling a little nervous.

'Would you like to escort me to the club, Harry?'

'Yes.'

Audrey moved away from the window and approached him silently, her head rocking slightly on her shoulders. Gubbs moved out of the way, shrinking back as she came right up close to Harry and inhaled the scent of his clothes. She felt the material of his suit and shirt and looked up into his eyes.

'Why do I have so much of your attention, Harry?'

'I've got something to tell you, Audrey,' said Harry. 'About an idea I've had.'

'Really, Harry? That sounds fascinating.' Audrey began playing with Harry's tie. 'Why don't you tell me *all* about it.'

'I think we should record your album.'

Audrey froze, her eyes narrowed suspiciously and then suddenly she backed away as if to avoid some awful disease. She only stopped retreating when she backed into one of the armchairs. She steadied herself on the back of it, seeming to shrink into the fabric.

'Audrey...'

'Stop,' said Audrey. 'Why are you doing this?'

Harry thought about approaching her, but there seemed to be something invisible between them, preventing him from getting close to her.

'Why, Harry?'

'I'm just trying to help, Audrey.'

'You think it's time someone exploited me do you?'

'Exploited?'

'Let's get this old freak show back on the road, is that it, Harry?'

'Audrey--'

'I'm not for sale, Harry.'

'I wasn't--'

'You can leave now.'

Harry desperately wanted to protest, to try and convince her that his intentions weren't the solution to some money making scheme, much less some kind of perverted attempt to make her look ridiculous. But Audrey had started to shake where she stood, head bowed, her legs barely able to keep her upright. Harry walked into the hallway and slipped on his overcoat. As he opened the front door, Gubbs was suddenly at his side, growling. Harry straightened his tie and plunged his right fist straight into Gubbs' guts. There was a loud burst of escaping air and Gubbs yelped like a puppy with its tail caught in a door. His feet lifted off the floor and he doubled up mid air before dropping down on the carpet. Harry, feeling the anger and frustration rising within him, went to kick Gubbs when he was down. But he stopped himself, only just. He felt his head pounding and took a step back from the scrawny little mess at his feet.

'Fuck off, Gubbs,' he spat before slamming the door hard behind him. He fled from the apartment block and ran to the end of the avenue, putting as much distance between him and Audrey Lee as possible. He entered the first pub he chanced on and ordered as he placed himself on a barstool.

'What can I get you?' asked the heavy set balding landlord.

'Brandy Alex--no, wait, pour me a gigantic slug of Black Bug.'

The landlord served up his drink and Harry downed it swiftly and smoked a cigarette. It was getting dark outside as the sun crash landed dying into the earth. He ordered another pint and smoked another cigarette. Nothing held any meaning anymore. He'd told himself that before, but now he finally believed it. From here on in, it didn't matter; he had nothing left now. He was just an orphaned common thief, full of half baked ideals and unworkable schemes. He drank a third pint under the watchful eye of the brutish landlord. He now saw how the rest of his life would be played out. He would sit amidst the dust of 77 Vancouver Hill, boring the furniture with tall tales of success and cackling as one by one his teeth fell out and his grey matter melted into nothing. In the end, he was ready and willing to accept his own invitation into the wilderness years of hard drinking and imaginary friends.

He drank a fourth Black Bug and didn't give the landlord a straight answer to several of his questions. The ashtray was emptied and he crossed the line with two mature women ordering drinks at the bar. They turned down his offer of a threesome in the pub car park but he told them with a nudge and a wink that he would be there waiting for them after chucking out time. He cheered on the plastic pop that came from the jukebox because everyone was his favourite and he knew the words to none of them.

He slipped across the sloping, uneven carpet and into the gents where he banged his head on the greasy tiles while he liberally urinated in the general direction of the bowl. Then he was spun around and hit hard two or three times in the face. His world exploded in a spray of bright red as he was spun around again and the vertical rectangle of the condom dispenser came towards him at the speed of light and seemingly struck him and kept on going through him. Harry's moist lips kissed the floor of the gents and he was aware that he was being kicked hard in the abdomen. He could feel his toes tingling and his nose burned from the smell of disinfectant.

'That's enough lads.'

'He ain't had enough.'

'You wanna clean up this fuckin' mess?'

'No one speaks to my bird like that.'

'Take the cunt out back and dump him.'

Harry saw the lights and smelt the stale aroma of empty bottles and rat piss. A cold blast of air gave him a second's worth of balmy relief before the rough sting of the gravel as he landed in a crumpled heap on the ground of the pub car park. Harry didn't want to move, but he knew he had to. If he was going to die tonight, he wouldn't die here.

25

Trent Seether put the phone down and turned to one of his colleagues.

'I'm going out, Mick.'

'Getting the first round in?' said Mick Crowley from Sports. 'Better take one of the photographers with you.'

'Piss off, Mick.'

'Okay, I'm in the chair first. Black Bug all round.'

'Later, I've got something on first.'

Trent turned his back on Mick Crowley to end the exchange and as he put on his coat, he rang Deborah's number. The call connected on the seventh ring and he didn't give her a chance to speak.

'Debs, it's me. Good news.'

'You've got a contact number?'

'Better, I've got a piece of paper here with his address on it.'

'Wow,' said Deborah, 'I hope you didn't have to call in too many favours for that.'

'Let's just say you're going halves with me on a case of champagne.'

'I think I can manage that.'

'I thought we could go along and tap the old fella's front door.'

'Now?'

'Why not? Then afterwards we could go for a drink.'

'Well, we'll see.'

'I'll pick you up in an hour.'

Trent hung up and took a small bottle of aftershave from his desk and slapped it on his neck. He caught the eye of the copy girl as she walked past. He gave her a friendly, tight lipped smile and she reciprocated purely out of courtesy. Copy girls will have to wait, he told himself as he took the back stairs down to the underground car park secreted beneath *The Edition* building. His vermillion red MG BGT was tucked away neatly between a Ford and a Citroen and he had just enough room to open the door and slip in behind the wheel. He lit a cigarette and checked his watch. If all went well, he'd help Deborah get what she wanted from Nigel St Davos; then he could get what *he* wanted. Finally. He wound the window down a couple of inches and watched his cigarette smoke float out through the gap. He thought of losing Deborah for the second time and brought his engine roaring into life.

26

The bedroom was exactly how he'd left it, garnished with the faint aroma of good booze. Having thrown enough hard cash at a cab driver to bring his body back to 77 Vancouver Hill, along with the necessary supplies of cigarettes and pornographic periodicals, Harry decided to spend the remainder of his semi conscious hours shaming himself into oblivion. A light rain was causing the accumulated dirt to dribble across the windows as he peeled away his clothes and fell back on the bed with a centrefold and a generous slug of whisky. Rub away the anxiety with "Edie From Cleethorpes". Edie's boyfriend Max wasn't letting her leave their flat of a morning until he'd eaten her out.

'Good work, Max, it's nice to see someone giving something back for a change.'

Harry was suddenly distracted by thoughts of Audrey and Deborah so he had a few more drinks. He glanced over towards the bedroom door as if half expecting one of them to burst in.

'Come on, Edie, do your stuff. Max has gone to work now so the rest of the day is ours and I want to show you how it's *really* done...'

Right at that moment, Harry mused, people all over the world were showing other people how it's really done. Right at that moment, while he lay there hard and ashamed with Edie at his side, thousands of sexual encounters were unfolding all over this murky brown city. In some beer-soaked corner of Finchley, a drunk nineteen year old political history student, hair pouring over her bulging, top heavy tee shirt would be succumbing to the greasy come-ons of a pot bellied, leathery middle aged rocker who, having been shot down in flames so many times before won't even pause to remove his cowboy boots. South London pub alleyways would soon fall host to the grubby closing time fumblings of erstwhile work colleagues caught up in the happy hour pay-off amidst the lager crates and dog-ends. In the deepest recesses of Clapham Common, a dissatisfied bureaucrat, disenchanted with the untruth of his domestic lot, would be illicitly sweating over the milky flesh of a jobbing northern runaway turning a trick for a fix. In a rundown bedsit in glorious Maze Hill, a tired divorcee would be slumped amid nicotine-stained wallpaper pasted on especially for QE II's coronation, furiously pumping away to an over watched recording. And out of all those festering, passionate moments, what would the yawn of sunrise leave? Pixellated recollections, sly finger pointing by the photocopier, guilt, the race-against-time dash to the nearest chemist for the magic pill, frantically-formed excuses that beg not to be scrutinised, and the optimistic and naive expectation that a new generation had been created to make this place a *better* place. A place that wanted Harry for a reason.

'*Look into my eyes,*' said Edie.

'I'm all yours,' said Harry

'*Are you sure you're up to it?*'

'Don't say that,' said Harry. 'Do you think I'm about to disappoint you?'

'*Did I say that?*'

'I chose *you*, remember.'

'*I know, honey.*'

'You'll always have Max and his dedicated jaw

muscles. I've only got you for now.'

'*Just relax and run yourself over my body. It's all for you now, honey.*'

'I want to, Edie.'

'*Have another drink, lover.*'

'I will,' said Harry and promptly acted on the advice.

'*Steady. Not too much.*'

'Don't worry,' said Harry, trying to sound reassuring. 'I think I've been pretty much drinking all day. I've reached my *plateau*.'

'*I don't want it to affect your ability.*'

'Tell me what you want.'

'*Go down on me now.*'

'You promise not to compare me with Max? Don't compare me with Max. Don't even score it in your mind.'

'*I won't.*'

'Promise?'

'*It's a promise, honey.*'

'Because I'll know.'

'It's a promise, honey.'

So Harry went down on her and he wondered if he was doing it the way Max did it. He did it until he could feel his head clouding over. He suddenly sat bolt upright on the edge of the bed and let Edie slip between his legs.

'*This isn't going to happen today,*' she said.

Harry pushed Edie to the floor and stumbled into the bathroom where he was violently sick.

An uncertain lifetime later, somebody knocked on the front door and Harry prised his right cheek free of the toilet seat. It had got darker and for the first time his whole body screamed at him to stop. He pushed his naked body into an upright position and caught sight of himself in the bathroom mirror. There was dried blood matted in his hair on his right temple as well as grazing along his jaw line. He tentatively caressed his torso, wincing at the slightest touch to his ribs. There was bruising there. He began to recall spilling out of a pub car park and staggering down a topsy-turvy, revolving high street. There was another knock on the door and he sighed heavily.

The door opened finally and Deborah instantly knew Harry had sustained injuries in some way. He stood in the doorway, not quite straight with his cute paunch teetering over the edge of a pair of black jogging bottoms. She could smell the booze seeping from every pore on his body. He held on to the front door as she stepped inside.

'Harry,' she said.
'I've had a hard day, Deborah.'
'It would appear so.'
'What time is it?'
'Does it matter?'
'I guess not. I don't think I have anywhere important to go to for the rest of my life.'
'Would you settle for coming round to mine?'
'Yours?'
'That's right.'
'What's going on next door at yours?'
'I have a friend over I want you to meet.'
'Do I have to bring a bottle?'
'Do you have any left?'
'Shouldn't think so.'

'Then don't worry about it. Just you will do.'
'Give me half an hour?'
'Half an hour.'

Deborah left and Harry closed the front door quietly. The headache was beginning to reach maximum intensity so he dragged himself up the stairs and threw himself under a boiling hot shower until he stopped shaking. He squatted down and pressed his back hard against the tiles of the shower, watching the seconds of his life washing away down the drain between his toes. The last time he had done this was in South America, the morning he decided he was going to go for it. He'd thought about lifting the information for the Treatment from Guillermo's safe for weeks and he knew that that day he would have the opportunity to do it. So he packed a hold-all and went into the office before his boss was due to arrive. There was Rosa in her bleached white blouse. There was the safe next to the drinks cabinet. Harry knew the code and he'd had a sudden choice to make; the technical information on the company's new wonder drug or the big brown envelope next to it stuffed with money. He'd had the big brown envelope out of there in seconds. He had been out of the main doors of Contact Chemicals and straight into a taxi to the airport. It had all been that easy.

'Sit him down before he falls down, for Christ's sake,' said Trent Seether from his position flanking the unlit fireplace. Deborah eased Harry onto the sofa and they waited for him to catch his breath. Harry tried to clear the fuzziness from his head. He wished there was no light.

'Harry,' said Deborah delicately. Her voice was close and Harry's eyes opened a little to see her on her knees right in front of him.

'I'm here,' said Harry.

'This is my friend I told you about. Trent, this is Harry.'

'Hello, Harry,' said Trent politely.

'Hello, Trent.'

'Look,' said Trent, 'is all this such a good idea, Deb? He doesn't look like he'll be able to contribute much anyway.'

'You'll be fine, won't you?' asked Deborah. To Harry, her eyes seemed to be imploring him to say yes. Harry smiled and gave her a wink that made his eyelid burn.

'I will for you, Deborah.'

'Thank you.' Deborah stood up and stood in the centre of the room. 'Now listen to what Trent has to say.'

'I've got a meet set with Nigel St Davos,' said Trent.

Harry achingly leaned forward on the sofa. 'You've spoken to him?'

Trent smiled to himself, 'Oh yes, Harry. I softened him up enough to get an interview with him at his country pile. He's keen to meet with Audrey Lee.'

'It can't be that easy,' said Harry, shifting position to ease the pain in his side.

Deborah studied Trent's face for a moment.

'Is it that easy?' she asked.

'Well,' said Trent, 'I will admit there is a slight *snag*...but nothing we can't fix.'

'What's the snag?'

'Nigel St Davos is currently under the impression that Audrey Lee is setting this whole thing up.'

'*Fuuuuck*,' sighed Harry and fell back into the sofa.

'Trent-'

'Everybody relax,' said Trent. 'I can read people, Deborah; you know that more than anyone. If I hadn't have gambled the whole thing would have come to nothing. I've done my bit, now it's up to you two to decide if you want to go ahead with this thing or not.'

An uneasy silence fell on the room as Harry realised that he'd have to step up to the mark and Deborah realised Harry was virtually useless in his current state. Trent knew what both of them were thinking and decided to leave them both to process the information.

'Be in touch,' said Trent, stealing a kiss on Deborah's cheek before heading for the door, 'and don't leave it too long.'

When the front door opened and closed, Deborah watched Harry sprawled on the sofa, head tilted back and one hand over his face blocking out the world around him. She sat down next to him and put a hand on his leg. Harry moaned quietly.

'Harry.'

'Hmm.'

'We need you in one piece, you do understand that don't you?'

'Perfectly.'

'This was your "epiphany" after all. We're all just passing through your life.'

27

Detective Inspector Kibber sat low behind the steering wheel of the unmarked police car, across the busy street from the entrance to the Otto Club, making notes for his continuing surveillance on Iain Gwynne. He held a deep-rooted disdain for these places. Influential people got away with stuff in places like this; deals worth billions of pounds that would cost thousands of innocent lives were brokered in places like this, all over a mature malt and a gentleman's agreement. There wasn't a gallows in the land that you couldn't dodge if you knew the right people. Kibber had never set foot inside one; he had always known that no matter how far he could have risen up the ranks of the New Metropolitan Police Service, his face would have always been seen to have an irregular shape. He took a sip from his hip flask, smoothed down his coarse moustache with a heavy, disgusted sigh and went through the notes that he had made so far that day.

Mr. Gwynne had left his house located at 39 Byron Gardens, W3 at precisely 9.37 am and proceeded by black cab into Central where he entered the publishing house of Rathbone & Kent. He was inside for just over an hour and a half. Kibber had attempted to get a closer inspection but the middle aged woman at the main reception desk had looked like a bit of a bruiser and had him on the back foot the minute he'd stepped through the revolving door. Surveillance had picked up upon Mr. Gwynne's departure from Rathbone & Kent Publishers at 11.14am when the subject took another black cab to Old Savile Row where he was seen being fitted for three new suits, the dark blue pin stripe being the favourite of his tailor. At 12.29 Mr. Gwynne caught a third black cab to the Otto Club where he remained until…

Kibber glanced at his watch. 14.48. He felt his joints groaning at his inactivity and so he took another drink from the hip flask and let his eyes follow the rear ends of two twenty somethings in knee length skirts. He reminded himself that he was on somebody's payroll and turned his attention back towards the Otto Club. As he put his hip flask to his lips, another female figure caught his eye, causing him to drop the flask onto his lap. It bounced into the footwell but Kibber didn't reach for it. He gripped the steering wheel tightly as he watched her walking amongst the other pedestrians, shielded by her designer sunglasses and the headscarf she'd got from that Morroccan John who used to visit her.

'Claudia,' he whispered.

As though she had heard her name in the wind, Claudia stopped dead in the middle of the pavement, causing the crowd to diverge around her. She took an uncertain look around her before pulling her shoulder bag across her torso and reaching inside to produce a manila envelope. She looked up towards the entrance of the Otto Club as a man emerged from it. The impeccably groomed man in the expensive suit trotted down the steps and as he pecked her on the cheek, Kibber felt his heart rise in his throat. The man took the manila envelope from Claudia and disappeared back into the club. Claudia adjusted her sunglasses and carried on walking. Kibber sank lower in his seat as she went by until he could no longer see her in his wing mirror. He sat up and retrieved the hip flask from the footwell, took a long drink from it, then started the engine.

He was already waiting for her in her apartment when she walked through the front door. She was forewarned by his distinctive smell but she was too slow to react. Kibber came from the side and jumped her, forcing her onto the living room floor. Claudia tried to wrestle him but one of her arms was caught in the strap of her bag and he had the other pinned underneath her. He got on top of her and put a rough hand over her mouth and gently lifted off her Gracci sunglasses with the other. Kibber leaned in close as though he was going to try and kiss her but stopped short. Claudia could smell the booze on his breath, so pungent it made her eyes burn.

'You've got some explaining to do, my lover,' said Kibber into her ear, easing his hand from her mouth.

'I don't understand what you're doing here,' said Claudia, remaining absolutely still so that he might relax his hold on her.

'Who do you know at the Otto Club?'

'What?'

'It's no good you playing dumb to me, my beauty,' said Kibber.

'You've been following me.'

'Not quite, lover.'

'You bastard.'

'Save the dirty talk for the mattress, girl. Now, you answer my question: Who do you know at the Otto Club?'

Claudia took a deep breath and looked him in the eye.

'I know Sir James Swaffham.'

A flicker of recognition crossed Kibber's face and he straightened up a little on top of her. He knew the name and he watched Claudia watching him working it out.

'Swaffham?...The minister for the government's space programmes?'

'That's right, Inspector,' said Claudia calmly.

Kibber detected the slightest sarcasm in her tone and took her face in his hand.

'What is he to you? I saw the envelope you gave to him so don't try and tell me he's just another one of your upper class Johns.'

'I gave him information,' said Claudia.

'What information?'

'Information about *you*.'

There was a pause and Claudia tensed even more as she waited to see if he had bought into the gambit she had just played on him. Kibber removed his hand from her face and got to his feet. As soon as she was free, Claudia stood and collected herself, keeping her distance from him. Kibber looked nervous as he paced back and fore, scratching his head. Finally he stopped moving and pointed a finger at her.

'What information do you think you could possibly have on me?'

'I know it was you who beat up Scottie,' said Claudia, trying to keep her rage at the thought of it in check.

Kibber remembered the girl in Claudia's bed and briefly entertained the idea of denying all knowledge.

'Just another dirty little whore.'

Claudia felt herself starting to shake with anger.

'Don't you talk about her like that,' she spat. '*You* don't talk about her like that.'

The penny dropped and Kibber broke into laughter.

'You and her? Oh, my lover, when will you end all this and realise your place is at my side?'

Claudia regained her composure enough to take a couple of steps towards him.

'Listen to me, *Inspector*. You will *never* know me again. Not today, not tomorrow, not ever. Do you understand me? And if you think for one moment you can try and force me, just remember what Sir James has in his possession. Not just the attack on Scottie, but information regarding "Balaclava".'

Claudia took a deep breath and watched Kibber's reaction. At first he seemed to do nothing. But then, the red blotches vanished from his face and he appeared to be looking through her at something beyond, something that spooked him. Claudia had played the only card she had ever held onto. She didn't even know what it meant.

'How…' said Kibber.

'You talk in your sleep sometimes,' said Claudia. 'I've told you about that before. Occasionally more than you should. And it's all in the hands of the space minister. I gave him instructions that if anything should happen to me, he will finish you.'

'Finish me?'

'That's right, Inspector. I don't think you need me to elaborate. Remember, someone like Sir James Swaffham is in the convenient position of knowing a lot more useful people than you.'

Kibber sat down on the sofa, clasping and

unclasping his fingers. He didn't know what to do, how to play this.

'Claudia,' he muttered finally, 'I don't want to be left alone by you.'

'You've got no other choice,' she replied firmly. 'Please leave now.'

Kibber looked up at her with pleading eyes but she did not waver. He rose to his feet and walked out of the apartment, hearing her close the door behind him. It was cold in the corridor and he pulled his rain mac tightly around him as he descended the stairs, momentarily seeing Scottie where she had tumbled and landed in an awkward heap. He was still trembling when he turned the corner of Concertina Street and climbed into his car.

28

Sir James Swaffham turned the brass key that locked the door to his private office deep within the bowels of the Otto Club. Crossing the polished floor to the vast mahogany desk, he sat on the edge, inserted a cigarette into an ivory holder, lifted the phone receiver from its cradle and tapped zero once.

'Secure line please,' he said as he lit the cigarette. The line clicked once and he tapped in a number. It rang once.

'Yes.'

Sir James instantly recognised the deep, monotone voice at the other end of the line. It was the operative he knew only as "O".

'This is S.R.H. I have an urgent assignment I wish you to carry out with immediate effect.'

'Yes.'

'The target is a Central Metropolitan Candidate so please apply relevant precautions.'

'Target identity?'

Sir James exhaled a long tail of dark smoke and inwardly detached himself from the reality of the sentence he was about to pass.

'The target is a consultant surgeon at St Marcus's Hospital. His name is Cromwell Rouse.'

'Rouse.'

'That's right. I would prefer a P77 Protocol to be undertaken. Please collate and advise as to the possibility as soon as possible. Limited involvement please.'

'Yes.'

The line went dead and Sir James replaced the

receiver. He smoked his cigarette in silent contemplation over the man whose fate he had just sealed. He went over to the sash windows that overlooked the inner Eden of the enclosed club gardens, wherein he had taken many such drastic actions before. He recited a silent, empty prayer for the dying in his head and then poured himself a large cognac from the drinks cabinet under the portrait of the Duke of Norringley, the founding father of the Otto Club. He raised his glass to the aged face on the wall and drank.

The telephone rang.

'Yes?'

'Good afternoon, Sir James, this is Gibbons.'

'What is it?'

'Very sorry to disturb you, Sir James, but Craven from security has just brought something interesting to my attention. Would you be able to come and take a look?'

'It had better be important, Gibbons.'

'Yes, Sir.'

Sir James put the phone down and drained his glass. Gibbons met him in reception and led him into the security office behind the main desk where Craven was stooped over a television monitor built into the far wall.

'Well,' demanded Sir James irritably, 'what's so bloody important?'

'Craven,' said Gibbons.

Craven, a middle aged hulk of a man, pressed a button and the monitor screen lit up with a monochrome image of the street outside the club. He stood aside to give Sir James a clear view.

'What am I looking at?' said Sir James impatiently.

'That car, Sir,' said Gibbons, placing a finger against the top left hand side of the screen.

'Well?'

'It was parked outside the club with the driver inside from 12.30 until just before three this afternoon. It drove away right after you stepped outside to retrieve the item from your acquaintance, Sir.'

Sir James glanced at Gibbons to see if he could detect any inference in the word "acquaintance". But the club's steward avoided any eye contact.

'Do we know who the driver is?'

'Yes, Sir. Craven?'

Craven cleared his throat and attempted to enunciate the way Gibbons did.

'Well, Sir, I ran the number plate and it's a police vehicle--'

'Police?' said Sir James.

'Yes, Sir,' said Craven. 'At the moment its registered user is a Detective Inspector of the New Metropolitan Police Service named Valentine Kibber.'

'Kibber...' said Sir James to himself. The name was familiar. And now it seemed there could very well be a link between this policeman and Claudia. He addressed Gibbons directly: 'Wipe the footage immediately and then I want the both of you to forget this conversation ever took place. Do I make myself clear?'

Gibbons and Craven looked at each other and then nodded a joint affirmative. Sir James exited the security office and returned hastily to his own inner sanctum. Again he locked the door and again he lit a cigarette as he dialled an outside line.

'Yes,' said "O".

'S.R.H. I have one more small matter I need you to look into.'

'Yes.'

'I request any information on an officer of the New Metropolitan. Rank of Detective Inspector. Name's Kibber, Valentine Kibber. Everything you can find please.'

'Yes.'

The line went dead and Sir James sank into the large leather chair behind the desk, lightly dusting the ceiling with exhaled smoke. He didn't like complications and operatives like "O" were conveniently installed to make sure there were none to worry about. As he finished his cigarette, the phone rang.

'Yes?'

'The show will be starting in fifteen minutes, Sir James, in the Scarlet Lounge.'

'Thank you.'

Sir James hung up and slowly loosened his tie. He silently lamented the glory days when dark matters were easier to keep wrapped up safe and warm in the murky gloom of bureaucracy. Televised capital executions were a handful of years away. Some local constabularies were already displaying the crude imposition of product placement on the sides of their police cars. On the way to chair a Commons select committee earlier that day he had told his driver to turn the volume up and had heard the latest jingle for the Harrow & Wealdstone Constabulary:-

"At Harrow & Wealdstone Police Service we pride ourselves on offering nothing but the best service to all our customers. We have a dedicated team of professionals eager to assist you in any way we see fit. Been a victim of burglary, street robbery or rape? No problem! At Harrow & Wealdstone Constabulary, 'Heinous' is our middle name. And starting next month we'll be offering our Harrow & Wealdstone Platinum Protection Plan where if you place at least three approved emergency calls within the first three months of signing up, you'll get the third callout free of charge! So don't waste time, stay ahead of crime with Harrow & Wealdstone Police Service. Harrow & Wealdstone Police - Making Crime Pay YOU."

It had made Sir James shudder and he'd instructed his driver to turn the radio off and raise the soundproof divider. All of this, he had decided over a corpulent back seat brandy, simply would not do. The Bowler Hats of Westminster, so keen to reap profit and power, had slowly taken their eyes off the ball. The whole country had seemingly been caught in the headlights of the Gregory Gem Supermachine as it bulldozed its way across the land, satisfying the population's unsettling thirst for mediocrity and ill-advised self regard. While, admittedly, Sir James had profited in the past from the misery and weakness of others, mostly in grubby foreign territories, this Gem apparition was profiteering greatly on behalf of others. Sir James had almost had the displeasure of meeting Gregory Gem once, but had refused with clenched politeness on the grounds of urgent affairs of state. There hadn't been any rumblings of ill feeling regarding the snub where their respective circles overlapped; in fact, when Sir James's nineteen year old Great Dane met with its unfortunate demise under the wheels of a cargo lorry, the enigmatic trillionaire had sent the most opulent wreath he had ever laid eyes on. A floral reworking of the Great Dane, each lily petal encrusted with an uncut diamond. Sir James had regarded the tasteless tribute with an acceptable level of visual grace before having the wreath separated and deposited in an off-shore account.

Sir James smoked a cigarette and changed into his regulation attire for the Scarlet Lounge. Black trousers, scarlet smoking jacket with matching tie bearing the emblem of the Otto Club, black shirt and black boots. He took the stroll along the circumference of the building until he came to the large double doors that carried the gleaming brass plate declaring the Scarlet Lounge.

Lords Trollope and Villiers were already inside, seated in their usual perch to the left of the dimly lit stage. They were implausibly old and dodged death as well as they dodged their hereditary duties. He gave them a cursory nod as he took his seat at the small round table towards the rear of the room. Sir Philip Gatland, uncouth businessman with as many fingers in the high street pie as any of the North American Corporations, was already on the very hard stuff; Sir James knew that within an hour of the show starting, this overweight oaf would be scrabbling to get on the stage to once again purge himself of his expensive attire that otherwise made him look like a gentleman to the casual onlooker's eye. Sir John Bletchley, a rare appearance since his son's Monaco overdose, was sitting just ahead and to the right of Sir James. He half turned and acknowledged him. Poor Johnny, thought Sir James as a steward set a Scarlet Cocktail down before him; lose a child and the world suddenly knows your name.

Sir James sipped his drink. He had long since given up wondering what the secret ingredient was that made the Scarlet Cocktail such an intriguing drink. It was a courtesy extended to the Head Mixologist, Herbie, that was universally observed within the Otto Club. The lights went down even further and the thick red curtains slowly retreated back across the stage to reveal a king size four poster bed, adorned in expensive linen. There was silence in the lounge and as Sir James lit a cigarette, two women emerged from opposite ends of the stage and stood together in front of the bed, silently acknowledging the audience with a curtsy. Sir Philip shuffled excitedly in his seat and clicked his fingers at the steward. The women had performed many times before in the matinee slot. Greta and Inga, Mother and Daughter supposedly, although Sir James deemed their passing likeness to be professionally engineered. They wore the familiar costumes of wealthy, widowed heiress and her young chamber maid. Greta sat on the edge of the bed while Inga proceeded to position herself behind her and start brushing Greta's long silvery hair. Sir James flicked ash from the end of his cigarette and noticed Lord Trollope's bony hands disappear below the table. Inga began to kiss the nape of Greta's neck. She allowed the heiress to lie back before straddling the older woman's face and raising her maid's outfit up around her waist to expose the white flesh underneath to the stage lights. Inga writhed back and forth as Greta's tongue acted with workmanlike precision. Sir Philip received his next drink and poured it into his face, slapping the table hard with his free hand. Inga pulled her maid's outfit over her head and threw it across the stage. Lord Trollope began to tremble, his shoulders hunched around his neck like a brace. Lord Villiers looked on, a gleaming strand hanging from the corner of his mouth. Greta's fingers slipped between her own legs, naked for the audience to see. Sir James finished his cocktail just as there was a cheer from Sir Philip. Somebody else had appeared on the stage, a strapping male model type with a ponytail and a gold chain. Sir James recognised him as Buddy Butch, the North American pornographic actor. Though he wasn't to his own finely tuned taste, Sir James had nevertheless viewed his work on the private screen and, on more than one occasion, previously witnessed him in live performance. He was dressed only in a velvet robe, loosely tied around the waist. He bowed for the audience and climbed onto the bed, disJamesg and exposing Inga to his critically acclaimed prick. Sir Philip was on his feet now, discarding his Scarlet Lounge fatigue with clumsy aplomb. Lord Trollope had fainted as usual, his right cheek flattened on the table. The steward brought a slip of folded notepaper and placed it next to Sir James's glass. Buddy Butch pushed Inga forward until her face was between Greta's legs. Sir James unfolded the paper and read the note. Buddy Butch got behind Inga. Sir James lit the note and let it crisp in the ashtray.

'Yes,' said "O".

'S.R.H. What have you got?'

'Detective Inspector Valentine Kibber.'

'Yes?'

'It seems he is already a monitored subject of the New Metropolitan Police and has been for several months.'

Sir James sighed and eased his feet up onto his desk.

'Very well,' he said. 'It probably wouldn't do to tread on the toes of the Blue Mice. Please disregard Kibber.'

'Yes,' said "O". 'Update for Professor Cromwell Rouse.'

'Yes?'

'P77 Protocol has been green-lit, providing there is an A1 Status. His work on the Treatment is a concern.'

'I can assure you the matter warrants A1 grading. Professor Rouse has put himself in a position where his involvement in the Treatment has, regrettably, become untenable as one of the country's leading medical minds. A replacement will be found for PR and accountability.'

'A solution has been recommended.'

'Go on.'

'Cromwell Rouse's former medical partner, Professor Andrea Sterling.'

'Of course,' said Sir James. He instantly recalled a mental image of Professor Sterling. 'There is a way forward there?'

'She is an equal authority on the mechanics of the Treatment.'

'Yes,' said Sir James, 'as I recall, probably more

so. There were mutterings once upon a time that the esteemed Cromwell Rouse had pulled a number on Sterling and taken the lion's share of credit for the research himself, although it was never proved of course. Where is she now?'

'She resigned any involvement in the Treatment. She has been a General Practitioner in Scotland ever since.'

'A professional with moral standards,' mused Sir James, 'how quaint. I take it therefore that she can be persuaded?'

'Every effort will be made to secure her as a replacement for Rouse.'

'Good. Please carry out your duty.'

'Yes,' said "O" and the line went dead.

As soon as Sir James replaced the receiver, the phone rang out.

'Yes?'

'Mr. Iain Gwynne has arrived, Sir James. He was wondering if you were available for a drink.'

Sir James loosened his Scarlet tie and dropped it on the desk.

'Tell Mr. Gwynne I will receive him in the Atrium shortly.'

29

Allen Wyngarde showered heavily and thought about his upcoming tryst with Ursula. He knew the sexual liaison with the wife of the man he was having tailed would be tense and awkward for him. He drank brandy as he towelled and sat at his writing desk with his dressing robe pulled tightly around his girth. He picked up the phone and dialled. It took thirteen rings.

'Yeah?' said the male voice at the other end.

'Mr. Kibber, please.'

'Wait one minute please.'

Allen waited and smoked and drank. Finally, a connection clicked and a gruff voice emerged from the earpiece.

'Hello?'

'Kibber?' said Allen. 'Allen Wyngarde here.'

'Hello.'

'Yes, hello. This is just a quick call to see if you have anything for me?'

'Well,' said Kibber, coughing heavily, 'I have a detailed list of Mr. Gwynne's activities. Pretty mundane stuff, to be honest. Nothing out of the ordinary. Spent a fair amount of time at the Otto Club.'

'Yes,' said Allen, 'I had expected he would. Did you see him meet with anyone at all?'

'No, nobody at all.'

Allen sighed. He wasn't gleaning anything that would help him understand why Iain Fucking Gwynne wanted him to read that manuscript of his.

'Alright,' he said, 'keep on it please, Mr. Kibber.'

'Yes,' said Kibber.

Allen was about to ring off when he heard a faint scratching sound at the other end.

'What's that?'

'Rats,' said Kibber. 'Bloody bastard rats. They're everywhere these days.'

The line went dead and Allen took a large cognac and his cigarettes into the bathroom with him. As he soaked in steam and smoke, he thought about Ursula and how he should break it off before everything started to get way out of hand. He barely noticed the cigarette ash mixing with the soap suds.

Ursula arrived on time and inside a taut white number that in Allen's opinion should give women her age a desperate look. But Ursula, so brazen in her sexual appetites, carried it off without so much as an exaggerated pout of the lips.

'Take some of my medicine,' she said as she straddled him on the chair and placed one of her little magic pills between his lips.

'Ursula…' sighed Allen, letting her poke it into his mouth.

'Surrender to bliss, darling.'

Allen swallowed the pill and drank some cognac.

'Your hair is still damp,' said Ursula, running her fingers through the unkempt sod. 'You'll catch your death of cold.'

'It's a popular myth,' said Allen, reaching for the zip on the back of her dress.

Ursula placed her hands on either side of his head and kissed him lightly on his nose.

'But I worry about you, my love.'

Allen looked at her face and she appeared, just briefly, to be attempting to make herself cry. He placed his thumbs under her eyes to prevent any potential welling up.

'Trust me, Ursula,' he said finally, 'when I die it won't be from the common cold.'

30

Audrey Lee, in her decades-old green dress, entered the Kommune Club at the usual time and seated herself in her usual place. Billy sat dutifully at the table with her and Rick had her Mint Sonata sent over. She caught Rick's eye while he serving behind the bar and he nodded, indicating that he would be playing her song shortly. Audrey sipped her drink and contemplated her performance for the evening. She would add an extra degree of melancholy this time; perhaps open her eyes a moment before the final verse and stare longingly beyond the walls of the club. The music faded and the opening bars of *Love Don't Fear Me* filled the room. She was about to start miming when she saw Harry across the room, sitting in the alcove at the other end of the bar. The vocals began without her. Harry was facing her, his Brandy Alexander in his hand. He raised his glass to her and drank. Audrey felt a sudden kick to the heart when she saw one of his two drinking companions, the aging dandy seated next to him.

'Nigel,' she whispered. Gubbs noticed her expression and spotted Harry across the room. He sprang to his feet.

'Sit down,' said Audrey.

Gubbs did as he was told and watched Audrey as she stared, unmoving, across the room at the figure sitting with Harry. The face was more gaunt, the hair white but still thick and moulded into position. The red cravat inside the open collar orange shirt. The black velvet jacket. The cheroot in the cigarette holder. There he was, staring back at her, his expression a mix of bemusement and regret.

The song kept running away from Audrey until she couldn't hear it anymore. She rose from the table and walked calmly across the floor of the club until she was standing before them. The other man, seated the other side of Harry, she didn't recognise. He got up and went to the bar without a word. Harry said something to her but she wasn't listening to him. All of her attention was fixed on the man she had known long before now. Loud music began to thunder through the room.

'What do you think you are doing?' she asked, her voice inaudible.

Harry didn't reply. His eyes were glazed over. Nigel St. Davos removed the cheroot from the cigarette holder and stubbed it out in the ashtray. He stood up and came around the table. Audrey watched him, uncertainly and scared. He kissed her gently on the cheek then took a step back. Audrey felt the chill rip through her at his touch and closed her eyes tightly for a moment. She wanted to cry but she didn't.

Harry watched her stand motionless, saw her open her eyes and stare directly at him. Nigel tentatively leaned in again and appeared to say something in her ear, but she didn't seem to be taking any of it in. Nigel stopped talking and took a step back, as if to check for any signs of life. But she didn't respond to him. Instead, she came around the table and seated herself next to Harry. She leaned in close and placed a hand on his cheek, easing him closer so she could speak in his ear. He heard her words clearly.

'You have just stabbed me in the heart.'

Then, without another word, Audrey stood up and

walked up the stairs at the end of the room. Harry sat there for a while, stunned by her words. Nigel was sitting next to him, talking urgently at him but Harry paid him no attention. He was looking towards the stairs that led up to the exit. He saw Gubbs leaving, making a throat-cut gesture at him as he went. Harry finished his Brandy Alexander in a daze.

Trent Seether had positioned himself at the bar and watched as the meeting fell apart. He considered Harry, sitting there drowning in his own drunken ideals. He knew that Deborah had a soft spot for him, like he knew that he would be wasting his own efforts pursuing her himself. He downed his pint, winked at Rick and left the club.

Harry smoked a cigarette, not knowing what to do next. He couldn't accept that he'd come to the end of the road. Nigel was still talking, screwing another cheroot into the cigarette holder. Amongst the booze and the smoke and the music, Harry felt that any second now his head could explode, spraying the crowd with splinters of bone and fragments of stewed brain matter. He could feel his heart's irregular rhythm rattling inside his chest cavity, at odds with the beat of the music. Harry placed a consolidatory hand on Nigel's knee, put out his cigarette and walked across the dance floor towards the stairs. Then he took a deep breath and ran up them to the street.

Amongst the people crawling along the pavement, there was no sign of Audrey anywhere. He moved along the pavement, expecting to be set upon by Billy at any moment. But the ambush never came and Harry found himself standing on the kerb at the corner of the street. He flagged a black cab and threw himself onto the back seat.

'St. John's Wood,' he said. 'Please hurry.'

Harry fell out of the taxi and stumbled across the pavement to the imposing gates separating him from Audrey. He felt out of breath, disorientated. He'd apparently seriously miscalculated things, but he couldn't leave it like this. If she was in there, he was going to make her talk to listen to him. He tried the buzzer several times, but nothing came back save for slight crackling sounds. Harry smoked a cigarette and contemplated the gates, stretching upwards into the gloomy darkness. He didn't know exactly what level of physical strength he possessed, especially considering the lamentable trappings of his lifestyle. And yet, he reasoned, if he really wanted to get to Audrey *badly* enough then he should be able to overcome any old run of the mill obstacle like gates.

Harry crushed the remains of his cigarette underfoot and rubbed his hands together to get his fingers moving. He took position before the left hand gate and gripped an ice cold vertical bar in each hand, sliding them up as far as he could stretch. Then he got a foothold on one of the curled strips of metal between the bars and began to pull himself up. He tried to regulate his breathing, aware of the large clouds of mist he was exhaling. He paused for a moment and stared up the path towards the apartment block. There were one or two lights on, but nothing from any of Audrey's windows, as far as he could tell. He kept going, an inch at a time. His body was starting to ache and he could feel the air getting colder, filtering into the sleeves of his overcoat. He suddenly longed for the humid confines of the Kommune, with its endangered soundtracks and its subterranean elite.

He peered down and estimated he was about a third of the way up. There was not much point in stopping now. He was starting to feel acute physical pain from and in every direction. With each traumatic pull up, his lungs felt like they were slowly filling with gravel. He managed to drag his right foot onto the lip of the magnetic locking box connecting the two gates and he squeezed his foot between the small gap above it as tightly as it would go, his arms gaining a grateful respite.

Then he heard a sound. Out there, in the shadows of the private grounds ahead of him. He froze, leaning his mouth into his sleeve to hide his clouds of breath. His eyes strained to pierce the darkness but he could make out nothing apart from the scattering of trees and bushes. It was then he noticed just how quiet everything was. For a moment, the only thing he was aware of was his anxious heartbeats coming through his overcoat. He shook his head, took a deep breath and went for the final push.

As Harry looked upwards to gauge the remaining distance, a boot came out of nowhere and caught him square on the forehead. He felt the connection, instinct causing him to let go of his grip on the railings. His body reclined backwards sharply, a sudden pain searing his right leg. His back crashed against the railings and he realised his foot was still jammed atop the magnetic lock. He flung his arms around wildly, trying to get a grip of the gate. His left hand made contact and he steadied himself just enough to see the wiry shadow of Gubbs sneaking like a spider down the gate railings towards him. Harry tried to swing his body around to get a grip with both hands so that he could at least pull himself into a horizontal position. But Gubbs had slid down far enough to start tugging at Harry's right foot, prising the shoe from between the bars. Harry was about to scream at him when the shoe came loose and suddenly he was plummeting, watching that sneering face shoot back into the darkness.

Harry hit the ground with a dull thud that made his ears ring. For a while, he couldn't feel his body at all; he could just feel the cold air on his face. But gradually, the acute sensation of universal pain began to attack every inch of him. He could feel his peripheral vision shrinking, sounds becoming echoes, what had been left of his sense of smell dialled back to zero. The last thing he saw before the lights went out was Gubbs' face, right above his, a smirking mask against the icy sky.

31

Special News Update: *A memorial service for the missing schoolgirl, Patience Sweetlove, is to be held next week. The announcement was made by Gregory Gem's PR Company through The Edition newspaper. Among the celebrities expected to attend are Viktor and Mitzy, last year's joint winners of 'Britain's Best Bathrooms'; teen pop sensation, Logan Wyre; Decathlon gold medallist Lindy Lucker and of course Rod Fortune, who has written the charity single which will be released next month. Fortune can currently be seen about town sporting a magnificent pair of pink Supertread XX trainers - a nod of respect to the missing girl whose own pink Supertread XX was recently found during a search. He is also expected to perform a solo acoustic performance of the song, said to be called* Have Patience (For Patience), *at the end of the memorial service. The big question, of course, is whether Gregory Gem himself will make an appearance at the service, but so far his people have not got back to us on the subject.*

Cromwell Rouse changed the station on the car radio as he navigated his way through the country lanes, the headlights bouncing from tree to hedgerow as he steered the huge car into the night. He found a rare piece of classical music on a medium wave channel and turned the volume up. He checked the little digital clock on the dashboard, sighing inwardly that it would take him another forty five minutes to get home. Cressida would no doubt be in bed by the time he got his key in the front door. He couldn't remember the last time he'd had a lustful thought about her, and he wasn't likely to at the moment, not with the reappearance of Guinevere. He could feel his pulse increasing just saying her name in his head. No matter how bitter their last exchange had been, it had felt like an electric shock to him. He was glad Cressida would be in bed when he got home; he would retire to his private study for the evening.

Just after passing through the quiet, dreamy little hamlet of Rent's Bastion, Rouse slowed the car to a stop at the traffic lights that he usually managed to dodge. He turned the music volume down halfway and strummed his fingers on the steering wheel to Gorecki.

The driver's door suddenly swung open and before he could react, an arm was around his neck, bracing him in a tight stranglehold. Rouse could feel the bicep squeezing his throat so that he could barely inhale. He heard the passenger door open and saw another hand closing in. He was being smothered; he instantly recognised the smell of chloroform. As his world began to mist and all the fight went out of him, Rouse heard the muted whispers and saw his car receding into the distance of his consciousness. He wondered if, sometime soon, Cressida would casually look at the clock and find it strange that he had not come home yet. The last thought he had was of climbing between the sheets of his own bed and wrapping his tired arms around his wife.

32

The first sensation Harry experienced as his consciousness took a shaky step into the light was that of being bathed. It felt warm and brought a smile to his face. He opened his eyes and immediately felt the sting of hot liquid that was projecting from the underside of the small, scruffy dog standing in the cocked position above his head. Harry squeezed his eyes shut and lashed out with a clenched fist, catching the animal right between the legs. There was a high pitched yelp followed by the urgent tap-tap of paws on paving stones. Harry sat up and wiped his face with the sleeve of his overcoat. His face felt like it had had acid sprayed on it. He brought a hand up and gently touched his head. Dried blood. He opened his eyes. It was still dark.

He was lying in a pile of bushes on the inside of the pavement, about ten yards from the gates to Audrey Lee's apartment block. He remembered Gubbs knocking him off. That little shit must have worked him over while he was lying out cold on the street. Harry's next thought was to rip Gubbs' body apart piece by scrawny piece, but that would require a certain amount of exertion that made him wince with pain. He pushed himself to his feet and checked his watch. Twenty past six in the morning. A black cab rattled past. Harry felt for his cigarettes and lit one, the nicotine going straight to his head. He began to walk awkwardly down the street, every inch of him aching and freezing cold. The smell of dog piss was overwhelming as it soaked into his clothes and clung to his hair.

As he passed the gates, he dared to take a look through them towards the shadowy apartment block beyond. Amidst the darkened outline of the building, he could have sworn he saw a stab of yellow light between shifting curtains, right where Audrey's apartment was. For a brief moment he entertained the idea of giving it another go; he was onto Gubbs and his dirty tactics now. But the pain and fatigue he felt made him think better of it. He had to stoically accept that whatever he thought he had with Audrey Lee was well and truly over. Now, Harry could only think of one other lady in his life. How he longed, right at that moment as he walked unsteadily through the overcrowded grime of this sinister metropolis, for the comforting figure of Deborah Flaxman. If she had somehow miraculously appeared before him right there and then, Harry would have gladly died in her arms.

33

Claudia sat patiently next to the bed and watched Scottie settle back into sleep. Only the angle lamp on the bedside cabinet was on in the private room, providing just enough light for Claudia to watch her lover's features. At around seven in the morning, the door quietly opened and Sister Clodagh entered the room.

'She's sleeping,' said Claudia.

'You look like you could do with some yourself,' replied Sister Clodagh, proceeding to check Scottie and consult the clipboard hanging on the edge of the bed.

'I am alright,' said Claudia. But she knew the nurse was right. She did need sleep and badly. 'Sister, when can Scottie come home?'

Sister Clodagh regarded the beautiful and exhausted woman sitting next to the patient. Then she cast her eye over the damaged, frail figure lying in the bed and wondered where the attraction lay.

'I will try and find out for you,' she said.

Claudia waited, but after twenty minutes she began to feel the stirring of impatience and so she kissed Scottie on the forehead and stepped silently into the corridor outside.

It was empty as usual, but at the far end and around the corner, she could hear something. As she walked towards it, she realised it was the sound of a television set, complete with the mutterings of whoever was there watching it. As she turned the corner, Claudia saw half a dozen people gathered in the nurse's bay, all huddled around the television that was bolted to the wall. They were all staff, including Sister Clodagh. As Claudia approached, one of the staff, a porter, said:

'There's more to this than they're letting on.'

'Oh, be quiet, Kevin,' said Sister Clodagh.

'Just sayin'.'

'Well don't. And I won't have any speculations flying around here either.'

Sister Clodagh noticed Claudia standing at the desk and put on her sweet smile for her.

'What's going on?' asked Claudia.

'Nothing important, dear,' said Sister Clodagh, coming around the desk and placing an arm around Claudia's shoulders to gently turn her away from the events unfolding on screen. 'Now, why don't we go and see if we can find out when Scottie can be discharged, eh?'

'That Rouse,' said Kevin, '*has* to be more going on.'

Claudia stopped and shrugged Sister Clodagh's hand away from her. She walked into the nursing bay and stood behind the others, looking at what was on the screen. A reporter was standing in the road of what looked like a small village. Behind him was a car with its front doors wide open.

"'…a search of the immediate area has so far failed to provide the police with any clue as to the whereabouts of Professor Rouse…'"

Claudia felt the small knot in her stomach tighten at the mention of his name. She knew instantly what had happened to him.

"'…there are no apparent signs of a struggle and so far no witnesses have come forward. Early indications suggest Professor Cromwell Rouse may have been drink driving…'"

So there it was then, Claudia thought. She felt a cold shiver course through her body, followed by the tingle of excitement.

'I'm sorry you had to see that, my dear,' said Sister Clodagh.

'It's quite alright,' said Claudia, stepping away from the group and walking away, 'I'm sure he will turn up sooner or later.'

Claudia returned to Scottie's side and opened the blinds, letting the first bank of early morning sunlight into the room. Then she sat at her side and held Scottie's hand in hers.

'Scottie,' she said gently.

Scottie stirred once.

'Scottie,' said Claudia again as she kissed her on the lips. Scottie's eyes opened and she looked up at her.

'It's time to go home,' said Claudia.

Scottie smiled.

34

Just after nine in the morning, Deborah Flaxman descended her stairs and prepared her coffee. It wasn't until she went to check for any post that she heard the gentle knocking sound against the front door. She pulled her dressing gown tight and slipped the safety chain. As soon as the door opened a tiny crack, a muddy hand slipped through the gap, fingers stretched as if desperately trying to get hold of something inside. Deborah knew, before she opened the door properly, that it was Harry.

He crawled across the threshold. Deborah carried him into the lounge and laid him on the sofa. His face was caked in dirt and dried blood. His breathing was heavy and his eyelids looked even more cumbersome. He reeked of alcohol, cigarettes and piss.

'Please tell me you haven't wet yourself,' she said, suddenly concerned for her furniture.

Harry shook his head and coughed.

'No. A dog pissed all over me.'

'Time to strip off, Harry.'

Harry exerted himself leaning forward and clawing his way out of his clothes. Deborah fetched a black bin bag and opened it while he dropped each item in.

'Underwear too,' she said.

Harry frowned, hesitated, then did as he was told. Deborah noticed the first stirrings of his uncontrolled morning glory and averted her eyes as he dropped his underpants into the bag. She went into the kitchen and dropped the bag outside the back door. Then she collected a tee shirt, an old pair of beige trousers and some sandals from the spare bedroom closet. When she returned to the lounge, Harry had curled himself up into a ball on the sofa with his back to her.

'Harry,' she said sharply, 'don't go to sleep. Turn around and sit up.'

Harry groaned and shifted himself around to face her.

'Put these on,' she said, dropping the clothes in his lap. 'You can wash and return them to me later.'

Harry considered the clothes.

'Any chance of a coffee?'

Deborah shook her head and knelt down in front of him. He smelled bad.

'What happened to you last night, Harry? Please don't tell me you got into a pub brawl.'

'No,' said Harry. 'It was Audrey.'

'Harry, are you trying to tell me that *Audrey* did this to you?'

'No,' said Harry, half smiling at the very idea, 'that skinny shitbag sidekick of hers. He caught me off guard, otherwise I would have unscrewed his head from his shoulders.'

'Sure,' said Deborah, 'but you must have provoked him.'

'Things didn't work out at the club, Deborah.'

'I know,' she said, 'Trent called me and told me Audrey walked out.'

'I fucked up, Deborah.'

'You didn't fuck up, Harry.'

'Yes I did. I thought I could do some good and bring somebody back in from the cold and I just made it a whole lot worse.'

Deborah saw how upset Harry suddenly appeared. She thought about putting a comforting arm around his shoulders but decided against it; she was still acutely aware of the slight and involuntary hardness under the neat pile of clothes in his lap. Instead she stood up and sat down in the armchair opposite.

'Now listen to me, Harry. I'm older than you and I'm also wiser than you. You may have had this strange notion in your head that you could help that faded pop starlet, but what you forgot was that it's you who needs saving first, not Audrey Lee. You're a complete bloody mess, an awful state and it's not particularly nice for me to have to sit here and look at you like this. You have a few issues you need to address and fast, Harry. I think the death of your parents has hit you a lot harder than you're letting on and it's not good for you to just brush it aside like it's something that just happened to two people you used to know. Whatever life you had, whatever you got up to before you came back to England, it's over now. It's time to grow up, Harry.'

Harry couldn't look Deborah in the eye. He got to his feet, the dizzying effects of sudden movement causing him to close his eyes and take a moment. He kept the clothes and sandals covering his middle as he sidestepped out of the lounge without a word, avoiding Deborah's observation. Then he went upstairs and locked himself in the bathroom.

Deborah poured herself a cup of coffee and stared out into the garden. She had seen that look of failure before; the resignation, the despondency. And she bloody well hated it. There was a heavy breeze whipping up the overgrown wildlife out the back. She wondered if Sara was out there somewhere, huddled perhaps between the fence and the greenhouse. She considered opening the back door and calling for her, but she knew better. Sara *never* came to her when she called her.

She heard the toilet flushing above her followed by disjointed footsteps on the staircase.

'How do I look?' said Harry quietly.

Deborah turned around and saw him standing by the breakfast bar, his face free of the mud and most of the dried blood. Nothing looked broken or too damaged. He seemed to be attempting to carry off a casual, debonair pose, one hand on the counter and the other in the pocket of her beige trousers. They were a little too short and he had just managed to squeeze into the navy blue tee shirt and brown sandals.

'You deserve to look a little bit foolish,' she said.

'Thanks,' said Harry, massaging his eyes. 'I don't think I've been too badly bruised. Got a slice above my hairline where that twat caught me with his shoe.'

Deborah felt a flash of concern for his wellbeing at that moment and placed her coffee cup on the side before approaching him and taking his head carefully in her hands, seeking out the cut amongst his scruffy hair.

'I see it,' she said. 'It's not too bad. I don't think it'll require stitches, just some antiseptic. I take it you'll have some of that next door?'

'Probably,' said Harry. 'Thanks, Deborah.'

'Don't thank me, Harry,' she said, letting go of his head. 'I'm not entirely happy about all this.'

Harry noticed the dark shadow of something from her past cross her face. It was melted away in an instant.

'That's what I mean,' said Harry. 'Thanks,

Deborah.'

'Alright, Harry.'

Harry suddenly placed his hands on her shoulders and tried to lean in to kiss her. Deborah put her arms up, preventing him from making contact. He backed off, his face suddenly flushed crimson red.

'I'm not sure why I did that,' said Harry.

'Please go home and do whatever you have to do,' said Deborah, feeling her own cheeks begin to redden.

'Deborah, I'm--'

Deborah put a finger to his lips to silence him. She shook her head slowly and Harry left without another word. As soon as she heard the door close, she went upstairs and ran herself a bath in which she remained for the next hour and a half.

35

The ringing telephone skewered Allen Wyngarde's ears at precisely eleven thirty. His head was swimming and he was naked and thirsty. He jolted forward in his chair and stared at it accusingly.

'Hello?'

'Hello, Allen,' said Iain Gwynne.

Despite the radiators in his apartment being turned up to thermonuclear, an icy shiver rippled through Allen's sagging body. He leaned back in his chair, staring up at the ceiling, stained brown by years of nicotine intake.

'Hello, Iain,' he said quietly.

'Have you read my manuscript yet?'

'Er…' started Allen, casting his eye over towards the safe.

'I'll take that as a "no" then, shall I?' said Iain. He didn't sound at all angry by Allen's stumbling response.

'Well, Iain,' he started apologetically, 'the thing is I really haven't had the time to sit down and read it all in one go. What with my own work and--'

'And fucking Ursula?' said Iain. 'Yes, I can see how it might be awkward to shoehorn me in, Allen. She does rather take it out of you, doesn't she?'

Allen felt the blood drain from his face and his hands start to tremble.

'Iain, I don't know what--'

'Allen, Allen, Allen,' sighed Iain, 'please spare me your half baked protestations, will you? Now tell me: Does she open that hole between her legs as often as she opens that hole in her face?'

'I--'

'Forget it, Allen,' said Iain, chuckling to himself on the other end of the line. 'I probably shouldn't ask but it's often the case that the wronged party wants to be told all the gory details despite knowing how upset it's likely to make them.'

'I'm so sorry, Iain,' said Allen. In a way, he almost felt relieved it was finally all out in the open. 'She's not here with me now, just in case you were wondering.'

'Oh, I know exactly where my beloved wife is at the moment, Allen,' said Iain and Allen could detect the sudden humourlessness in his voice.

'What do you mean by that?'

'Listen, old boy,' said Iain purposefully, 'unless you want Ursula on your conscience, you'd better knuckle down and read my manuscript by midnight tonight, alright? That should give you ample time, I should think, don't you?'

'Well--'

'And then when you've read it, I want you to bring it to me over at the Otto Club, where I will quiz your experienced literary brain about it. Does that sound like a plan, old boy?'

Allen placed a sweaty hand on his forehead and shook his head miserably from side to side.

'Alright, Iain,' he said. 'I'll see you at your club later.'

'Splendid,' replied Iain Gwynne and hung up.

Allen left the receiver off the hook and let his head drop forward onto the bureau. He remained in that position for several minutes, ruminating on the current fate and condition of poor Ursula. He questioned whether or not he was man enough to fight for her, to rescue her from the clutches of her twisted husband. Allen knew he had been cursed at an early age with acute cowardice, a condition that had reverberated throughout his entire life. Most notable decisions he had ever made had been out of fear rather than gutsy determination, the desire to be accepted rather than to challenge. His output of telemovie scripts had been precise, production line fodder, by the numbers and enough to guarantee cheques from the studios. His private life had been choreographed by his dear, departed Barbra; a series of concessions and concurrences that did little to earn her respect. And now here he was, being verbally -and later, in all likelihood, physically - manhandled by a loathsome poet who considered himself the very cream of the literary universe. Had Allen been half the man he knew he should have been, he was sure he would have put Iain Fucking Gwynne in his place a long time ago.

Allen opened up the safe in weary resignation, like a condemned man loading the executioner's gun himself, and settled onto his small leather couch with his cigarettes and a large cognac.

Four hours later, he dropped the manuscript to the floor and staggered into the bathroom where he positioned his aching head over the toilet bowl and tried to make himself sick.

36

Harry lay on top of the mauled bed sheets in his old bedroom, staring through the ceiling. He saw a thin trail splitting the azure sky turning from a brilliant white to an ominous grey. At its head, the shape of an aeroplane, crazed by a restless amber glow as it twisted like a drill bit across the heavens, slowly tearing itself apart into tiny flailing shards of burnt metal. Harry shut his eyes tightly to block out the vision, but it still remained, scoring a downwards trajectory amongst the ebb and flow of the dead cells punctuating the darkness behind his lids. He had another drink and pondered his next move. He would sell 77 Vancouver Hill; better still - he would raze it to the ground and free himself of any connection to his past. Eventually he nodded off into a fitful slumber for the rest of the day, waking every half hour or so until the room began to fill with dusky hues.

He tried thumbing through some porn but found little in the way of relief. In the end he made his way downstairs and picked up the phone.

'Listen, Deborah,' he started awkwardly, 'I'm truly sorry for being a pain in the arse and I just want you to know that I shan't be troubling you again. I'm selling the house and going away forever.'

'Shut up, Harry,' said Deborah calmly, 'and come over. Trent's here.'

Deborah hung up on Harry.

Harry lingered about in the hallway for several minutes, on the brink of another whisky. Instead, he went into the kitchen and boiled himself up a scolding cup of coffee and then dressed silently upstairs in a sombre black three piece suit from his father's wardrobe. It almost fitted, although he had to leave the trouser button undone and suspended by braces to accommodate his paunch. He ignored the completion of a tie and slipped on a pair of his own brown shoes and took the short walk to Deborah's front door, the alcohol in his blood chilling his insides.

'Come in, Harry,' said Deborah. She was wearing a tightly drawn scarlet dressing gown and nothing else. Harry followed her into the living room where Trent Seether was sitting in the armchair, nursing a cigarette over an ashtray on the arm of the chair. He acknowledged Harry with a reserved nod.

'Trent's got some news,' said Deborah, sitting down next to Harry on the sofa.

Trent took his cue and stubbed out the cigarette.

'This morning I had a meet with Nigel St Davos,' he said. 'He gave me the master tapes of Audrey Lee's music. With the specific instruction that you pass it on to the lady herself.'

Trent brought two flat, grey boxes from the side of the armchair and placed them at his feet.

'Why?' was all Harry could find to say.

'He didn't want to go into specifics about his motivation,' replied Trent. 'I suspect it's the guilt that's suddenly hit him after seeing her at the club last night. Who the fuck knows? I'm due to phone him tomorrow anyway.'

'But Audrey didn't take seeing him again very well,' said Harry. 'Why should this make her feel any differently?'

'Maybe it won't,' said Trent, 'but it's what you wanted, Harry.'

'I know,' said Harry, falling back into the sofa, 'and that's just it, isn't it? It's what *I*, selfish old Harry Brewer wanted. I can't even remember if I gave her feelings in this any thought at all. It's my motivation we should be questioning, not Nigel's.'

'Whatever,' said Trent.

'Look Harry,' said Deborah, 'it was bound to come as a big shock to her, seeing him again so unexpectedly after all these years. I doubt the attack on you was sanctioned by her. You can't possibly know how she feels about it by now.'

'I haven't the heart to even find out,' said Harry in defeat.

'Well, you'd better make up your mind and let me know,' said Trent. 'I do have other work to be getting on with.'

'Wait a minute,' said Deborah. She turned to Harry and placed a hand delicately on his leg. 'Harry, think about this very carefully. Even if she is upset with you now, at some point she will know that whatever you did or tried to do was as much for her as it was for you. If you give up now, you're just leaving a bad taste in everybody's mouth.'

Trent saw something that the others didn't see at that moment. It was subtle, barely perceptible, but he saw it. He collected his cigarettes and rose from his seat.

'I'll be off then,' he said. 'Let me know the state of play, eh?'

He left the room and heard Deborah following him to the front door.

'Thanks for everything,' she said.

Trent turned to her and placed his hands on her

shoulders.

'He fancies you, Deborah,' he said quietly.

Deborah sighed, 'Really. Your journalist's eye has lost none of its acuity, has it?'

'I'm serious,' replied Trent. 'I've seen that look before. When I was with you, every time I looked at my reflection in the mirror. Trust me.'

'Jesus, Trent--'

'And I'll go you one further: You feel the same way about him. Bye, sweetheart.'

Before she could reply, Trent gave her a heavy kiss on the forehead and walked through the front door. Deborah touched her forehead lightly where he'd left his farewell kiss and then she returned to the living room. Harry was not there and she heard the clinking of bottles coming from the kitchen. She found him there, struggling to uncork a bottle of pinot. She remained in the doorway, unnoticed by her guest and listening to him swear as he managed to cork the wine.

'I thought you'd have been a past master at that kind of thing by now.'

Harry turned around and held the bottle up slightly, 'I thought maybe we could toast your reasonable assumption of success.'

'You've decided then.'

'Why not, hey.'

'I'll have mine in a glass, please.'

Harry poured them both a generous helping and they silently saluted each other before drinking.

'My god, that's good plonk,' said Harry. 'Shame I corked it.'

'It's expensive plonk,' said Deborah.

'Sorry.'

'That's life.'

'Yes.'

Deborah seated herself at the breakfast bar and spun her glass slowly around between her hands.

'Harry?'

'Yes?'

'How often do you fall for someone?'

'Fall? In love?'

'That's right, Harry. In love.'

Harry didn't reply; he had been visibly caught off guard by the question.

'Let me put it another way,' said Deborah in a cool, measured tone. 'Do you fall in love with someone easily? And if you do: Are you certain that it is indeed love? Can you tell the difference between that head-over-heels, all-or-nothing feeling and just one more throbbing crush to squeeze into your no doubt extensive wank-bank?'

Harry tried to reply, but instead knocked his glass against the work surface sending red wine across the laminated covering.

'Shit,' he said and turned away to the sink to grab a cloth. He mopped the spillage up nervously, unsure as to where she was taking him with all this talk. He rinsed the stained cloth out and hung it over the tap. When he turned around, Deborah was standing closer to him, her scarlet robe discarded on the floor behind her. What he saw of her body, he had seen before but now he felt as though he was seeing her like that for the very first time and it left his eyes with nowhere else to go. She watched his face intently as he poured over her, seeing the conflicting emotions of uncertainty and lust in his expression. They stood there for several long and intense moments before she broke the silence.

'I'm going to go upstairs.'

Then she was gone, leaving Harry bemused and semi-erect in the kitchen, his addled brain desperately trying to process this unexpected sequence of events. Then, he downed both glasses of pinot and bounded out of the kitchen after her. She had already ascended and he broke into a shaky, nervous run as he started onto the stairs, pulling off his clothes as he went. As he neared the top, his ankles became entangled in his trousers, causing him to lurch forward with a heavy thud onto the landing. He got to his feet, freed one of his legs and again lost his balance, collapsing back onto the wicker laundry basket. It toppled over and a few items of clothing spilled out. He freed himself of his clothing and found himself pausing for a moment to have a quick look at a pair of Deborah's knickers. He felt the smooth, slight texture of the silk before rising to his feet. The doorway to the roof was ajar and, fully erect, he ran through it.

He reached the top, the evening air at first antagonistic then soothing. His eyes darted across the roof terrace, desperately trying to seek her out. For a brief, dreadful moment he suspected she might be performing some cruel act of humiliation upon him; a mean-spirited "that'll teach you" for the drunken impositions he had subjected her to. But then he heard movement, there by the chimney stack and he saw her, half submerged in the shadows. She was leaning back, pressing herself against the brickwork of the chimney and looking at him intently.

He approached, wanting to get on with what they

were about to do but at the same time trying not to appear too desperate. He stood before her and without a word he felt her hand around him, pulling him closer to her so that her breasts nestled in his chest hair. He was privately relieved that he hadn't lost any of his hardness. After a few minutes, Deborah wrapped her arms around his neck and kissed him full on the mouth, her tongue forcing its way in. Harry's fingers grabbed her breasts roughly, then he let his right hand glide down over her middle to the hair between her legs. She opened them a little and his fingers clumsily found their way inside. He had always been bad at this act of fumbling, having nowhere near perfected any kind of technique since the seamy explorations of his teenage years. After a while she removed his hand and her lips pulled away from his. She was breathing heavily, staring into him. She turned around to face the chimney and guided him between her thighs. Harry bent his knees and somehow managed to get inside her on the first attempt. She spread her legs wider as he found his momentum, holding onto her waist to keep his balance. Deborah pushed back and fore against him, her head bowed between her shoulders. Harry could feel his calf muscles burning and just before his legs were about to buckle he came. He began to shudder, folding his arms around her navel and feverishly kissing the back of her neck. He felt her contracting around him, holding him, twitching inside her. He was panting heavily, unable to catch his breath. They remained there in that position for a while, until he felt the blood receding and he took a few steps back. Deborah slowly turned around, her hair hanging loosely around her flushed face. She pressed herself flat against the wall and stood motionless as a statue. The whole thing had been clumsily executed and yet for the first time in as long as he could remember, it felt like something had *actually happened*.

'I should have come outside,' said Harry apologetically, 'sorry about that.'

Deborah gave him a surprised stare, then began to laugh; a schoolgirl's giggle at first which then developed into something louder. Harry looked around him. Suddenly self conscious of the glowing windows of the surrounding suburbs. Deborah pulled herself together and held out her hand.

'Come here, Harry,' she said. 'Let me see your eyes.'

Harry took her hand and she drew him to her, their faces inches apart.

'What?' said Harry.

'How do you feel, Harry? How do you *really* feel at this very moment?'

Harry swallowed, blinked twice and he knew the answer she was looking for. And he knew that because it was the truth.

'Love,' he said. She gave him no reply and he suddenly imagined he may have been wrong. 'Or *in love*...is that what I'm supposed to say? I mean, you wouldn't mind me saying something like that, would you? I wouldn't want you to think I was just saying that because we just had it off up against your chimney stack. Not that if I *didn't* feel as though I was in love, it wouldn't mean that I *didn't* feel anything more substantial than mere fantasy. I mean, you *were* in my wank bank, *are* in it...sorry, I probably shouldn't have said that, any of it for that matter. Christ, Deborah, could you please help me out here!'

'You're shivering,' she said. 'Let's go to bed.'

37

Trent Seether, having finally witnessed the inevitable final nail hammered into the coffin of his relationship with Deborah Flaxman, got loaded in the Cloisters on more rounds of Black Bug than he could cope with and drove his sports car across town and made an untidy attempt at parking on Adam's Brook Road. He wrenched himself from behind the wheel and crossed the street to the old Victorian building, violently kicking in the main front door. As he entered, he heard movement coming from one of the ground floor flats. But he was pounding his way up the darkened stairway before anybody could come out and complain. He reached the fourth floor and threw his entire body weight against the door. There was a loud crunch as the lock gave way in a flash of splintered wood from the rotting door frame. Trent entered and crossed the long corridor towards the solitary light coming from the room at the rear of the apartment. He could hear no noise and as he walked in, he saw Super G lying on the floor, flat on his back and staring wide-eyed at the ceiling. All of the electronic equipment in the room was switched off now. Trent stood over him, staring down at the slender, weak body beneath him. Super G didn't even seem to register his presence.

'Time to wake up,' said Trent.

'It's coming,' whispered Super G.

'*What's* coming?'

'*It's* coming.'

'You little prick.'

Trent reached down and grabbed the neck of his tee shirt, shaking him violently from side to side.

Super G didn't resist. Trent pulled him up off the floor and threw him against the wall, holding him against it with his hand around his throat. Super G's eyes grew wider still, but Trent could see he wasn't frightened of him.

'It's coming,' said Super G.
'Tell me...'
'You're powerless.'

Super G was pointing again, up towards the ceiling. Trent relaxed his grip a little and turned to look up. All over the ceiling, he could make out Super G's scribbles and equations. Every inch was covered in his writing and diagrams and Trent couldn't understand any of it. He began to grow even more agitated by all of it. He turned back to Super G and got him on the floor, slapping him around the head lightly at first.

'Tell me--'
'It's coming--'
'Tell me--'
'It's coming--'
 The slaps got harder.
'Tell me.'
'You're powerless--'
'Why?'
'We're all powerless--'
Trent hit him harder.
'Why?'
'We're all--'
Harder again.
'Why?'
'--'
'*Why?*'

But Super G was unconscious.

Trent straightened up, the Black Bug playing havoc with his head. He lay on the floor, next to Super G and stared up at the seemingly unintelligible scrawls above him. He found he couldn't take his eyes off the image of the spaceship at the heart of it all.

'This is the end,' said Trent.

He piled into his car and forced his way into the mess of traffic heading back into the square mile, the beating, greedy heart of the Capital. He could feel his pulse, heavy and throbbing and tense in his neck. He fumbled with the cigarette pack against the steering wheel and dropped most of them on his lap and in the foot well, but managed to retain one which he lit and drew heavily on as he searched for a space to pull in near The Cloisters. He squeezed his car in at an acute angle between a hatchback and a Transit van and eased himself out of the driver's seat. He considered the pub, where he had spent almost his whole working life since becoming a paper man, listened to the dulled noise pounding against the distorted, mottled windows. He knew that he would also end his career here. He allowed a brief thought for Deborah and their Judy and how he'd really, sensationally screwed everything up. He knew that it would end in The Cloisters one day, one night, maybe tonight. Trent Seether knew it and it made him smile.

To the north, Deborah Flaxman awoke to find herself alone in her bed. She assumed for a moment that Harry was, at that moment, submerged in her wine rack and drinking her dry. But something outside caught her attention. A flickering glow was dancing its way through the crack in the curtains and it made her sit up. She listened intently and heard the quiet crackling coming from down below. She slid from the bed and crossed the room to the window. At the far end of the garden, beyond the overgrown weeds and stacks of pottery, stood Harry.

He was facing away from her, staring at the large black chiminea she had bought years before in Venezuela. He had got it going and now, dressed in the clothes he had arrived in, watched the glow increase inside the grate. He took a few steps closer to the pot and it was at that moment that she saw what he was clutching in both hands.

Deborah stepped out into the garden, pulling her night robe close around her neck. As she approached, Harry heard her footsteps and half turned. She came along next to him and stared into the flames.

'More second thoughts, Harry?'

Harry nodded and raised the two flat grey boxes, contemplating what was contained inside.

'This just feels like the right thing to do, Deborah.'

'Why?'

'If I destroy the tapes then I destroy the physical past of Audrey Lee. Then, her past will only exist the way she wants it to; sitting there night after night in that basement club, listening to that same song over and over. Who the hell am I to interfere?'

'It's not your decision to make. Not anymore.'

'I'm holding the tapes. It's my decision alright.'

He took a step forward. A few embers spat out of the chiminea and landed on the tapes. He lifted the lid, revealing a large spool inside.

'Don't do it, Harry,' said Deborah, almost in a

whisper. 'just come back inside and I'll make us some coffee.'

Harry didn't reply at first. For a while he just stood there, holding the master tapes near the fire grate. Deborah was about to turn and leave him to it when he gave a heavy sigh and reached for her hand.

'I'd rather have a glass of red.'

38

Detective Inspector Kibber sat back in the driver's seat of the unmarked squad car and took a drink from his hip flask. It was closing in on midnight and there had been more members leaving the Otto Club than arriving over the past hour or so. The interior of the car was getting stuffy and Kibber could feel his joints beginning to seize up from hours of inactivity. He longed for the sanctuary of his room, watched over by Claudia's eyes as he slept. He was about to call it a night when he saw a familiar face stepping out of a taxi at the steps of the club. Kibber, now wide awake, sat up behind the steering wheel and watched as Allen Wyngarde, looking like he had the world's troubles on his shoulders, walked heavily in through the doors of the club. Kibber was also alerted by the package his client had wedged under his right arm tightly, as though he were trying to keep it concealed from uninvited eyes. Kibber waited for a few minutes, topping himself up from his flask and massaging his thighs to get some blood circulating. At exactly midnight, Kibber stepped from the car and crossed the street towards the Otto Club. At the unwelcoming and over-ornate doors he pressed the buzzer.

'Yes?'

'My name's Detective Inspector Kibber of the New Metropolitan Police Service.'

'Yes?' came the indifferent response.

'Would you mind letting me into the club, please?'

'On what business?'

Kibber counted a beat in his head as he felt his agitation clawing its way up inside him.

'I wish to speak with somebody inside.'

'I presume you have brought some type of warrant with you?'

'I'm not here in an official capacity. I wish to speak with Mr. Iain Gwynne. Now kindly let me in.'

There was a click from the intercom speaker followed by silence. Kibber blew into his hands to warm them up against the midnight air. Eventually, the voice returned.

'You have identification on you?'

'Of course I have bloody identification on me,' barked Kibber.

'Then please hold it up to the camera above you.'

Kibber removed his warrant card from inside his jacket and held it up towards the small security camera perched next to the top left hand corner of the doors. There was another break of silence before the lock mechanism clicked and Kibber pushed his way through into the club. There was a scrawny, smug looking man behind the main reception and the way he looked over at him as he approached confirmed to Kibber that this was the one he had just been talking with. The man stood up as he approached, head held high so he could stare down his upturned nose.

'Mr. Gwynne,' said Kibber, placing two heavy hands on the counter. 'If you don't mind.'

The concierge, whose name Kibber read as Gibbons, picked up a phone.

'I shall have to see if he's free.'

'You do that, Gibbons,' said Kibber, allowing an intimidating grin to upset the fault line of his mouth. Gibbons lifted the receiver to his ear and pressed a button. He tried to avoid Kibber's stare.

'Mr. Gwynne, sir? I'm terribly sorry to disturb you but I have a Policeman here at reception who would like to have a word with you...What did you say your name was?'

'Detective Inspector Kibber.'

'Detective Inspector Kibber, sir...What is it regarding?'

'It's a private matter between myself and Mr. Gwynne.'

'It's a private matter, sir...Very good, sir.'

Gibbons put the phone down and pressed a button on the small console next to it. A few moments later, just as Kibber had outstared the concierge, an elderly steward arrived.

'Jeffrey,' said Gibbons in a manner which betrayed his relief, 'please escort this police officer to the Bull Room.'

Jeffrey nodded and Kibber winked at Gibbons as he followed the steward away from reception and down a narrow, wood paneled corridor that only seemed to become visible when they were directly in front of it. There were portrait paintings at exact intervals all the way along on both walls. Old men in an older world. The steward stopped at a door, seamless with the surrounding walls, and opened it. Then he stood aside and waited for the Inspector to enter. Kibber hesitated, then went inside. There were no windows, the light coming from a large, square panel set into the ceiling. Otherwise, it was colonial and out of date; bookcases and trophies, wall-mounted heads of long-deceased wild animals snatched from their homelands, paintings and photographs of the Empire's late and great.

'Would you care for a drink, sir?'

Kibber turned his attention to the steward.

'Yes, Jeffrey. I would like the largest glass of Black Bug you can find. No ice.'

'Yes, sir,' replied the steward with a curt nod and left, pulling the door closed as he went.

There were two taut, studded leather sofas facing each other in the middle of the room and Kibber took a seat on the nearest one. Several minutes passed, during which the steward brought him his drink on a silver tray and left again. Kibber drank his drink in long, drawn out slurps, running his tongue across his moustache between every mouthful. He was just reaching the end when the door opened and in strode Iain Gwynne. Kibber got to his feet and by the time he did, Iain Gwynne had come to a stop barely a foot from him. Kibber could see him sizing him up instantly and tried to straighten himself out.

'Detective Inspector Kibber,' said Iain Gwynne, over-enunciating every consonant. What can I do for the police at this hour I wonder?'

'Well, sir,' said Kibber, clearing his throat, 'I'm not here in an official capacity…'

'Really, Inspector,' said Iain Gwynne with a knowing smirk, 'you do surprise me.'

'Well, sir,' continued Kibber, 'I have reason to believe that your life may be in danger.'

Iain Gwynne's eyebrows rose slightly.

'In danger?'

'Yes, sir. That's right.'

'Well, Inspector, that sounds terribly intriguing.' Iain Gwynne sat on the sofa opposite and waved for Kibber to sit down also. 'Tell me, Inspector; who am I to be afraid of on a dark night such as this?'

'Well, sir,' said Kibber, shifting uncomfortably on the hard leather, 'are you familiar with a gentleman by the name of Allen Wyngarde?'

'Allen? Of course I am, we've known each other for years.'

'In what way, sir?'

'Well, we're both writers; he writes telemovie scripts and I write poetry.'

'I see, sir.'

Iain Gwynne leaned forward, his eyes narrowing.

'Inspector Kibber; are you trying to imply that Allen Wyngarde is out to cause me some harm?'

'Why is Mr. Wyngarde here at the Otto Club tonight?

Iain Gwynne hesitated for barely a second, but it was enough for Kibber to pick up on.

'He's here at my invitation, if you must know.'

'And the purpose of your invite?'

'Nothing sinister, Inspector. Just a spirited literary discussion, that's all.'

'I see.'

Iain Gwynne studied the beaten, weathered features of Kibber's face. He had smelt the stale odour of yesterday's booze the moment he had walked into the Bull Room. An out-of-date copper from the bad old days, he decided. Extinction was the only feasible outcome for somebody like Detective Inspector Valentine Kibber.

'Tell me,' he said, 'why do you suspect Allen is in some way involved in a plot against me?'

'Well, sir,' replied Kibber, running a finger around the inside of his dirty shirt collar, 'the New

Metropolitan Police Service pays me to discover such things.'

'Really? And do they also pay you to spy on innocent members of the public in your spare time?'

Kibber, visually taken aback, began to play with the empty whisky tumbler between his fingers. Iain Gwynne sat back on the sofa, arms folded.

'What do you mean?' said Kibber.

'It's time to put those grubby hands of yours up, Inspector. I've found you out. I know you've been tailing me all over town these last few days and our mutual connection is, obviously, Allen Wyngarde. Therefore, one can only assume that he is paying you to do it. So I'm going to ask you a very simple question: *Why?*'

Kibber didn't say anything, choosing instead to stare at the bottom of his glass.

'Perhaps another drink would oil your vocal chords.'

Iain Gwynne went over to one of the bookcases and depressed a button. A row of books flipped back to reveal a well stocked drinks cabinet. He selected a bottle of Black Bug and returned to top up Kibber's glass.

'Now then,' he said as he sat back down. He watched Kibber drain half the whisky and wipe the tiny golden droplets from his bristles. 'Let me lay it all on the line for you, Inspector. The Otto Club wields enormous power and influence due to the wealth of its membership. We all have our connections, our methods of information and our ability to control and destroy as our common goal for survival continues. I know you, Inspector Kibber: You're a marked card in the deck of your superiors. You should have kept your nose a little cleaner than it has been.'

Kibber was feeling acutely uneasy. He drank his drink, conscious that his hand was shaking slightly. As he swallowed, he managed to regain some of his composure.

'Look, sir: Even if I was hired by Allen Wyngarde, I still did the right thing by risking blowing my cover to come here and inform you of my suspicions about the possible danger you could be in.'

'From *Allen*?' Iain Gwynne let out a loud chuckle. 'That washed-up old hack? Oh please, Inspector, do tell me another one. An amusing thought, I'll grant you. Still, I wonder how he would have done away with me in here? Hmmm? Strangulation maybe or a swift falling axe to the back of my neck?'

'I have reason to suspect he arrived here in possession of a weapon.'

'The manuscript?' Iain Gwynne laughed again, this time louder. 'My dear fellow, as a weapon that manuscript is likely to have done him more harm than it has me. Now, Inspector, if there are no other matters - police or otherwise - outstanding, I would very much appreciate it if you would leave the Otto Club and go and have a long, hard think about your future.'

Iain Gwynne stood up. Kibber lifted the glass to his mouth and tipped it upside down against his lips, letting a single drop of Black Bug to roll down onto them. Then he stood up and faced Iain Gwynne.

'That was a nice drop of whisky, Mr. Gwynne.'

'Indeed,' said Iain Gwynne. He picked up the bottle and handed it to Kibber. 'With compliments of the Otto Club. Savour every drop as though it were your last.'

Without another word, Kibber walked out of the room and back down the narrow corridor. As he passed the reception area, he noticed Gibbons there, staring at him with an expression of victorious self-satisfaction. Kibber briefly contemplated grabbing him and beating his head to a pulp with his own switchboard console. Instead, he waited for the concierge to release the inside lock and then he was out of the door and into the chilly night. He stumbled down the steps, in his mind resolving to steer clear of the Otto Club and Allen Wyngarde. K.D.A. was over, closed for business. He made it back to his car and he sank into the seat, drawing a huge gulp from his hip flask and staring up at the many floors of the club, darkened windows hiding their many, many secrets. When he had regained his composure, he started the engine, shoved the bottle of Black Bug into the glove compartment and slammed the unmarked squad car's gearbox hard into first.

Iain Gwynne entered his office and locked the door behind him. Allen Wyngarde was seated exactly where he had left him in the chair before his desk. Allen turned around and watched him return to his seat. Iain rested his elbows on the desk and studied Allen's tired features.

'You look terribly ill, old boy.'

'There's a lot of sick people around,' muttered Allen, fumbling for another cigarette.

'Would you like an aspirin?' said Iain, ignoring the remark. 'No? Alright, you old fashioned fossil. You just sit there and man in out.'

Allen lit the cigarette and took several long puffs.

'I've just met a friend of yours, Allen.'

'How?' said Allen.

'How what? How did I know you had hired a clapped-out policeman to tail me?'

Allen flashed Iain a glance at the reference to Kibber. So, that was that then.

'Actually,' said Allen, 'I meant how did you get your hands on that?'

He nodded towards the manuscript on the desk between them.

'Ah...' said Iain, smiling and drawing the manuscript closer to him. 'Well, I'm not sure I should tell you. I wouldn't want to be the ruiner of your love life.'

Allen tried to decipher what Iain was talking about. Then it dawned on him.

'Ursula.'

'That's right, Allen. My darling treacherous wife. Society slut and expert copyist. It's fortunate for me that you are such a heavy drinker that you pass out the moment you come. Enough time for Ursula to get to work copying your masterpiece for me.'

Allen felt himself physically shaking as he continued to smoke his cigarette. He felt hollow inside. Iain Fucking Gwynne had set him up and taken the very thing from him that was to be his legacy after he left this rotten dirty world.

'But *why*, Iain? For Christ's sake *why*?'

The mocking temperament suddenly went out of Iain. His features darkened and his voice became deeper.

'Because of you, Allen. Because of what you are.

For years I have put up with your snobbery, watched as your work was lauded whilst mine was largely ignored. And then I looked on as you squandered what talent you had inside bottles of expensive cognac. And most of all, Allen, I'm doing it because of Barbara.'

The image of his late wife flashed in Allen's mind. 'Barbra?'

'That's right, Allen. Supposedly the love of your life and unequivocally the love of mine.'

'*You* and *Barbara*?' Allen's voice was barely above a whisper.

'There was no time, Allen. I gave up any hope of something happening the night she decided she could no longer put up with your slow, painful demise and swallowed the contents of your pill drawer. Tell me, Allen; how does it feel to know you killed your own wife?'

'You bastard,' snarled Allen.

'Save your anger for your own reflection.'

There was silence between them for a while. Allen seemed to shrink in his seat, staring at the floor as though it had opened up and was about to take him.

'You don't understand, Iain,' he said finally. 'I need my manuscript.'

'You mean *my* manuscript,' said Iain, the sneer returning to his face.

'It's the only thing I have left,' said Allen.

'You owe me that manuscript, Allen. However, it also happens to be incomplete,' said Iain. 'Which is the other reason why I asked you here. I want you to tell me how your masterpiece ends.'

'You can't possibly get away with all this, you know.'

'I already have, old boy.'

'What do you mean?'

'A copy of your original treatment is currently in the hands of another of our mutual acquaintances; your literary agent.'

'Henry,' said Allen. So there it was, the cruel irony there for him to see. The very manuscript that Henry Meyer had been fobbing him off for was his anyway. He recalled Henry's excitement at "the literary milestone" that was on its way. It almost brought a smile to his face.

'I've won, Allen,' said Iain. 'And if you think you can out me, you'll find I have enough weight behind me to bury you under a mountain of sleaze that even you could not climb out from under. The raconteur, womanising cheat, widower of the woman who couldn't stand by and watch her beloved husband self destruct and father to an estranged daughter who can't even stand the smell of him.'

Allen, now broken down by the harsh reality and the cruel twist of his situation, sighed heavily and then looked him straight in the eye.

'I have two endings prepared,' he said quietly.

'I want them,' said Iain.

'They're in my safe at home.'

'Then we shall have a drink and go and get them.'

39

The kettle reached its boiling point with a shudder and snapped Claudia out of her trance. She had been out of sorts since she had brought Scottie home and took her into the bedroom. Scottie was still very weak and not really saying much. Claudia had fluffed the pillows and made sure the central heating was sufficiently on to keep her warm. She'd asked Scottie if she would like anything to read and Scottie had said no, telling her that keeping her eyes open for too long made them burn. So Claudia had dimmed the light in the bedroom to the lowest possible setting and pulled the door to.

Claudia had assembled the medication that she had brought back with her from the hospital, arranging them on the work surface in ascending order of size. There were the little blue pills that would ease Scottie's bowel movements, elongated orange pills that would stop Scottie's brain from grinding against her skull, grainy blue pills that would keep the peace between Scottie's red and white blood cells and finally those nasty looking yellow pills that would keep her veins from shrinking. Claudia would need to administer the pills every few hours, according to Sister Clodagh's instructions as dictated by Cromwell Rouse's notes. Claudia considered the surgeon who had given her girlfriend the Treatment. *Poor Wellie,* she thought without spite, recalling her meeting with Sir James Swaffham and the solution she had sought from him. For the briefest of moments, Claudia felt a pang of guilt; but not for Cromwell Rouse: he was a soul beneath contempt. No, she suddenly felt a momentary sorrow for his wife and she silently thanked God that she had never met her.

She added the water to her coffee and stirred it softly before turning the stove off and preparing the soup she had made for her patient. She could feel the strain of recent days crushing her into exhausted submission and she knew that she would welcome it very soon. She carried the soup on a tray, along with a glass of water, some pills and her coffee along the hallway and into her bedroom where she set it down on the floor next to the bed.

'Scottie,' she called gently. There was no reply.

Claudia eased herself onto the bed and positioned herself as close as possible behind the sleeping figure under the blankets. She listened as Scottie's breathing altered at the mild disturbance next to her. Claudia smiled as she watched her and at one point she dared to run her fingers along the sleeve of her nightie. *It was all over now,* she thought, a warm glow spreading through her body.

Claudia forgot all about the tray she had brought with her. Instead, she closed her eyes and curled up alongside Scottie. It only took a matter of moments before she sank into a deep, dreamless sleep.

40

Iain Gwynne followed Allen Wyngarde through the latter's apartment and into the dusty, stale study at the front of the building. He had spent the entire taxi ride from the Otto Club basking in his absolute glee at the discomfort and despair he had caused his loathsome companion. How long he had waited for this moment when he could make him wither and die before him and claim the glory for himself. The man was a pig, snout troughing desperately amongst the tattered remnants of the talent he had once possessed. *And for you, Barbara,* he thought to himself as he watched Allen light a cigarette and open up the safe.

Allen, his back to his tormentor, fumbled around inside the safe and pulled out a handful of loose paper. He arranged it neatly into a pile and turned to face Iain. Iain's face visibly lit up when he saw the pages.

'Give them to me,' said Iain feverishly.

'Would you care for a drink, Iain?'

'Give them to me, Allen. Give them to me right now.'

Allen sighed and without another word, held out the papers. Iain took a few steps forward and snatched them impatiently from Allen's grasp. As he hastily scoured them for information, Allen turned to his writing bureau and poured himself a generous slug of Cognac. He downed it in one just as Iain spoke.

'What the hell is this?' he said, holding up the pile of pages even though Allen once again had his back to him.

'What's wrong, Iain?'

'This is *not* the ending to your book,' hissed Iain.

'What kind of pathetic stunt are you playing?'

'Who's playing?'

'Give me the real ending, Allen. Right now.'

'Alright,' said Allen heavily. 'Alright, Iain. If you want an ending, then I'll give you a fucking ending.'

Allen turned around. Iain saw the World War Two service revolver first, the defiant glimmer in Allen's eyes second. There was an intense, kinetic silence between the two men for a while. Finally Iain, his armour slowly beginning to shatter around him, spoke:

'Do you honestly believe you have the bollocks to shoot me?'

'Ordinarily no,' replied Allen, feeling the change in the balance of power giving him a renewed resolve. 'But there's little ordinary about this now, is there? This is my late father's service revolver, you know. I've been keeping it until I finish my manuscript. Afterwards, I was going to put the barrel in my mouth and decorate my study with the contents of my head. So killing you first wouldn't really make much of a difference to me now, would it, Iain?'

The colour had begun to drain from Iain Gwynne's face.

'But you see, now that we've had this little episode and I've seen you for what you really are, well, I'm not sure what to do now. Maybe I'll just have another few drinks and see where my mood takes me. How does that sound to you, eh?'

'Allen--'

'The truth is, Iain; I'm dying, in the literal, physically terminal sense of the word. There's nothing the top people in the white coats can do for me, although my specialist has waxed medical about this amazing treatment you can get if your wallet's big enough. But I'm not sure I want to put myself through any more of this terrible place, with its terrible people and their terrible conceits. But I think if I have to, I will put a bullet in you. So you see I can't possibly let you have my manuscript, Iain. Firstly, because it's for my daughter and secondly, because I haven't even written the ending yet.'

Iain Gwynne, hands held at his sides and away from his body, sat down deflated on the sofa behind him. He knew his gambit had failed. He looked on as Allen downed another Cognac.

'So what now, old boy?'

Allen put his glass on the bureau, picked up the telephone receiver and levelled the revolver at his foe.

'I'll tell you what, Iain: You're going to make a late night phone call to Henry Meyer and tell him the whole dirty story.'

41

The Kommune was full and the music pounded Kibber's brain as he sat hunched over a large drink at the far end of the bar. He massaged his temples, regretting his decision to go into the club in the first place. He hadn't been there before and he'd felt like he needed to go someplace he could feel anonymous. Looking around him, it seemed to him that he was more obvious than ever. He'd used a bit of warrant card leverage to gain access, telling the bloke on the door that he wasn't official but if he couldn't have a quiet drink downstairs then there was a possibility he could return mob-handed another night and give the management a bit of grief. The punters in the Kommune all seemed far too slick to share any common ground with an ungroomed mess like him. He drained his glass and felt the hardness of the bottle of Black Bug that Iain Gwynne had given him earlier. He would make a start on that later, he decided, when he returned home to his room at Eiderlands. He would also make an appointment and go and see Chief Superintendant Annabelle Stoking and lay his cards on the table. Straight to the top, that was the way to go. Cut out all the middle-man shit. He'd tell the Chief that he'd fallen off the wagon, taken his eye off the ball, let the team down and so on and so on and so on and then he'd tell her that in spite of his severe shortcomings he was determined to prove himself to her and the rest of the Force - sorry, ma'm...*Service*...and then he'd throw himself to the floor and pray for mercy. He would also make it up to Claudia too. He had no choice, aware as he now was just how much of a bastard he had been. He wanted her to understand that she wasn't going to have to worry about him anymore. Besides, she was bad for him too, an unhealthy reminder of the past. She didn't need anything from him. Yeah, cut her out.

Kibber ordered another drink and took a look around. He hadn't heard music like this in a while and clearly there were a lot of regulars here. It was giving him a searing headache but he found himself unable to move from the barstool. He carried on drinking and at that moment he noticed a figure at his side.

'Sergeant,' he said, coughing into his glass. 'What are you doing here?'

Detective Sergeant Sam Keady rested his elbow on the bar next to Kibber and looked down at him, smiling.

'I've been looking for you, Sir.'

'Let me get you a drink, Sam,' said Kibber. 'You should try going off duty once in a while.'

'No thank you, Sir,' said Keady.

'Suit yourself,' said Kibber gruffly. 'You won't mind if I have a couple more?'

'Well, Sir, I'd much rather you didn't if it's all the same.'

Kibber set his glass on the counter and half turned to confront his subordinate.

'Say that again, Sergeant?'

'I'd rather you didn't have another drink, Sir.'

'Now listen to me, Sergeant,' said Kibber tersely. 'I may be off duty but I am still your immediate superior officer, understand?'

'I'm sorry, Sir,' said Keady. He leant in a bit more. 'But it might be the best opportunity to save yourself.'

This caught Kibber off guard and he tried to read Keady's face, but there was nothing there to read. He felt himself slowly slipping off the bar stool and walking with him into the crowd. He was starting to feel lightheaded and he pulled his rain mac closer around him. Keady was ahead of him and Kibber felt as though he was being left behind.

His left shoulder connected hard with somebody and he stopped as he recognised the face. It was that bloody Harry Brewer and it looked like somebody had given him a right working over since their last meeting. Harry Brewer immediately recognised Kibber and the look of sickening recollection flashed in his eyes. The two men stood there, staring at each other, not quite sure what to do or say next. Kibber suddenly blurted:

'Have a drink with me.'

Harry Brewer shook his head and mouthed the word "no".

'Have a drink with me,' shouted Kibber louder over the throbbing music.

Harry Brewer shook his head again.

Kibber closed in and held Harry Brewer's overcoat by the collar with both hands. His face came in close to Brewer's ear.

'You can forget about trying to fuck Claudia again.'

He stepped back to gauge the reaction but Harry Brewer appeared confused.

'*Who?*'

This made Kibber's blood boil and he pulled back to throw a punch. He suddenly felt his arm become immobile and as he twisted he saw that Keady was holding his wrist in a vice-like grip. People in the crowd were beginning to stare and at first Kibber tried to shrug his Sergeant off but Keady wouldn't let go. In the end, Kibber relaxed and Keady finally released him from his grasp. Kibber saw that Harry Brewer was nowhere to be seen.

'Let's go, Sergeant,' he said as he continued to follow Keady out. 'You can drive me home.'

Rick saw Harry step up to the bar and drop a bag on the counter. The guy looked like shit.

'What the hell have you been up to, friend?' he said as he poured Harry a Black Bug.

'It'd hurt just to tell you about it,' replied Harry, staring at the glass Rick was sliding his way.

'This one's on me,' said Rick.

'It'll have to be one for the road, cheers.'

'Not stopping then?'

'Audrey's gone already then?'

'You know the drill, my friend. The lady doesn't do encores.'

'Sure.'

Harry drank his drink.

'So what's in the bag?'

'It's for Audrey. Will you give it to her for me?'

'No problem. What's in it?'

'Recordings, Rick. Her recordings.'

'Wow.'

Rick placed a hand on the bag. Harry placed his hand on Rick's.

'To Audrey only, Rick. No one else. Especially that little fuck she travels with. Got it?'

'I got it,' said Rick coolly and Harry let him go. 'Is

there a message to go with it?'

'Yeah,' said Harry, finishing his drink and sliding the empty glass back across the bar. 'Tell her Harry said when the walls are closing in, there's only one way out: Up.'

'What the fuck does that mean?' said Rick.

'I don't know yet,' said Harry, 'but it sounds better than fucking "sorry".'

Harry left the Kommune Club for the last time.

42

Kibber came around in the unmarked squad car, his head resting hard against the steering wheel that was damp from the drool gathering at the corner of his mouth. He sat up straight and saw that he was parked outside the Eiderlands guest house.

'I thought I told you to drive me home,' he said, his voice hoarse.

'You insisted, Sir,' said Keady, seated patiently next to him.

'Yeah, well,' said Kibber. 'How long have I been asleep?'

'Half hour or so.'

'What are you still doing here?'

'I've got time, Sir.'

Kibber mulled this over as he watched Keady staring out of the passenger window at the darkness outside.

'Well,' said Kibber, opening the car door, 'I'm going to go in. You're welcome to join me for a nightcap.'

Keady turned to him and smiled politely.

'No thank you, Sir. I'd best be going.'

They both got out of the car.

'Goodnight, Sir,' said Keady.

'Goodnight.'

Kibber stood by the bonnet of the car, watching him walk away into the shadows. Then something struck him.

'Sam!'

Keady paused and turned around.

'Sir?'

'How did you know where I was tonight?'

Keady smiled and turned his coat collar.

'I always know where you are, Sir.'

Then he turned away and disappeared into the night.

Kibber walked through the doors of Eiderlands and as he approached the stairs he noticed Mr. Sisk, seated behind the reception counter. The sweaty guest house owner looked up and smiled his dirty, mahogany smile.

'You have a nice evening, Mister Kibber?'

'One of many,' said Kibber.

'I too have a nice evening.'

Kibber paused and looked at Mr. Sisk. He was still smiling and still looking directly at him. Kibber approached the counter.

'What's so funny?' he asked calmly.

'I had to go into your room today, just to check for radiator keys.'

'My room.'

'Yes,' said Mr. Sisk, his smile getting wider and dirtier, 'many photos of very pretty girl.' He held his hands up and waved them in a circular motion. '*Everywhere.*'

Kibber could feel himself start to sweat.

'You stay out of my fucking room,' he said through gritted teeth, 'you got that?'

Mr. Sisk's smile diminished slightly as Kibber began to turn aggressive.

'Hey, Detective Inspector, there is no problem. No problem.'

'You'd better hope so.'

'No problem.'

Kibber walked sharply away from the reception and straight up the stairs, his key in his hand already. If he didn't get into his room very soon, there was a good chance he was going to go back downstairs and knock every decaying tooth in Sisk's mouth straight through the back of his head.

He shut the door hard behind him and rested flat back against it, fumbling for the light switch on the wall. As the room lit up, a thousand Claudias greeted him. It wasn't the same feeling this time. Everything had changed and he knew this was the last time he would see her face. He pulled the bottle of Black Bug from the pocket of his rain mac and unscrewed the cap. It bit hard as it melted through him, working its way into his stomach like a meteor splitting the sky before ploughing into the ground below. He took off his rain mac and threw it on the bed and, filling the tumbler up to the brim, began to pull down every picture of Claudia. One by one, she dropped onto the lino, swept by a shaky foot into a pile in the corner. It took him no more than a half hour and as the last picture of her, taken from afar as she crossed Concertina Street one windy April morning, Kibber sat back on the bed and drank. The room looked larger now that the faded, grazed wallpaper was allowed to breathe once again. He decided that once he'd drank down to the label, he'd collect the pictures up and take them outside to burn them. And fuck Sisk. He would move out of Eiderlands.

As he lay back on the bed, tumbler on his heaving chest, Kibber heard the rats scratching in the attic again. They were directly above him. He stared blankly at the ceiling, waiting for it to stop but it continued; scratch-scratch-scratch. He downed his glass and staggered unsteadily to his feet.

'Bastards,' he muttered as he bowled over to the wardrobe and flung open the doors. He dragged a dark blue hold-all from the bottom and opened it on the bed.

'Bastards.'

From it he extracted a long, black police torch and a hammer.

'Bastards.'

He made himself smile at the thought of what he was about to do and went out onto the landing. He reached up, stretching as far as he could and testing his sense of balance to the limit. His fingers caught the small hook screwed into the attic hatch and he yanked it. The hatch swung down, followed by a set of ladders attached to the other side. He just managed to catch them before they struck him in the chest. He set them down and flicked the torch light up into the black hole above his head. The beam danced off the cobwebs hanging from the wooden support beams of the roof. He could hear the low whistling from the draught sweeping through the attic space. He listened for any sound of movement coming from downstairs. Satisfied that Sisk wasn't coming up, Kibber put the hammer between his teeth and began to ascend, one slow step at a time. As his eyes came level with the hatch, he heard the scratching again, coming from somewhere behind him. He went up one more step and steadied himself, taking the hammer out of his mouth and setting it down on the floor of the attic. He began to sweep the torch beam along the floor of the attic, gliding over old packing cases, stacks of newspapers and boxes.

Then, something caught his eye in the far corner, just beyond a dusty old tea chest.

'Bastards,' he whispered. He climbed up until he could get onto the attic floor. He crouched there, trying to control his amplified breathing and pointing the beam straight ahead. He heard the scratching sound again, louder. He picked up the hammer and moved forward on his hands and knees and he was aware that there was comparatively little dust on this section of the floor. He reached the tea chest and gripped the hammer tightly. Then he counted to three and pulled the chest out of the way.

There were no rats to be found. Instead, Kibber saw a dirty old single mattress, shoved into the corner and on it, wide eyed and petrified, lay Patience Sweetlove. Her mouth was sealed with a long strip of silver insulation tape that went right around her head. Her wavy blonde locks, caught by the tape, were hanging and spearing messily in all directions. Her face seemed greasy and drawn in the torch light. Her hands were bound behind her back and the collar of her school shirt was blackened. Her ankles too were bound, and he could see that both these and her wrist bindings had been laced together. Kibber could feel his heart pounding faster by the second. The little girl's face was a mask of horror.

'It's alright, Patience,' he said as reassuringly as the booze would let him. 'I'm a policeman, okay?'

Patience Sweetlove still appeared absolutely numb with terror.

Kibber realised he was still clutching the hammer and lowered it from her field of vision.

'You don't have to worry anymore, Patience,' he said. 'I'm here now and I'm going to get you out of here, alright? Nod if you can understand me.'

He saw her nod, a scared, barely imperceptible but enough to tell him that she believed what he was telling her.

'Good. Now I just need you to be brave for a little while longer, alright? I'm going to get something from my room and then I'm coming back for you, alright?'

Patience Sweetlove nodded again, more clearly this time. He tried to give her a solid smile of reassurance before retreating back as swiftly as he could so that she couldn't see the anger in his eyes.

Kibber began to descend the stairs, the hammer once again between his teeth. He decided he would arrest Sisk, but only if he happened to survive the beating he was about to administer.

He was two steps from the bottom when he was suddenly grabbed around the waist and yanked backwards. Kibber had the brief sensation of flying through the air, cut short as he landed flat on his back on the floor of the landing. He let out a moan of agony and the hammer dropped from his mouth.

'I'll kill you, you fucking pig!'

He saw Sisk standing over him, dirty smile more of a grimace, the eyes burning with intense anger. He also noticed that the landlord was now holding the hammer. Kibber rolled onto his side to get to his feet but Sisk delivered a heavy kick to his back that made Kibber think for a moment that his spine had been broken. He jerked forward into the banister and lashed out with one hand, finding Sisk's leg. Sisk came down with hammer, striking Kibber on the bicep. Sisk's arm swung up and came down a second time; this time the hammer's claw dug into Kibber's neck, the detective didn't let go. Instead he pulled hard and Sisk lost his balance, falling back into the ladders and then down the side onto the floor.

'*You fucking pig!*'

Kibber scrambled to his feet amidst a wash of his own blood and launched himself into his room, trying to find something he could use as a weapon. Sisk got up and raised the hammer up over his head as he marched towards Kibber's room.

'I'm going to kill you, pig! And then I'm going to kill the little bitch!'

Sisk reached the doorway and the last thing his eyes saw was the bottle of Black Bug coming towards him before it smashed into his face. Kibber stepped around the corner as it struck. The bottle shattered as it connected with Sisk's head, erupting in glass, booze and blood. Sisk's body jerked, he let out a gargled scream and toppled backwards against the banister. He brought his hands up to his face to try and brush the glass away. Kibber grabbed Sisk's claret stained shirt collar in his own bloodied hands and pushed him back over the banister railings. Sisk, frantically searching blindly for something to hang on to, suddenly gripped Kibber's sleeve as he toppled over the railings, pulling the Inspector with him. The two of them dropped through the air before hitting the stairs heavily and awkwardly.

Then, save for the quiet, irregular breathing of Patience Sweetlove up in the darkened attic, Eiderlands fell silent.

43

Special News Update: *A press release has been issued by Gregory Gem's PR Company following the rescue of missing schoolgirl Patience Sweetlove. In the statement, sent to The Edition, it is revealed that the recording and release of the charity single,* Have Patience (For Patience), *will go ahead. This is apparently due to contractual obligations. The statement also went on to state that should her abductor, widely thought to be the Albion Snatcher, be handed the death penalty then Gregory Gem's media company will be seeking to secure the live screening rights.*

The soft, bleached corpse of Professor Cromwell Rouse washed up on the Dorset shore in the early hours, just as Claudia was awakening from her night of uninterrupted slumber. She stretched out her legs under the covers and stared up at the ceiling, stained white by the early daylight coming in around the curtains. She was thinking of what she would make for breakfast when she rolled over to see Scottie, still sleeping in the same position she was in when Claudia had curled up beside her. Claudia propped herself up on her elbow and gently shook Scottie's shoulder.

'Wake up, my love,' she said in her soothing voice.

Scottie didn't stir so Claudia repeated the action.

'Scottie,' she said, 'it looks like a beautiful morning outside. I was thinking I might go out and get some bagels and yoghurt.'

Scottie remained oblivious. As she leaned in and

kissed her shoulder, she felt the coldness of Scottie's skin and immediately began to panic. She threw off the bed covers and got to her knees, rolling Scottie onto her back. Straddling her, Claudia leaned in and heard the breathing, slow and irregular. Without thinking, she shook her harder this time. When still Scottie failed to respond, she ran into the lounge and grabbed the phone, dropping the receiver at first before clumsily managing to get a grip on it. Her hands were shaking violently as she dialled. Her legs were turning to jelly and she dropped to her knees on the floor before she fell down.

'Emergency Hotline, please state your preferred department.'

'Ambulance please.'

'Location please.'

'93 Concertina Street WC1.'

'Redirecting you to Gemergency Metropolitan Resources. Hold please.'

'Fuck you!' screamed Claudia into the receiver.

'Gemergency Metropolitan Resources. You're through to Miranda.'

'I need an ambulance now! It's a fucking emergency and I don't want to answer any of your stupid questions!'

'What is the nature of the emergency?'

'My partner is dying,' said Claudia, trying to hold herself together. 'Can you understand that? My girlfriend is *dying*.'

'Is your partner conscious?'

'No. No no no!'

'An ambulance will be despatched to you as soon as possible. I would just like to do an assessment first.'

Miranda the Operator carried on talking, but Claudia wasn't listening. Instead she was screaming; screaming into the shoulder of Scottie, begging her to open her eyes and bring an end to it all.

44

Sir James Swaffham strode purposefully into the outer office of The Box and barely acknowledged the Prime Minister's aide. He placed his hat and umbrella on the desk and awaited the expected reply.

'The PM is waiting for you, Sir James.'

'Thank you.'

Sir James Swaffham strode purposefully behind the bespectacled aide through the corridor below Number Ten towards The Box. He left his hat and umbrella on the stand and let the aide usher him inside the private room.

He found the Prime Minister not sitting behind the huge desk but standing before the large portrait of the London skyline at sunset. Sir James had always privately despised its old fashioned ugliness, pining for the old Empire that was never to return.

'Damn good result that,' said the Prime Minister.

'I'm sorry?'

'That missing schoolgirl turning up like that. Good work. Was it this Albion Snatcher who had her?'

'It looks very much that way, yes.'

'This result will help convince some of our naysayers that the reinstatement of capital punishment is the way forward.'

'Yes.'

'After all, the public voted a majority.'

'Indeed they did.'

'He must hang, James. Whatever it takes.'

'Yes, Prime Minister.'

'Good show being rescued by a copper, too.'

'Yes, Prime Minister. Detective Inspector

Valentine Kibber.'

'How is this Inspector Kibber? Still laid up in St Marcus's is he?'

'Yes, Prime Minister. Took a pretty nasty strike in the neck and he still hasn't regained consciousness.'

'I see. Tell me, James, what's all this fuss surrounding this Kibber?'

Sir James adjusted his tie, unsure how much, if anything, his superior knew about his operations.

'Well,' he said evenly, 'Inspector Kibber has been on "soft duty" for some time.'

'Soft duty? For what reason?'

'Almost a year ago, Kibber and his sergeant, Samuel Keady, were on an operation in Soho. Operation Balaclava, to give it a name.' He paused to see if there was a flicker of recognition in the Prime Minister's eyes; there wasn't. 'They were pursuing a sex trafficking ring and there was a violent encounter. Sam Keady was fatally stabbed.'

'I think I recall,' said the Prime Minister. 'Am I right in thinking no one was brought to justice over this Sergeant Keady's murder?'

'That is correct, Prime Minister. It was a messy affair with an untidy conclusion. The police made several arrests for pimping and other milder charges, but Keady's murder was never pinned on anyone.'

'I see,' said the Prime Minister quietly, head slightly bowed.

There followed a brief period of silence.

'If I may, Prime Minister,' said Sir James at what he considered to be the opportune moment, 'Inspector Kibber remains somewhat of a loose end in all of this.'

'What do you mean?' the Prime Minister's eyes

narrowed.

'It has come to my attention that he has been of some nuisance to certain ladies of the night variety. It could get ugly.'

'Hmm,' said the Prime Minister with a sudden undertone of distaste. 'Putting noses out of joint at that club of yours is it?'

'He has also been in contact with Sergeant Keady's widow several times since the tragedy. Part of the emotional trauma, no doubt.'

The Prime Minister leaned forward a little.

'Swaffham, are you implying something?'

'Mere speculation on my part, Prime Minister. But there may be a logical explanation for the severity of Inspector Kibber's rather lax psychological grip.'

The Prime Minister considered what Sir James had just said.

'What to do…what to do indeed…'

'Prime Minister,' interrupted Sir James, 'I suggest that it may bolster support for your cause if a policeman was added to the Albion Snatcher's list of unfortunate victims. Especially if it happened to be the very same policeman that had caught him.'

The Prime Minister shot Sir James a distasteful look, but also saw the advantage it would give the government and their New Directives.

'If it has to be done, I want it done clean. Do you understand?'

'Of course, Prime Minister. There will be no comebacks.'

'Alright.'

The Prime Minister sighed as if purging any responsibility for the fate that awaited Inspector

Valentine Kibber and said:

'You have something for me?'

Sir James placed the document on the desk and sat down without asking. The Prime Minister turned around and for a moment addressed the impetuousness with a look of disdain, before taking a seat behind the desk.

'So this is it then.'

'Yes, Prime Minister.'

'Is there anything you want to add?'

'It's all pretty self-explanatory, I'm afraid.'

'I see.'

It was clear to Sir James that the leader of the British Government didn't want to touch it.

'Perhaps,' ventured Sir James, 'the Right Honourable leader would prefer some privacy at this delicate time?'

The Prime Minister glanced up at Sir James.

'I think that might be appropriate.'

Sir James nodded curtly and stood up. As he opened the door, he heard the PM call his name. He hesitated, then turned.

'Yes, Prime Minister?'

The Prime Minister leaned forward on the desk, bracing Sir James with a steely stare.

'If I were you, I'd better hope there isn't a candy trail that leads anywhere near your door.'

Sir James smiled, but not a sneering smile, more of a smile that suggested that very little mattered anymore, no matter what politically coloured shroud you wrapped yourself in. He knew that he would be leaving the Box for the Otto Club where he would make the necessary arrangements to sever his ties with

Contact Chemicals and all of their interests in the South Americas. He left, and the Prime Minister picked up the document and sat back in the chair. It was stamped simply with the words "North Angel".

Thirty minutes later, The Prime Minister buzzed the aide and told them to hold all calls and appointments. Then, she rose from her chair and walked back to the painting, trying to rationalise what she had just read. A shadow was about to fall across England's nucleus. The Prime Minister shivered inwardly in spite of the fire that was licking away beneath the marble mantle shelf. She returned to the desk and pressed the intercom.

'I want the whole cabinet in attendance in one hour - no exceptions and no excuses. Is that understood?'

'Yes, Prime Minister.'

'And when they have arrived I want you to take the rest of the day off.'

'Thank you, Prime Minister.'

The Prime Minister picked up the document papers once again and returned to the final pages, headed with the sub-title "Hangman Beetle Treatment And Its Effects On The Human Subject In Outer Orbit Conditions", reading the transcript over and over again until her hands shook.

45

At the moment Claudia stood looking through the glass of the operating theatre as Dr Andrea Sterling undid Cromwell Rouse's deliberately incomplete handiwork on Scottie and administered the full, correct Treatment, the phone rang in Allen Wyngarde's study. Its shrill tone made him jump. He hadn't been asleep, hadn't even had a drink since he'd thrown Iain Fucking Gwynne out. He'd more or less lay down on the sofa and gone into a quiet, peaceful transcendental state. It was almost disconcerting to see everything in full focus after so many years.

'Yes?'

'Dad?'

'*Dee*,' he said almost disbelievingly.

'How are you?'

'I'm actually pretty good.'

'Still writing?'

'I'm close to finishing my book. I was struggling with the ending for a while, but now I think I've got it all worked out.'

'Oh good. That's good. Listen, Dad, do you mind if I come around later on this evening? Only I'd like you to meet my partner and I thought we could drop by after dinner.'

Allen allowed himself a smile.

'I would really like that.'

'Great. I'll let you know when we're on our way. And Dad?'

'Hmm?'

'Don't call me Dee. It's *Deborah*. Bye.'

'Bye.'

The line went dead and Allen sat down. He picked up his father's service revolver and gripped it tightly for a few moments. Then he emptied the bullets from the barrel and put it away in the drawer of the bureau, resolving to never load it again. He massaged the worn features of his face, for a moment thinking some of the creases had faded away. The end for him would come as sure as nightfall; but for now, his world had suddenly began to feel a hell of a lot lighter.

Deborah Flaxman returned to the lounge where Harry was finishing his glass of red. She suddenly noticed how smart he looked in the black three piece suit and combed hair. He smiled at her as she checked her purse and smoothed out her long azure blue evening dress.

'I think you'll get on with my father,' she said. 'He smokes and drinks too much, just like you.'

Harry put the empty glass down and walked across the room to her, placing his hands on her shoulders.

'I don't think I need any more kindred spirits.'

They kissed and then she tapped his chest with her purse.

'Come on.'

Standing on the doorstep, as Deborah locked the front door, Harry gazed up into the early evening sky. It appeared quite unblemished, save for one tiny circle of bright light. At first, he assumed it was an aircraft. But it didn't seem to be moving and there was no giveaway white trail. It was just there, like a hole in the sky.

'What are you looking at? said Deborah

'Oh, nothing much,' sighed Harry. 'Just the

future.'

'Come on.'

Deborah put her arm around his and they went down the garden path, pausing only once as Sara suddenly darted out from under the siding and bolted across and up over the garden wall. The jet black cat stood there for a few moments, observing the stranger that was linked to her master. The stranger leaned in as if to stroke her but Sara hissed and retreated under a rose bush.

'How odd,' remarked Deborah.

As they reached the pavement, a black cab pulled up alongside them and the door swung open. Harry and Deborah stood and watched as Audrey Lee stepped out of the cab and walked slowly but purposefully up to them.

'Hello, Harry.'

'Audrey,' replied Harry, 'I didn't think I'd see you again.'

'Neither did I,' said Audrey. She acknowledged Harry's companion. 'Ms Flaxman.'

'Ms Lee.'

'How did you find me?' said Harry.

'That journalist friend of yours. Nigel was good enough to ask him for your address.'

'Nigel?'

Just then, Nigel St Davos stepped onto the pavement and joined them, standing just behind Audrey.

'No Gubbs?'

'One can have too many friends,' said Audrey, a glint in her eye.

'I suppose,' said Harry, inwardly hoping Gubbs

was, right at that moment, having an exceptionally hard time dealing with rejection.

'You were right, Harry,' she said, smiling. 'You were so right about everything.'

She came close and gave him a lingering, heartfelt kiss on the cheek. When she pulled back, Harry was about to say something but Audrey placed a finger across his lips. Then, without anything more to be said, both she and Nigel got back into the cab and it pulled away from the kerb. Harry and Deborah watched it rattle away down Vancouver Hill and for a moment he found himself feeling that odd sensation of fulfillment mixed with loss, like the expression he had seen on his mother's face the day he'd left the family home for university. Yet there was something else…a sense of foreboding perhaps. Sara had sensed it and now he was sensing it too. He thought of his parents and it suddenly hit him for the first time that they really weren't there anymore and that there was no point in looking back for them. And then he noticed the unmarked white van drawing slowly onto the street and heading at a crawl towards where they stood. The slide door on the side opened up slightly and he saw the slender black cylindrical protrusion looking straight at him. Once more he thought of his parents, lying on the mountainside in South America. He almost felt a wave of relief as he knew that there could now be closure.

'It's all over then,' said Harry to himself.

Deborah gently tugged on his arm.

'Harry, is that a tear I see welling in your eye?'

46

Miles above the world, Captain Ione Blanchard sat in the pilot's chair, staring through the viewport at her home, wishing she had had more time, wishing even more that the rest of the crew of the *North Angel* had survived long enough to see it too. She sipped the tepid coffee and pulled her space suit tighter. The craft's heating system was starting to fail now. She had been left all alone for a day or so, after jettisoning the body of her pilot, Nathan Bloom. She was far beyond exhaustion and caught up in euphoria. She knew she was hallucinating, knew that the accident had exposed them to toxins that had rendered herself and everyone on board incapable of sharp judgement. There was nothing left to fear, nothing left to decide and nothing left to fight for. She picked up her journal and reread her final entry that she had sent to Greenwich. And when she thought of Greenwich, she thought of her mother. She hoped that she had been able to receive it.

It is with a heavy heart that I have to inform you that we failed. That is to say that our belief in ourselves as a dominant species has been dealt a fatal blow. I am alone about this ship now and in full acceptance that I shall never hear another human voice.

Please know and believe that we tried. We tried to warn you in time of what waits for us out here. Please know also that I am sorry and, at the very end of things, all I can add is that I love you all.

Ione Blanchard,
Captain, North Angel

Captain Blanchard closed the journal and stared out of the viewport once more at the world in all its tragic beauty. And as she did, finger hovering over the magic button, she smiled a final smile.